ASHWOOD'S GIRLS

A TROUBLED SPIRITS NOVEL

J.R. ERICKSON

COPYRIGHT

DEDICATION

For Rayna Chapman. The newest member of our tribe.

AUTHOR'S NOTE

Ashwood's Girls is inspired by a true story. To avoid spoilers, that story is briefly retold at the end of this book.

1

"It's really happening," Holly said, smiling as she surveyed the stretch of ten acres they'd purchased that morning.

Tall gray maple trees lined one edge of the clearing where they'd build their house. The trees stood watch like guardians over their future home.

"No turning back now," Adam murmured.

Holly had taken off her coat and stood with her arms stretched wide as if she might take flight. Above them lay a cloudless sky. Sun lit the grass, damp and brown from the long winter, casting the stalks in crystalline sheaths.

Adam watched as she twirled, face tilted up, long dark hair swishing. His heart swelled against his ribs. Buying the property had been the right thing to do. He'd worried for months about the decision, about the risk with Holly's heart condition, but now with Holly in her pretty peach-colored sweater, her face awash with midday sun, it had all been worth it.

She bent over and picked a sparkling weed. As she straightened up, her face paled and she frowned, lifting one hand to her chest.

"What is it? Your heart?" Adam stepped to her, weaving an arm behind her back.

She smiled, but didn't answer right away. "Just got… a little short of breath. I'm okay." She leaned heavily against him, resting her head on his shoulder.

"Let's head back to the hotel, grab some dinner, sit in the hot tub," he said. "This has been a big day."

"In a minute," she murmured. "Let's just breathe this in a little longer."

~

One Week Later

Adam drove along the Lake Huron coast passing through the small town they'd soon call home. It was little more than a grocery store, a diner and a gas station. He turned west on a county road that took him away from the water and into the woods.

Their property on Black Mountain Road was isolated, a factor that still gave him pause. He'd argued with Holly about choosing something closer to a major hospital due to her heart condition, but she'd been adamant about the ten acres they'd bought. She'd loved it on sight.

Adam turned his truck, which hauled the trailer carrying the excavator he'd rented onto the two-track that would soon be a paved driveway to their new home. It bumped over rocks. As he covered the last stretch, the trailer sank into the soft earth and tugged on the truck. He shifted into four-wheel drive, hit the gas, and maneuvered it the last ten yards.

A crew had cleared a section of trees, but Adam and Holly had chosen their building location in part because it was a spacious field surrounded by forest.

The architect had drawn up the plans more than a year earlier and the permits were in place. If all went according to plan, Adam and Holly would move into their new house in six months, catching the tail end of a northern Michigan summer.

Adam parked his truck and walked to the excavator, removing chains and straps that held it in place. He backed the machine down and guided it toward the space where the house would stand. He hadn't operated an excavator in years, but he'd grown up on the machines working with his dad and uncle, and the memories of their operation remained.

Adam dug into the ground, pleased when the grass split to reveal lush black soil—perfect for Holly's garden. As he dug, scooping out great mouthfuls of dark soil and piling it to the side, something pale stuck from the base of the hole. He switched off the excavator and swung open the door, jumping down from the cab. He walked closer.

A tattered bit of once-blue cloth clung to the object. Frowning, Adam dropped into the hole. Something crunched beneath his foot. A leg bone jutted from the dark earth, a skeletal foot askew on the ankle.

"Holy crap," he muttered, stepping close to the dirt wall.

He knelt and brushed the dirt away to reveal more of the skeleton, the ribcage beneath a blue dress, a skull above that. His mouth turned dry. As he looked at the ground around the skeleton, he noticed more bits of pale bone and colored cloth. He got on his hands and knees and gently swiped at the dirt, revealing a second skeleton and a third. The bodies lay stretched out long. Someone had folded their arms across their chests.

His stomach twisted and his mind jumped to warp speed.

"It's a cemetery," he murmured.

Two hollows that had once contained eyes gazed up at him.

A chill came over Adam and for a sickening moment he thought the skeleton could see him, was watching him.

Adam scrambled out of the hole, jogged to his truck and jumped behind the wheel. He slammed the door closed and stared through the windshield at the hole.

The land had once been a graveyard, perhaps a family burial place.

He had to call someone. Who? The sheriff? The county land permit guys? They'd stop the construction. Some local group might insist the land was sacred ground and protest any future developments.

Adam thought of Holly standing there the week before. The way she'd grown breathless and pale. It was possible that her new heart was failing. It was possible that her days were numbered in months, not years. He had to give this to her, this one dream they'd imagined for so long.

Silencing the voices in his head, he opened the door to his truck and stepped out. He grabbed suede work gloves from his tool box and climbed back into the hole. He'd simply remove the skeletons and bury them elsewhere. No harm, no foul.

He reached for a skeleton partially submerged in the dense earth. As he pulled on the shoulder girdle, a tiny clavicle bone snapped in his fingers.

He shuddered and took several deep breaths, looking at the sky.

Staring into that blue void, he could almost imagine what lay beneath him, around him, didn't exist at all.

He hauled the bones out and piled them to the side of the clearing. A hank of dark hair slipped from one skull as he pulled it free and he shrieked, dropping the bones as the hair fell on his shoes. He stared at it, pulse pounding. It was dark and thick, but embedded with wriggling pinkish worms.

He couldn't do this. Couldn't just move these bones and carry on with business as usual.

But again, he thought of Holly and how her face had filled with hope when he'd plucked the 'for sale' sign from the ground.

No. He wouldn't call anyone. They were dead. Skeletons probably buried a hundred years before in a forgotten graveyard.

In total, Adam unearthed five skeletons though they were no longer intact. As he carried two handfuls of short bones from the hole, a ring dislodged from the pile and landed in the grass. He picked it up and stuck it in his pocket.

As the sun set, Adam moved the excavator to the edge of the clearing and dug another hole next to the enormous pudding stone Holly insisted stay where it was. As the last glimmers of sun faded from the sky, he nudged the bones over the side of the hollow.

He stepped from the excavator and paused at the tangle of skeletons, wondering if he should say something, a parting prayer, but he doubted anyone was listening.

"It's just us and the birds out here," he muttered.

He took the ring from his pocket and dropped it in the hole.

Adam returned to the excavator and covered the bodies with dirt.

2

Six Months Later

"Oh, Adam," Holly murmured. "It's actually real."

They sat in the van in the circular driveway facing their new home.

The ranch had a bright blue aluminum roof sloping over white wood siding. Windows stretched floor to ceiling along the front of the house. A low wooden porch wrapped around two sides. Adam had installed a hanging swing with a thick cushion and pillows for Holly to sit on.

Holly climbed from the van and slipped off her sandals, walked barefoot across the yard. Adam let Marshmallow, their one-hundred-pound Pyrenees, out of the back of the van. He ran to Holly and she knelt beside him, wrapping her arms around his fluffy white neck. "What do you think, Marshmallow? Isn't it perfect?"

"Here, come on, let me show you the little touches."

Adam had been on the property helping the building crew nearly every day since he'd broken ground the previous spring, but Holly had only accompanied him a handful of times. She hadn't been to the house in nearly three weeks. During that time the furniture had been delivered, the garden fence had been erected and Adam had hung all her photos and her mother's paintings.

"Hold on." Adam put a hand on Holly's arm as she started to open the front door. He swept her up, propping the door open with his hip, and carried her inside.

She laughed. "Isn't that for newlyweds?"

"Every day with you is like the first day." He kissed her temple and stood her on the ground.

She moved slowly into the living room, trailing her fingers over the series of paintings he'd hung. Each depicted the same tree during different seasons. Holly's mother had painted them in watercolor and their branches and leaves merged with the sky above and the earth below.

Holly's eyes sparkled with tears. "Oh, Adam," she murmured. "It's more beautiful than I imagined."

"You deserve it, Holly."

She ran her hand along the burnt-orange suede sectional, heavy with down pillows, that stretched along one entire wall.

"I like to call this the lounge room," Adam told her, flopping down on the couch.

She fell down beside him, laughing, and moaned. "It's so soft."

"Wait until you try out the new bed."

She squealed and stood up.

The master bedroom held a king-sized memory foam mattress atop a navy-blue upholstered bed frame. Adam had special-ordered the bedding. It depicted Marshmallow as a puppy lying on a red and black checkered blanket.

"Oh, my gosh. I love it!" She laughed.

Adam held Holly's hand as he guided her out of the bedroom. "The study and the guest bedroom are right down…" He froze, staring at the heather-gray runner that ran the length of the hall. Red-brown footsteps marred the fabric, as if someone had walked in mud and then run across the carpet.

"What the hell?" he muttered.

"They look like bare feet," Holly mused beside him. "Who would have been barefoot in the house?"

He shook his head, furious, trying to think of which workers had been at the house in the previous days. "It must have been the painter. He came in for final touch-ups after the furniture and appliances got delivered."

"He has very small feet."

Adam considered the prints. They were small. More like Holly's size or smaller. "He must have brought his kid. That would explain why they're bare. I'm going to call him. He'll be replacing that rug."

Holly tilted her head and then stepped beyond the rug, eyes still trained on the floor.

"What?" he asked.

"Well, look at them. There's no trail. They just stop at the end of the rug and begin there too. It's odd, isn't it?"

Adam saw what she meant. The footprints didn't appear on the wood floor on either side of the runner. "He must have cleaned up the hard floor and couldn't get the prints off the rug."

"It doesn't look like he tried on the rug. If he'd wiped them, they'd be smeared."

Adam sighed and took Holly's hand. "I'm sorry. I wanted it to be perfect."

She gave him an exasperated look and laughed. "It is perfect, you fool." She hugged him. "It's a few footprints on a rug. A little soap and water and that thing will be good as new."

"Yeah, you're right." He glared at the rug for another moment before following Holly toward the kitchen.

"I'll get the sandwiches from the van," she told him. "I'm starving."

"Okay. I put some paper plates in the pantry. I'll meet you on the porch."

Adam flipped on the light in the pantry and the bulb crackled and went dark.

"What the hell?" he murmured, flicking the switch a few times. He reached up and unscrewed the bulb.

The electrician had left a few replacement bulbs for various fixtures in a hallway closet. Adam retrieved one and screwed it in place, turned on the light and grabbed the stack of paper plates.

They ate the sandwiches sitting on the porch and watched the light drain from the sky. At dusk the lightning bugs appeared and with them a racket of crickets and frogs.

"Good grief, they're loud." Adam chuckled.

"It's decadent and wild, this place," she murmured. "A concert every night. How did we get so lucky?"

Adam bent down and grabbed the bottle of sparkling water. He refilled Holly's glass and then his own.

"To living our dreams," he said, holding his glass up.

She clinked her glass against his. "To living," she breathed.

He wrapped his arm behind her on the swing. Her feet were propped on the porch rail, which kept them from rocking. He kissed her neck. "No regrets then? About selling the coffee shop, leaving Grand Rapids, turning our world on its head?"

"Not a one. Well…"

"What?"

"I miss those old ladies who used to come into the coffee shop."

Adam laughed. "The Black Hat Ladies?" He thought of the group of five women who came in every other Friday, donning their witchy black hats. One of them said they were the Red Hat Ladies' nemeses.

"Those are the ones."

"We'll find you a new set of old ladies to chat with."

"Oh, good. We can invite them to our housewarming party—merge our two worlds."

They made love in their new bed, in their new home. Afterward, Holly lay facing him.

"You did it," she murmured. "You made the dream come true."

"We did. It never would have happened if you hadn't imagined it."

She smiled. "I'd hoped to help more. To leave our names in the concrete footpath and hang some of the drywall with my own hands. This shortness of breath thing has really knocked me down a few notches."

Adam reached a hand to her chest, resting one palm against the steady, albeit weak, thrum he felt beneath her ribs. She was on her third heart. The first had been her own, the second two were transplants. In the previous two years he felt as if they'd been living on a rollercoaster. The heart attack, the first transplant, Holly's body rejecting the heart, the second transplant. Before the first attack they'd been floating along, unaware that they were in the cart slowly clicking toward a peak, and when they went over the edge, they'd never be able to get back off.

The scar that stretched from Holly's throat to her breastbone gleamed in the lamplight. He traced one finger down the raised pink skin.

"I saw a magazine the other day with scars turned into tattoos,"

Holly told him. "A man with a transplant had his scar tattooed into a zipper."

"A zipper?" Adam shook his head. "That sounds a little creepy."

Holly laughed. "Yeah. I thought mine would make a pretty stem for a flower."

"You want a tattoo?"

She smiled sadly. "I don't know. Sometimes when I look at it… I wish it looked… different."

"I think it's beautiful." He kissed the raised flesh. "How do you feel right now, honey? Do you feel as if…?"

"My body will keep this one?" She rested a hand over his. "I'm not sure yet. I hope so."

Adam closed his eyes when the emotion started to slither up. He didn't want to cry, to reveal the fear that crept around in his head every waking moment.

Adam knew grief. He'd watched his own mother perish from breast cancer, listened at night as his father wept at her bedside, begging her not to leave them, to please stay and fight. And she would have. Joan Tate had always been a fighter, a woman who, though barely standing over five feet tall, stared into adversity like a knight approaching the fire-breathing dragon, shield high, sword at the ready, unwilling or unaware of the odds.

But chemo had eroded her stubborn strength. It had happened slowly and then all at once. The gradual wasting of her muscles, the eventual spread of tumors to her vital organs and then one day Adam had run into her bedroom triumphantly displaying his soccer trophy and she'd been unable to lift her head from the pillow. Blood had beaded at the corner of her mouth and strands of her short dark hair clung to the pillow behind her.

"I won," Adam had announced, though his enthusiasm had drained at the sight of his sickly mother, who he'd realized for perhaps the very first time was dying. It was apparent on that day as it had been on no other day before.

His father had fallen apart after Joan died. His grief had been too much. The years of Adam's life after his mother's death all seemed to be tinted in blues and blacks.

"It's going to be okay," Holly whispered, drawing him back into the moment. She traced her finger along his jawline. "This is just a body. I will go on and eventually you'll meet me on the other side."

Adam's chest constricted and he closed his eyes. He couldn't tell Holly that he didn't know if he believed that. "What scares me most of all is how quiet, how gray the world will become. How, when I see the first golden leaf of autumn, I won't have you to call or to drag onto the porch to look at it with me. You've brought the life into my life."

Holly kissed his chin. "The life is there, Adam. It's in you, it's all around you. I might label it, I might point it out, but it's there. And someday, rather than lying here beside you, I'll be out there. I'll be in every golden leaf and in the iridescent wings of every dragonfly, in every whip-cream cloud. I'll be everywhere."

Adam burrowed his face into the crook of her neck. He breathed her in, the scent of her sweat and her medicine and the shea butter lotion that kept her skin from cracking.

"I am not sure I can make it without you," he whispered, and he wished he hadn't said it because Holly carried so much already.

She ran her fingers through his hair and kissed the top of his head. "We'll make it together. I'll be just behind you. But I'm very clever and when you turn, I'll slip quickly away and you will never see me, but I swear I'll be there."

"Promise?" he asked, fighting against the dark thoughts swirling, the secret fears that Holly would fade into the black and someday years on he would as well.

"I promise."

"I love you, Holly."

"I love you more."

"Reading time?" he asked, leaning over to his nightstand and grabbing their paperback copy of *The Great Gatsby*.

They'd started reading to each other years before, taking turns night after night reading a chapter from a book. They tried to stick to the classics, but had often wandered off the path, reading the Lord of the Rings series, Anne Rice's Vampire books, and even the sultry pages of more than a few romance novels.

Holly rarely read the chapters now. After the heart attack, she'd begun to have trouble with her vision at night. Her eyes grew tired quickly.

Adam cracked the book and looked for the page he'd dog-eared.

"I swear to God if Gatsby doesn't make a move on Daisy soon, I'm chucking this book out the window," Adam said.

Holly smiled and combed the curls of hair on his chest. "Let's hope it happens in the next three minutes because my eyes are already getting heavy."

As Adam read, Holly fell asleep on her stomach, one arm flung above her head.

He kissed her arm, flipped off the light, and closed his eyes.

Adam woke to a sound that had vanished before he became conscious. He lay and listened. Holly was still beside him and he stared hard at her back for a moment until he saw the gentle rise that signaled her breath.

From somewhere in the house, he heard a click as if a door had been closed. He sat up, swung his legs over the side of the bed and eased quietly to his feet. He cocked his head, listened, but heard no further sound.

Once he'd slipped into the boxer shorts he'd discarded that evening, he crept from the room and looked down the hallway, first toward the study and then swiveling in the direction of the kitchen and living room. Something knocked in the kitchen.

He considered arming himself, grabbing the letter opener on the desk in the study, but decided against it. As he walked down the hall, he waited for another sound, but heard none.

He stepped into the kitchen.

A white shape hulked in the corner and Adam froze.

3

Adam stared through the gloom at the white thing crouched near the pantry. It growled and Adam's breath left in a rush.

"Marshmallow," he whispered, his taut muscles slackening within him. "Hey, boy, what's up?"

The dog didn't turn.

Adam flipped on the light.

Marshmallow held his position, his head sunk low toward the wood floor near the opening into the pantry.

Something clunked against the wood beneath them and then suddenly a sound like footsteps pounded across the floor as if someone were running full speed along the kitchen floor, but not on their side, on the underside where a child could barely stand between the boards and the dirt floor beneath. It wasn't tall enough for someone to stand, not to mention they'd have to run upside down.

"What the...?" Adam recoiled from the sound, stepping toward Marshmallow.

The dog, as if hearing him for the first time, spun and bared his teeth, barking viciously and lunging at him.

Adam fell back, bumping his back against the counter and holding up his hands.

"Marshmallow, no!" he shouted, blocking his face from the dog he suspected was about to clamp sharp teeth onto his arm.

No attack came and when he moved his hands, Adam found Marshmallow hanging his head and whimpering. He slunk towards Adam with his tail between his legs. Adam held out a shaky hand, and the dog licked it.

"There, there, it's okay buddy. Spooked ya, did I?" Adam patted the dog on the head.

When Marshmallow calmed down, Adam returned his attention to the kitchen floor, trying to make sense of the sound. Was something in the crawlspace? Access from the house went through a trap door in the pantry.

Adam stepped into the pantry and flicked on the light. The bulb crackled and extinguished with a tiny burst.

"Seriously?" He flipped the switch several times, though he knew it would make no difference.

He returned to the kitchen and shuffled through drawers until he found a flashlight. He flicked it on and returned to the pantry, squatted and prised up the trap door. A blast of cool, damp air rose from the hole. It had a slightly rancid smell, and he wrinkled his nose.

Marshmallow hovered behind him, eyes glued to the opening.

Adam trained the light into the hole. He needed to crouch lower, drop his upper body into the cavity to see beneath the house, but something in him resisted. He didn't want to put his head down there. Shifting the light back and forth, he searched for any movement and, when he didn't see any, he quickly shoved the trap door into place and stood up.

Adam slumped into a kitchen chair and considered the trap door, waiting to hear the strange sound again.

Marshmallow curled into a ball of white fur beneath the table, picking his head up now and then to look quizzically at Adam as if he too was contemplating the origin of the sound.

After a half hour, Adam's eyelids drooped and he struggled to stay awake.

"Let's concede defeat, Marshmallow." Adam stood, turned off the kitchen light, and walked back to the bedroom. Marshmallow followed, settling on the floor on Holly's side of the bed.

~

Adam spent the next morning rototilling the area where Holly wanted to plant her garden. He'd already installed the posts and chicken-wire fencing, which might keep critters from gobbling up her lettuce and tomatoes.

Holly pulled a wagon from the garage filled with the potted plants she'd dug up from her own garden in Grand Rapids weeks before.

"I'd like to find a nursery in the area," she told him, wiping her dirt-streaked hands on her already stained garden apron. "I thought I'd get some mums and a few cool-weather vegetables."

"Great. I'd like to check out the town. We can have dinner out tonight."

"That sounds nice. Hey, did you clean the footprints off the rug?"

He frowned and shook his head. "No. I figured you did it."

"I planned to this morning but the rug was clean. Maybe they just… faded. Weird."

"Yeah, weird. I thought I'd hike around the woods a bit too," Adam said, shielding his eyes and looking toward the towering maple trees.

His eyes passed over the large pudding stone and his stomach lurched as he remembered the bones he'd moved six months before. He hadn't told Holly about them, or anyone. He'd been doing his best to forget it had even happened.

"Go for it," Holly told him. "I've got this. Marshmallow will keep me company."

"Marshmallow will need a bath if you let him in the garden."

Holly rubbed the dog's head. "Maybe we'll take him to the beach and he can have a lake bath."

Adam grinned. "He loves a swim." He blew Holly a kiss. "Okay, I'm off to explore."

Adam hacked at the invasive vines with his machete, tearing them down from the tall trees they strangled. The woods were dense and the mosquitoes ruthless as he moved deeper into the vegetation. Sweat poured into his eyes and he yanked his t-shirt up to wipe it away. He'd imagined a leisurely stroll through the woods, but discovered instead a mission into a northern Michigan jungle.

A sharp bramble caught him on his side and he winced, looking down to find he'd walked into a blackberry patch. A branch of thorns stuck through his t-shirt into the soft flesh of his abdomen. Holly would be excited about the berries. He'd tell her when he got home. He carefully removed the branch and pushed it away, maneuvering out of the thorny bushes.

As he shuffled away from the tangles of vine and bush, he noticed a clearing ahead of him. He pushed through and stepped onto an overgrown piece of property. A white farmhouse stood on the far side of the clearing. The same invasive vines had attacked the house, snaking up the wood and the deck.

The lawn was overgrown, and the house in disrepair. The only signs of life appeared as a swarm of gnats aiming for his eyeballs as Adam shuffled across the weedy lawn.

A tire swing hung from a tattered rope suspended from a tall oak tree beside the house.

He gave the house a wide berth as he walked the perimeter. As he came around the back of the property, he caught a scent, a swampy smell, and the culprit stood before him. An old in-ground pool filled with mossy black water occupied a portion of the backyard. More vines and vegetation crawled over the stone rail that surrounded the pool. A weeping willow stood at the far end, its snake-like tendrils sweeping the dark water.

Adam picked up a stick and walked to the edge of the pool. He poked at the slimy topcoat, swirling it away to reveal the murky water reflecting the blue sky above him. As he gazed into the dark surface, he realized a figure suddenly loomed over his left shoulder. The pale face of a woman watched him.

Adam jumped and spun around. "I'm sorry," he started, ready to apologize for trespassing, but the woman was not there. The abandoned yard stood empty.

Adam's heart hammered in his chest. He searched for her in the woods beyond the yard. Nothing moved. No figure retreated toward the trees. He'd merely imagined her.

Beyond the pool, he discovered a series of stables, a faded red barn and a once-white fence. The home had clearly once been an expansive homestead, but it looked as if no one had visited it in decades.

A gnarled apple tree squatted halfway between the stable and forest. Dozens of apples, spoiled and brown, lay in heaps in the overgrown grass. A mass of bees hovered over the putrid fruit, releasing a droning buzz.

A tennis shoe stuck up from the fruit, weathered and gray, partially buried by apples. A large black and yellow hornet landed on the toe of the shoe.

Still jittery after seeing the woman's reflection, Adam turned to go home. As he walked toward the forest, something caught him hard in the forehead.

"Ouch, shit." He pulled back and squinted. He'd walked into a grimy string. "A laundry line," he muttered, pinching the string between his thumb and forefinger. As he looked down its length, he noticed several wooden clothespins, time-worn, the tiny metal hinges rusted. Two of the pins held tattered pieces of fabric. He kicked at the grass beneath the tatters and discovered dirty sheets embedded in the foliage.

Adam trudged out of the yard, rubbing his forehead, troubled by the house, most of all the laundry line that had held sheets never taken down. He'd seen neglected houses in his day, homesteads abandoned when the town factory closed and the money dried up, but people usually took their things. Who moved away and left their sheets hanging on the line?

4

Adam found Holly in the kitchen, dirt-streaked and washing her hands.

"How was the adventure?" she asked, surveying his scratched arms and face.

"Well, I had a fight with a blackberry bush and the bush won."

"Ooh, blackberries, really?"

He laughed. "I knew you'd say that. Yes, lots of them. We'll have to go pick some, but I need to take some heavy-duty clippers out there and make a path. Those woods are treacherous. Did you get everything planted?"

"Yep. Oh, and the bulb blew in the pantry," Holly told him, drying her hands on a dish towel.

"What? I changed it again this morning. That's the third time it's blown."

"Really?"

"Yeah."

"Hmmm, probably a bad pack of lightbulbs. Hey…" She walked to the table and grabbed a clipboard.

"What do you have there, my lovely wife?" He peered at the paper. The title read 'Five Wishes Living Will Document.' Holly's doctor had given them the document so they could record Holly's end of life desires in terms of care, resuscitation orders, and burial preference.

"I don't want to do that right now," he said, retreating to the cupboard to grab a glass. He took the water pitcher from the refrigerator and filled it.

"We have to do it eventually, Adam. And sooner is probably better."

He kissed her shoulder. "I know, but not today, okay?"

She sighed and put the clipboard down. "Okay."

"Guess I'll run into the hardware store. Need anything else?"

"We might need paper towel, want to double-check?"

Adam peered into the pantry, dim without the overhead light. He scanned the shelves and spotted a single paper towel roll. As he ducked out, something scratched at the floor beneath him. He squatted close to the floor and listened. It stopped, but the moment he stood up, it came again.

It sounded as if something were scratching the floor from beneath the house. He thought of the sound from the night before, like something thumping along the underside of the kitchen floor.

"Great," he muttered.

"What?" Holly asked, opening the dishwasher and loading their breakfast dishes.

"Have you heard a scratching in the kitchen? Under the floor?"

"Scratching? Gosh, no. You don't think an animal got in there somehow?"

Adam sighed. "Maybe. I'll check around the perimeter and see if I find any holes, but that's wilderness life. Those little buggers can fit through a hole the size of a pea."

Holly smiled ruefully. "What little buggers are we talking about exactly?"

"The usual culprits: squirrels, raccoons, possums."

"Possums can squeeze through a hole the size of a pea?"

He chuckled. "Or more likely a rat, but I didn't want to use the 'r' word and have you refusing to walk into the kitchen."

"Oh, quit it." She laughed, slapping his arm. "I have one rat scare and I'm forever labeled a rat-phobic."

"You did nearly crush Duke's kitten with a lamp."

Holly groaned. "It rubbed across my leg in the middle of the night. He didn't tell me he'd gotten a kitten." She shook her head. "I'll never live that down."

Adam grinned. "I have to heckle you about something." Adam grabbed his phone off the counter, glanced at the battery icon and scowled. "What the heck? I charged this all night and the battery's almost dead."

"Might need a new battery."

"Which means a trip to a cell phone store, which is God knows how far from here."

~

Adam parked and walked into the hardware store, grateful for the blast of air conditioning. He closed his eyes and sighed.

"It sure is a scorcher out there today," the man behind the register commented, looking up from a display of bug spray he was arranging on the counter.

"Yeah, it is. My car thermometer said eighty-five, but I'd swear it's past ninety."

"Got some cold drinks in the cooler there." The man gestured at a tall refrigerator with the Coca-Cola label on the sign. "Water, Cokes. My grandson has started stocking energy drinks too. I told him we'd be lucky to sell one. Instead, we can barely keep 'em in stock." He shook his head, as if struggling to make sense of it. "Back in my day, an energy drink was a cup of coffee."

Adam laughed. "That's still my preferred energy drink. Can you point me to the lightbulbs?"

"Yep, two more aisles down on your left. You can't miss 'em."

Adam walked into the aisle and surveyed the rows of bulbs, grabbed a box of compact fluorescents and a box of plain white bulbs. He started toward the front and then turned back, scanning the aisles. He spotted a live animal trap and grabbed it.

As the man rang him up, Adam added a bottle of bug spray. "Have you been in this area long?" Adam asked.

"I'm as old as some of the trees around here. At least that's what my grandson tells me. Born in the same house I live in today, five miles out on White Pine Road."

"My wife and I recently built a house on Black Mountain Road, quite a ways back in the woods. I found an old house about a half mile from our place. Any idea who that belonged to? It looked like a nice place once upon a time—horse stables and a big in-ground pool."

"Sure, yeah. That was the Ashwoods' place."

"And what? They moved and just left it?"

"Nope. Big tragedy for the Ashwoods. It happened in 1956. The girls took the boat out for a sail on Lake Huron and all disappeared. Boat must'a gone down, but they never found it."

"There was a group of girls on board?"

"Yep. The Ashwoods had a whole gaggle of girls livin' there. Some people called it a finishing school. They were teenagers, usually four or five at any given time. Sometimes they stayed for a summer, sometimes for years. Alice Ashwood was a sailor, her and the husband both. Back in those days, I worked on the family farm, so I didn't see folks like I do now, but my ma ran our little country store where we sold the eggs and milk, beef, pies and whatnot. She used to tell me I needed to ask one of them girls out on a date. They were real pretty, most of 'em. I saw 'em around town a time or two, always walking in a group, so you didn't dare speak a word to 'em."

"And they all died in a sailing accident?"

"Yep. Alice used to take 'em out for a weekend sail two or three times a summer. They left on a Friday morning and neither the girls nor the boat was ever found."

"Still, to this day, they've never found the boat?"

The man shook his head. "Not a shred. Weird too, because usually something comes drifting up over the years or divers come across her."

"They searched for it, though? The police or whatever?"

"Oh, yeah. Course, it shifted from a saving mission to a body recovery mission after that first week—though you never know, sometimes people can float out there in a little lifeboat for weeks, especially if they have provisions. The weirdest thing is there wasn't a storm that weekend, pretty low winds, relatively calm waters. Police figured there was some fatal flaw in the boat that no one was aware of until they were too far out to do anything about it."

"Is there anything that would happen so fast they couldn't send out a distress signal or—"

"A fire, for one. I've seen that before. If they were far enough out, nobody from the shore might have seen it. A fire might have taken hold quick. Those old boats could go up in a flash and… I don't know. I hate to think they went that way. It would be a terrible death for sure."

"But wouldn't there be pieces of the charred boat floating in the water?"

"You'd think so, but the Great Lakes are funny places. Anybody that's worked around them learns a certain respect and a bit of fear, too.

Planes flying overhead disappear, boats, people. Some of 'em turn up, some of 'em don't."

"Did you know the Ashwoods personally?"

He shook his head. "I was young then, barely sixteen, working on the farm, like I said. I saw the sailboat once or twice. She was a beauty. *Darling Marilyn,* they called her. Alice Ashwood was a beauty as well. You noticed them, her and this group of beautiful girls. You couldn't help but notice them."

"Was she a good sailor?"

"Oh, yeah, she sailed circles around a lot of the guys in town who fancied themselves experts. It was a shame, that's for sure. People talked about it for years. The husband survived—Michael Ashwood—because he was on a business trip that weekend."

"And the husband abandoned everything?"

"Seems so. Grief-stricken and all. He moved on, probably intending to come back, but we never saw him around again."

"Who owns it now?"

The man shrugged. "I'd reckon someone in the Ashwood family. I never heard of it goin' up for sale."

~

Adam returned home to find Holly napping on the couch. He changed the bulb in the pantry and then pried open the trap door that led into the crawlspace. The dirt floor was dry, which was good, but cramped and claustrophobic. Adam hunched down and set the trap. He climbed out of the hole, closed the door, and checked on Holly one more time. She was still sleeping soundly. He slipped out the door and cut a path toward the Ashwoods' house.

5

1956

10 Days Before the Sail

Unlike most of the girls who lived at the Ashwoods' house, Mildred didn't have a nickname. They simply called her Mildred, not Millie, as she'd attempted more than once to fashion for herself by signing her cards 'Millie' with a flourish or even referring to herself in the third person: *Millie's happy to help set the table or feed the horses.*

Still, everyone persisted in calling her Mildred, which sounded like both 'mildew' and 'dread.' Not an ounce of romance existed in such a name. How then could she ever live up to any romantic potential? There were no film actresses called Mildred, no princesses, no stars.

Even in the books she devoured, rarely did she discover a character who reflected her either in name or personality. Even the wallflowers, the shy girls with their noses stuffed in a book, were beautiful, or magic, or secret heiresses to wealthy fortunes. Mildred was none of those things.

All the other girls had pretty nicknames. Margaret was Margie, Florence was Cocoa, Nellie was Nell. Even Bertha, whose name seemed a blight on any woman's reputation, was Bitsy. All the girls, save

Mildred, had a fun, special name that lent a certain intimacy to the friendships.

Even Mrs. Ashwood used the pet names on the girls or made up her own. She'd even embroidered their special pillows with their nicknames. But again, Mildred stayed just plain, dull, sad, sloppy, no-good Mildred. But she was good. She was good at collecting things, mostly secrets. She was helpful, pointedly so, and she always volunteered to wash the supper dishes and muck the horse stalls and to skip her free time on Saturday to grade the other girls' papers if Alice didn't have time. Perhaps most important of all, she was smart. But no one noticed. No one saw all the things she did.

In the books she read, girls like Mildred always had someone on their side. The hard-nosed teacher who recognized the secret genius in the quiet homely pupil who sat in the back of class. The son of the duke who saw through the girl's frumpy clothes and plain face to the jewel beneath.

Not for Mildred. No one took a special liking to her. She understood the saying that the opposite of love was not hate but indifference.

She would have almost preferred the girls to pick on her—to single her out as the ugly one, the dull one—but they never did. Some days they brushed past her as if she didn't exist at all, as if she were little more than a ghost passing them in the hall. But no, even a ghost would elicit a response, a startled look, a gasp. Mildred inspired no reaction at all.

Mildred peeked through the cracked door into Nell's bedroom. Nell sat on her bed, legs bent, her diary propped on her knees. Her silky dark hair cascaded over her shoulders. Mildred felt a tremor of jealousy.

"Nell, look at this stone I found," Mildred announced, pushing into the room and opening her furled fingers to reveal a glittering blue pebble. "Doesn't it remind you of the sea? I've only seen the ocean in pictures, of course. I've heard Cocoa went to the ocean as a child, but I've never seen any photographs, so it may not be true. Have you seen any photographs? Don't you think this is the exact color?"

Nell barely looked up from the journal she wrote in with a lovely gold pen. After Mildred continued, Nell shot her an exasperated look.

"Mildred, can't you see I'm writing? I would like some privacy, please."

Mildred, wounded, smiled brightly. "Oh, sure, yes. I didn't even realize you had your journal there all tucked up behind your knees like a secret treasure. What do you write in there anyway? Letters home, or are you musing about your hopes and dreams? I like to write too, but sometimes my thoughts spill so quickly I can't catch them with my hand. I'll write like the devil's on my tail for an hour and then I go to read what I've written and realize I've just scribbled bits and pieces of my thoughts and it's hardly a story at all, simply a big mixture of half words and exclamations."

Nell sighed loudly, but didn't meet Mildred's eyes.

"I've read the entire collected works of Charlotte and Emily Brontë. They were writers, and voracious readers, of course. You can't truly be a writer if you're not a reader, wouldn't you say?"

Nell said nothing. She bit her lip and her pen was poised over her diary, but she'd not written a single word since Mildred entered her room.

Mildred stepped closer, angling to see what Nell revealed in the pages, but the girl slammed the book shut and gave Mildred a pointed look.

Mildred shrugged and backed toward the door. "Okay, well, never mind. Maybe later you can look at the stone and perhaps we can all go down to the beach. I heard Margie talking about playing Scrabble this evening and I think Mrs. Ashwood is making ham for dinner, which is just divine. I love ham the most out of all the meats."

Mildred had barely made it through the doorway when Nell jumped up and practically slammed the door in her face. There were no locks, but she heard Nell dragging a chair across the room and stuffing it under the knob. Though Nell shared the room with Cocoa, the two girls seemed to have a sixth sense regarding when the other wanted to be left alone.

"How rude," Mildred sniffed, sulking back down the hall to the narrow set of stairs that led to her own room in the attic.

Alice Ashwood listened to her husband on the porch swing. Six, seven bottles of beer down. They clinked together as he rocked.

Chink… chink… chink.

A sound that could drive her mad, drive her to do things no sane woman would do. How much could any one woman take?

What was the final straw after nearly twenty-five years of a sham marriage, the loss of a child? His leaving their bed to slip off to some other woman's apartment, some motel, some midnight rendezvous in the backseat of his car.

"Women," she muttered, shaking her head because that was giving him more credit than he deserved. They weren't women, not all of them. Girls, little more than girls.

Perhaps Alice had been destined for life with an unfaithful man. Her mother and her mother before had been submissives to their domineering husbands, men who tilled the soil, reached into the bitter earth and dug out stone and sand in search of the black dirt that might give rise to a crop to feed their family for a year. It rarely did. There was no tilling bad ground, but they were stubborn men who, once rooted, refused to pull up and seek life down the road. They dug deeper and deeper, drank moonshine, and used their fists to quell their raging resentment of a land that never wanted to give back.

Alice could not remember her mother without a black eye, without a purple yellowing bruise on her shoulder where her father had grabbed her and squeezed and squeezed until Alice thought that little bone in her mother's shoulder would snap. A chicken bone, she called it when she gave Alice and her brother a bath, tickling their shoulders and necks, a wishbone.

Alice had wished on the bone often, touching it as she lay in bed, wishing for another life, for a wealthy man to take her away from her sad, insignificant life. Sometimes Alice touched the bone and marveled at how fragile it was. How had her father not broken her mother's in two? How had it borne the brunt of his fury?

Perhaps her wishes had been granted, for Michael had come along with his winning smile and his big ambitions. He wasn't a farmer, but a businessman who'd provided Alice with all the things she'd believed mattered.

But that had been before… before she'd had Marilyn and understood that nothing mattered more than her daughter. And then Marilyn had disappeared and all the joy had left the world.

Even before Marilyn vanished, Michael had been unfaithful, but Alice had turned a blind eye. He'd always come back to her. Men were predictable that way, but women were not. They wore a mask of calm, of placidity, as people saw it, but beneath the surface a maelstrom was forming, spinning and gathering its strength. It could haul a ship to the sea floor if it unleashed its deadly wrath.

6

Adam stepped across the invisible barrier between the forest and the yard of the large abandoned house. Unlike most lawns, no clear distinction divided wild from civilization in this place. The forest spilled out, took back what had once been hers.

Vines slithered onto the porch; waist-high weeds grew through the spokes of a bicycle leaning against a tree. Bulbous white mushrooms grew from the rotted wood at the base of the house.

Some urge compelled Adam forward—a sensation he would have been unable to find the pulse of even if he'd paid attention to it.

His heavy boots sank into the sagging wood porch steps and he tried to move lightly for fear of falling through a rotted board. Adam tore at the vines that devoured the front door. He ripped the vegetation away and came to boards nailed crisscross over the entrance.

He hesitated for only a moment. Someone had closed this house off, didn't want people inside.

He set his jaw and jerked off one side of the top board. It tore away easily. The opposite side stuck, and he gritted his teeth and yanked hard. The board came off, nails poking like rusted fangs. He dropped it behind him and started on the board beneath. This plank refused to budge. He shook and tugged at it. It broke loose suddenly, and Adam stumbled back, tripping over the uneven boards and landing on his backside. A sharp poke stabbed through his forearm. He whipped his arm away and looked down to see he'd punctured it on one of the rusted nails. Blood oozed from the wound and he used his t-shirt to blot it.

It stung. He needed to go home, rinse it with peroxide, and cover it with a bandage. He probably needed a tetanus shot. Instead, he held it against his shirt until the bleeding stopped.

He stood and reached for the handle on the door, expecting it to be locked, to have another barrier to enter, which might prompt his better sense to kick in. It turned easily and, with a little push, the heavy wooden door swung into the murky interior.

Don't go in.

The thought arose, and he overrode it as quickly as it appeared.

Soft floorboards groaned beneath his footfalls as Adam stepped into the foyer. A long dark hallway stretched before him, a mildewed rug ran the length. Dust bunnies and mouse poop speckled the floor. The mice had left trails of their sharp little footprints in the dust.

Adam turned into a sitting room, furnished haphazardly, as if someone had taken a few pieces, but left most of it behind. A settee upholstered in faded pink fabric faced the hollow of a long-cold fireplace. The fabric was streaked and dirty, and the legs were pocked as if an animal had chewed the wood. Other chairs and a larger couch were angled toward an empty corner where the wood floor had faded. Adam suspected a television had stood there.

Paintings of sailboats hung from the walls, some of them drifting on tranquil waters and others getting tossed in storm-racked seas. He wondered if any of the images portrayed the sailboat the Ashwoods had capsized in.

Adam moved back into the hall and through an archway that led into the kitchen. The kitchen cabinets, once painted an eggnog color, flaked to reveal dark wood beneath. The wallpaper, a medley of lemons, limes and other fruits, peeled in curls from the wall. A large round kitchen table stood in front of a bay window. A vase, thick with mold, that might have once held water and flowers created a disturbing centerpiece.

Adam opened a drawer filled with cobwebbed silverware. Another drawer contained spatulas and wooden spoons. A third drawer held a stack of letters in yellowed envelopes.

The cupboards contained dishes. The vintage refrigerator held a can of coffee and a box of baking soda.

As he moved through the kitchen, eyeing the contents, a veil of disquiet settled over Adam. He stared at the single white coffee mug in the sink, a silver spoon resting inside it. Had it been the last cup of coffee ever sipped in the house?

A family had occupied the now empty chairs, a wife had cooked at the stove, a husband and a group of girls had eaten at the table. He ran a finger along the counter, examining the coating of fine dust on his fingertip.

The house was a time-capsule, largely preserved save for the grime and the havoc wreaked by whatever animals had gotten inside. He could almost imagine stepping back fifty years into the kitchen with sun streaming through the window and the smell of bacon sizzling in a frying pan. It seemed so wrong, this place, the contents of all those lives simply abandoned.

Adam returned to the hall and walked deeper into the house. Besides the living room, the first level held a study that also appeared to serve as a game room. A tall bookshelf held stacks of board games, along with a set of encyclopedias butted by ivory bookends. A desk, clear except for an amber-shaded lamp, faced a window overlooking the backyard and pool. Two loveseats occupied the room, along with a round wooden table surrounded by matching chairs. Beside the window stood a tall china cabinet. Double glass doors protected stacks of delicate-looking plates and teacups.

A bathroom and laundry room were the final two rooms on the lower level. Tiled in the unpleasant avocado-green color that had been popular at the time, the bathroom was large with a deep bathtub, double vanity and toilet. The laundry room held old-fashioned laundry basins. A wooden table sat next to the machines, a stack of folded women's clothing on top.

Adam returned to the hall and paused at the stairway. Yellowed photographs hung on the wall. The largest was a wedding photo depicting a handsome couple flanked by family. The bride wore a layered white dress, the long train held up by a woman with a brittle smile. The bride looked no more than nineteen or twenty, fresh-faced with long golden hair. The groom wore black. He was tall with a square jaw and blue eyes. They were an attractive couple, her petite and shiny, him tall and chiseled. The family surrounding them seemed to fade from their brightness.

There were photos of horses and photos of girls lined up in pretty dresses. Each photo seemed to include different girls, and he thought of how the man at the hardware store had described the home as a finishing school for girls. He wondered which group of girls had been on the sailboat that fatal day.

Adam walked up the stairs, each wooden plank groaning beneath his heavy footfalls. A net of spiderwebs caught him in the face and he recoiled, swiping them away.

He stepped into the first bedroom. It contained two neatly made twin beds on opposite sides of the room. Matching wood nightstands and dressers were also twin sets. Stuffing from a mattress trailed onto the floor. On each bed, an embroidered pillow stated a name. One pillow read 'Cocoa,' and the other said 'Nell.'

On the dresser next to Cocoa's bed sat a round silver jewelry box. A white plastic disk decorated in red flowers adorned the top. Adam lifted the lid, and a melody played from the small box. A jumble of costume jewelry lay inside. Like the downstairs, the upstairs held furniture and personal belongings. Mildewed clothes hung in the closet and lay neatly folded in dresser drawers. Colored perfume bottles stood along the edge of Cocoa's dresser. Nell's nightstand and dresser were clean except for a single photograph in a tarnished silver frame. A woman wearing a polka-dot dress stood beside a new-looking Buick Skylark.

He returned the photo to the nightstand and wandered into the next room. It was a carbon copy of the first—two twin beds, two dressers, two nightstands. The pillows on these beds read 'Margie' and 'Bitsy.'

The third bedroom was larger than the others, with a four-poster bed. Beneath one window stood an antique Singer Sewing Machine, black with gold lettering.

It was nearly identical to the sewing machine that once stood in his aunt's bedroom, passed to her by his grandmother. After his aunt died, it had moved to his house. Adam's mother had chosen a spare bedroom for the machine. More than once, he'd carried his G.I. Joes into the room and used the machine as a tank heading into battle, putting one man in charge of maneuvering the large wheel on the back of the machine. Adam hadn't seen one since the day over twenty years before when he'd watched one of his mother's friends carry the sewing machine out of his house and drive away.

Adam gazed around the rest of the room, wallpapered in pale blue paper lined with rows of tiny white flowers. The wallpaper peeled from one wall and lay on the wood floor. One strip of wallpaper lay curled over a dresser. Adam gripped the edge of the paper and ripped it free, letting it drift down. Framed photographs lay on their sides on the surface. A single candle melted to a stub stood in a pressed aluminum dish.

He opened the top drawer of the dresser to reveal women's undergarments, once white, now faded and yellowing. In the drawer's corner, he spotted a stack of photographs, but didn't take them out.

What he was doing was wrong, searching through the belongings of long-dead women, and yet he couldn't bring himself to leave the house.

Adam moved to the closet, opened the door and peered again with wonder at the rod filled with hanging clothes. Pleated full-skirt dresses, wool and knit cardigans and silk blouses occupied the space. Shoes stood in a line beneath the clothing. One side of the closet stood empty save for a wool suit coat and a single man's white dress shirt.

"Bizarre," he murmured, easing the door shut.

The husband had taken most of his own clothing, it seemed, but his wife's items remained, as did the belongings of most of the girls.

Adam turned back to the room. An end table stood on each side of the bed. He walked to the table that held a glass, empty. He picked it up and thought he could see a smudge of pink on the rim of the clear glass. The place where lips had last touched it, probably Alice Ashwood's lips.

A sound echoed up from downstairs and Adam jumped, dropping the glass. It struck the edge of the nightstand and shattered. He leapt back as bits of glass skittered across the wood floor.

The noise came again, and he hurried to the door and listened. It sounded as if someone were retching. Someone was not only in the house; they were throwing up.

7

Adam ran down the hall and took the stairs two at a time. In the distant back of his mind he thought he could be in trouble for trespassing, that he'd be better to go out the window than face the person in the house, but the upheavals were violent and followed by a woman's moans.

Adam skidded on a threadbare rug at the bottom of the stairs and caught the banister before he went down on his butt. He turned for the living room where he was sure the gagging originated. He rushed in and scanned the room, but saw no one.

"Hello?" he called out. "Please don't be afraid. My name's Adam Tate. I own a house nearby. I didn't mean to break in." Obviously, he *had* meant to break in, but he couldn't think of what else to say.

No one stood up or slipped out from behind a doorway. The gagging had stopped, and a muted quiet fell over the house.

Legs trembling, heart thundering in his chest, Adam moved from the living room into the kitchen. "Hello?" he called again, expecting at any moment a woman to step from a room, to respond or, worse, get sick again.

No one. He walked warily from room to room, peeking behind doors, but found no sign of her.

Everything in the house looked eerily the same. Nothing at all seemed changed. Even the front door, which he'd left slightly ajar, seemed open the same amount.

Disturbed, Adam returned to the front porch. The heat of the day enveloped him. He walked down the steps and scanned the yard, but saw no sign that a person had been there.

He thought of the vomiting and imagined Holly at home. Could it have been Holly getting sick? And somehow, he'd sensed it? Heard it in that strange way he sometimes detected when something was wrong with his wife?

He broke into a run, smashing through the woods back to his own property. Adam was halfway across his lawn when he spotted Holly lying in the grass beneath the shade of a drooping maple. Legs crossed at the ankle, head propped on a crumpled-up blanket, she stared into the tree above her. Marshmallow lay beside her, head resting on his front paws. Adam slowed and stopped, panting, watching her.

Holly reached for a glass and propped herself up on her elbow for a sip. She looked up and smiled.

He waved and started over, forcing his breath to slow, wiping quickly at the sweat beading on his hairline.

"Getting some fresh air?" he asked her.

"Getting to know the earth in this place," she told him. She patted the grass. "Sit with me. I'll make salad and we can have a lazy afternoon. Where did you wander off to?"

He sat, but his eyes trailed toward the path that led to the Ashwoods' house. "Just poking around in the woods." He didn't tell her about the house. "I'll make the salad," he said.

"Oh, no, you don't." She bounced to her feet too quickly, and put a hand against the tree.

He stood, but she shook her head. "Sit your butt back down, Adam Tate. You're going to relax today if I have to staple your pants to the ground. Now lie back and marvel at the maple leaves. You won't believe how each one has its own little quirk."

Before she walked away, he grabbed her hand. "Are you feeling okay today, honey? Light-headed?" Dizziness, shortness of breath, swelling feet, nausea. All potential signals that her body was rejecting the new heart.

"I feel great. If I didn't know what I know, I'd think everything in this body was healthy as a horse."

"Okay. Good." He kissed the back of her hand.

Holly walked into the house, Marshmallow trailing behind her.

Adam picked up a fallen maple leaf, but he didn't contemplate its beauty. Instead, he found himself back in the Ashwoods' house startled by the sound of a woman vomiting downstairs. The sound had been unmistakable. Someone had been in the house and they'd been terribly ill and yet... there'd been no one at all.

What could have caused the noise? Some kind of animal who'd taken up residence in the walls? He considered a bird. He'd encountered a few with strange cries. The forlorn screech of the barn owl had scared him more than once as a child when he'd gone to visit his grandparents. Ravens were said to have dozens of cries, including the ability to mimic human sounds.

Holly returned with two bowls of salad, and Adam stood to help her. She wrinkled her forehead, gazing at his arm. He'd forgotten he'd stuck it on the nail and the memory of it caused an immediate throbbing pain.

"What happened? You got hurt?"

"Jabbed it on a stick out there." He hooked a thumb back toward the woods.

"I'd say we better move this lunch inside then." She started back toward the house. "Come on. We'll get you patched up."

She cleaned the wound with peroxide and put a bandage over it. Her fingers moved deftly across his arm, and his eye caught on a ring Holly wore on the middle finger of her right hand. A white stone sat in a nest of silver leaves and vines on a twisted band. Adam stared at it, frowning. It took a moment for the memory of where he'd seen the ring to come back. It had been on the bony finger of a skeleton he'd discovered when digging the foundation for the house.

Holly noticed his gaze and wiggled her fingers. "Isn't it pretty? Mother of pearl. It looks like an antique. I found it in the yard this afternoon, came in and polished it with toothpaste. It looks brand new."

Adam wanted to insist she take the ring off, but knew how the demand would sound. He'd told Holly nothing about the unmarked graves and he would not tell her now that they'd moved in. His window for revealing the secret had passed.

Each day he'd withheld the discovery was another nail in the proverbial coffin. The thought almost made him laugh out loud. Imagine how much work it would have been if the skeletons had been in coffins? He'd have been digging for days.

He frowned, wondering for the first time why they hadn't been in coffins.

"It's like looking into the reflection of moonlight on a lake," Holly said, rubbing her thumb across the pale stone.

"It is," Adam said, but he shifted his gaze away from the ring. He didn't want to look at it for another moment.

~

"It's too hot to work around the house," Holly announced the next day. She held up a bowl of bright lemons. "I'm making lemonade and sandwiches and we're going to the beach."

Adam yawned. "The beach, huh?" He glanced at the pile of mail he'd picked up from their PO box several days before.

"Nope." She swept over and stuffed it in a folder. "Don't even look at it. We're having a beach day."

"Can I have coffee first?"

She grinned. "I guess we can make time for that."

~

Sand blazed beneath his feet as Adam trundled to where Holly stretched towels and jabbed a bright turquoise umbrella into the sand.

Two dozen other camps of sun-worshippers dotted the beach. They played music and drank cans of pop and beer from floating coolers. A teen boy with white-blond hair ran along the frothy water's edge, jumped on a wooden board and skimmed across the glassy surface.

Voices, waves, the far-off cries of a beach volleyball game offered a backdrop of sound.

"Did you get the lemonade?" Holly called, tilting the brim of her wide straw hat to reveal starlet-sized sunglasses perched on her freckled nose.

He held up the metal canteen. "Got it."

Adam climbed under the umbrella and squatted, half-falling into the too-low beach chair. The canvas sagged beneath him all the way to the lumpy sand and he wondered about the point of a chair that left its occupant sitting on the sand with only a swath of fabric between butt and beach. He didn't mention this to Holly, who looked fiercely happy.

Holly's illness had formed her into a person who reveled in the small things—the smell of rain-soaked grass, the softness of Marshmallow's fur. She saw every sunrise and sunset as a reason to celebrate. Adam wanted to feel Holly's joy, but when it arose within him, the fear of the pain that followed caused him to shy away from it.

"How's your arm?" she asked, gesturing at the white bandage covering his forearm.

His eyes flitted over the ring she still wore and he looked away. "It's better, I think." It did feel better, though he vaguely remembered it pulsing the night before.

"Look," Holly murmured. She gestured toward the water's edge where a toddler girl in a ladybug bathing suit waddled down the beach. Her mother and father trailed her. As she walked, her dark curls bounced. She bent to pick up a stone and nearly toppled over, saved from a face full of sand by her father, who reached out and grabbed the straps on her swimsuit to steady her.

"She's a beauty," Adam said, sensing that Holly, like him, was thinking of the children they'd never have—children that were impossible because of Holly's heart condition.

Adoption, fostering—there were options, but the hourglass was ever-present, sand slipping down faster than seemed possible. How much time was left, they did not know—could not know, but both he and Holly suspected it was far less than even the doctors told her.

"I've been searching for the words to describe this peach," she said, holding up a plump, round peach. "It reminds me of summers at my nana Hazel's farm. Every morning she'd pick peaches fresh from the tree in the back yard and slice them into a bowl. She'd add a dollop of chilled hand-whipped cream. They were fragrant and juicy and the perfect texture, somewhere between firm and soft with that velvet skin. They melted in your mouth. I bit into this a moment ago and it transported me back. It was so good I closed my eyes for a second and half expected to open them and be back at the grooved wooden table with my bare feet dangling above the yellow linoleum as Nana Hazel watched my face to see my reaction after the first bite. Here." She extended the peach to Adam.

"I want you to enjoy it. You're loving it."

"And I love you. My pleasure in this peach will be tripled by sharing it with you. Much like it was for my nana."

Adam took the peach, so soft and fragile his fingers immediately dented it. He lifted it to his lips.

"Close your eyes," she told him. "And tell me the first word that pops into your head when you take a bite."

He let his eyes drift closed and bit into the peach, barely needing to chew the flesh of the fruit as it dissolved on his tongue.

"Exquisite," he whispered, knowing his own description paled in comparison to hers.

Holly chose the perfect words to encapsulate a moment. She described stars as glittering immortality, chocolate as smoky, bittersweet bliss, and campfire smoke as the spirits of the trees rejoicing in being set free.

Adam had begun to find such experiences aching—the wonder of Holly's words had become tinged with sorrow, with missing Holly even though she was not yet gone. He felt terribly guilty for the reaction, as if he were awaiting her death, squandering the time he had by grieving what would one day become absent. He knew the hole would be gaping, unfathomable, and when the abyss rose in his mind, he wanted to grab Holly and crush her against him and try to somehow change her destiny—both of their destinies.

The sweet fruit slipped down Adam's throat and he knew from then on, whenever he ate a peach, he would imagine Holly as a child dipping a spoon into a bowl of fresh peaches and cream as her nana Hazel looked lovingly down at her.

"Ready for a sandwich?" Holly asked, patting the cooler.

He turned and shook his head. "Not yet."

Lake Huron stretched glistening and calm to the opposite horizon. Adam tried to imagine the sailboat that had carried a woman and a group of girls across the water. How close were they to the beach where he and Holly now sat? The wreckage, the bodies? How had they never washed ashore? The tides perhaps had taken them elsewhere.

"The sign in the parking lot said at its deepest point, this lake is more than seven hundred and fifty feet deep. Isn't that wild?" Holly asked, as if reading his thoughts.

Adam nodded, trying not to imagine the sunken sailboat resting in those icy black depths.

8

After they returned from the beach, Holly grabbed a book and headed out to one of the two hammocks Adam had hung between the line of maple trees at the edge of the property. Adam changed from his sandy shorts into mesh hiking shorts and a clean t-shirt.

"I wanted to run some errands. Do you want to come with?" Adam asked Holly.

She didn't open her eyes, draping her hand out of the hammock and giving the ground a little push to send her rocking. "Why don't you skip your errands and hop in that other hammock over there?"

"No, I'd feel better getting these things done. I've had enough relaxing today."

"Tell me about these oh-so-important errands."

"Well, for starters, I want to drive over to the Alcona Health Center and give them your file."

Holly opened her eyes. "I haven't even gone to an appointment yet. Can't we take the file when I go for my first visit?"

"I just want them to be aware ahead of time, just in case."

"Just in case I have a heart attack while I'm relaxing in a hammock."

"Holly, it's not a joke."

She smiled. "My mom liked to say leave the serious stuff for the taxmen and the reaper. All the rest of us should just enjoy the ride."

"Holl..."

"Honey"—she tilted her head to look at him—"you do what you

need to do, okay? I'm going to lounge in this hammock. If you want to be busy, be busy. I'll be fine right here."

"It's not that I want to be busy. I'll just feel better once we have a plan."

"Plans are for breaking, my love. Pick up some ice cream while you're out, will you?"

He sighed, wanting to argue with her, but also wanting her to enjoy her afternoon in the hammock. "What flavor?"

"I'm thinking something dark and decadent and so rich my toes curl when I take a bite."

He leaned to the grass and picked up her phone, checking that it was fully charged. "Okay, full battery. If you need anything call me, and don't… do too much. Okay?"

"Oh, don't worry. I don't intend to."

Adam drove to the health center with Holly's file and delivered it to the receptionist, who promised to give it to the doctor, asking him several times if he wouldn't have just preferred to send an email. He'd been hoping to speak to the doctor but learned the man was out of town until the following afternoon.

As he drove back toward home, he passed the small local library and abruptly swung his truck into the parking lot.

Neither he nor Holly regularly used the Internet. They'd never created personal social media accounts or laptop computers. They'd owned a desktop computer at the Daydream Café for accounting and a Facebook page, but they'd sold it when they sold the business.

Unlike most libraries, this one was bustling. A group of elderly women sat at one table knitting and chatting. Another table held teenagers in what looked like a game of Dungeons and Dragons. The library was not large, contained to a single room with tables, a circulation desk at the front, and stacks of books running down the middle and lining the walls.

The librarian's desk stood empty, but as Adam made his way past the knitting ladies, a man with a name badge stopped him. "Welcome to Social Saturday. Are you here for the shipwrecks talk?"

Adam blinked at the man. "I'm sorry, the what?"

"Arnold and Julia Cooper. The marine archeologists. They're here today speaking on the shipwrecks in the Great Lakes in conference room B." The man gestured at a door. "Or did you need to check out a book?"

"Umm… no, or yes. I'd like to hear the talk. Can I just go in?"

"You sure can. They started about twenty minutes ago."

Adam slipped through the door into a dim rectangular room with three rows of cushioned metal chairs containing less than ten people. A man and woman stood at the front on either side of a projector screen. An eerie blue photo of a ship resting on a sandy floor was displayed.

"The SS *Regina* went down in what has been called the worst storm the Great Lakes has ever experienced," the man explained, clicking to another image. "Here's an image of her before that trip, which occurred on November 9th, 1913. The *Regina* started out going north from Point Edward, Ontario, when it ran into some of the largest waves ever recorded, as tall as thirty-eight feet high. This was a very large, very heavy ship. Two hundred and forty-nine feet long, weighing one thousand nine hundred and fifty-six tons. The captain attempted to make it to a safe port, but could not do so. The crew anchored and got some lifeboats in the water, but the ship ultimately capsized and sank. Though some of the crew made it into lifeboats, none of them made it to safety. There were zero survivors from the SS *Regina*."

The woman stepped forward as the image changed to a grainy photo of a rusted hunk of a ship in the blue-green water. "The *Regina* was not discovered for more than seventy years. A Canadian firm funded the team of divers, some of whom were from right here in Michigan. They discovered the ship between Lexington and Port Sanilac, Michigan, in nearly eighty feet of water. It was an astounding find, and they salvaged more than ten thousand artifacts, including some items you see pictured here." The image on the screen changed again. A line of vintage glass bottles filled the screen. "These are full intact bottles of champagne and Scotch, which were found on the ship."

The presentation continued for another half hour, and Adam listened, rapt. Nearly all the shipwrecks had been caused by volatile weather.

When they concluded, the husband-and-wife duo announced they'd be selling signed paperbacks in the library. Adam trailed out with the rest of the group but lingered outside the door. When Arnold and Julia stepped out, he stopped them.

"Hi, great talk today. That was really informative."

"Thank you," they both said.

"It's been a passion of ours for many years," Julia explained. "We're finally at an age where we have time to write the books and do these speaking engagements. We dreamed about it for a long time, but work and children took precedence."

"Do you mind if I ask a quick question about something?" Adam asked, noticing several attendees of the talk queued at a table stacked with paperback copies of the Coopers' books.

"I'll get started over there," Arnold told Julia.

"Sure, what would you like to know?" she asked.

"Well, there's a bit of a mystery in these parts. Maybe you guys have heard of it. A sailboat carrying a group of women disappeared off the coast here in Lake Huron in 1956."

"Really. It disappeared?"

"Well, they went out for a sail and neither the boat nor any of the women were ever seen again."

"Did they run into foul weather?"

"It doesn't seem so. The forecast for the weekend was pretty calm according to locals."

"Hmm… that is strange, isn't it? There are many boats that have wrecked and never been found. That always adds a hint of mystique, but nearly all of them succumbed to the elements. The Great Lakes are a force to be reckoned with."

"But is there any reason a sailboat would go down on a perfectly nice day?"

"There are many reasons. It might have been taking on water through a hole. It might have run aground or hit some piece of debris. There might have been some issue in the boat's structure."

"But if the boat was taking on water, the women on board should have had plenty of time to signal for help."

"That's true and, in most cases, that's what happens, but we can never account for how people will react in such instances. People panic. They might all climb into a lifeboat rather than calling for help. Their radio might have been damaged or not working."

"But none of them ever washed ashore. No sign of the boat or the lifeboat."

"I wish I could offer more guidance, but…" She shrugged. "Part of what drew both myself and Arnold to underwater archeology was the mystery at the heart of these shipwrecks. There's something about being out on these giant bodies of water that makes you realize how powerless we are. I accepted a long time ago there would always be catastrophes that defied logic. Someday the sailboat will likely be recovered, and that's when the answer will come. Until then... there's only the mystery."

"Thanks, I appreciate your taking the time to talk with me."

"My pleasure. If you ever find out, send me an email. I'd love to hear the story." She produced a business card from her bag and handed it to him. He slid it into his back pocket and walked to the circulation desk where the man who'd greeted him earlier sat.

"Do you have computers for public use?"

"Yes, we do. Follow row A to the end and there are three computers in the back. I believe only one of them is occupied."

"Thanks."

Adam walked to the back of the library and sat at one of the empty kiosks. He opened an internet browser and typed in 'Alice Ashwood sailboat, Michigan.'

A single news article, archived in the *Alpena News* from August 16th, 1956, came back.

The headline read 'Sailboat Still Missing.'

The search resumes for the missing sailboat named Darling Marilyn, *which vanished somewhere off the shores of Lake Huron on last weekend.*

Michael Ashwood, the owner of the boat, contacted local police on Monday when his wife Alice and the five girls on board, wards of the Ashwoods, did not come back from their weekend of sailing. He had been out of town on business the Friday they sailed and expected them home on Sunday. Assuming they'd docked late and stayed on the boat for an additional night, he didn't contact authorities until the following day, last Monday.

Bill Jessop, Kurt Jones and Ralph Thompson, stationed at the Coast Guard station, executed a search by water. Local police and rescue did a ground search on the shoreline for evidence of the boat. There have been no signs of the Darling Marilyn *or her passengers.*

Forecasts over the weekend of the sail did not indicate high winds or stormy weather and Alice Ashwood was reportedly an adept sailor.

Searches will continue through the upcoming weekend.

Adam found only one more article that referenced the disappearance of the *Darling Marilyn*.

'Boat Sinks on Anniversary of *Darling Marilyn*'s Vanishing.'

A small boat capsized and sank Tuesday morning approximately two miles from the shore of Alpena. An ominous occurrence, as yesterday marks the one-year anniversary of the disappearance of the sailboat Darling Marilyn, which vanished last year. Neither the sailboat nor any of her six passengers has ever been recovered.

Fortunately for the Hobart family, whose boat sank Tuesday, they were able to radio for help before their boat sank.

He scrolled past several articles about shipwrecks and then his eye caught on another headline.

'Police are seeking the public's help locating the family of Marilyn Ashwood, who vanished in 1946.'

Marilyn Lee Ashwood disappeared in the summer of 1946. Last year, skeletal remains were found in a mass grave in the Manistee National Forest. Based on a unique piece of jewelry, a locket engraved with the initials M.L.A, discovered with one skeleton, investigators believe the body belongs to the missing twelve-year-old Marilyn Ashwood. Police have been unable to locate her mother or father.

If you have any information about the Ashwood family, police ask that you please call the Manistee Police Department.

Adam read the article a second time. Marilyn Ashwood. It was possible that she was only a distant relative of Michael and Alice, but he didn't think so. After all, they'd named their sailboat *Darling Marilyn*.

As the librarian passed him, Adam waved to get his attention. "Excuse me."

The man veered away from the shelf he'd been walking towards. "Yes?"

"I'm looking into a sailboat that went down in Lake Huron in the fifties. Do you keep old newspapers from the area here at the library?"

"We do. Unfortunately we had a big fire in '67 and our entire archive was destroyed. You might go directly to the papers, but the trouble you'll likely find is a lot of the presses that were running back then closed up years ago."

Adam sighed. "Okay, thanks. Can I print a few things?"

"Yep. It's ten cents a copy. The machine there takes cash or cards." He gestured at the large printer abutting one wall.

Adam printed the few articles he'd found and headed for his truck.

9

1956

9 Days Before the Sail

Nell gazed into the garden where Mrs. Ashwood worked in a fury, tearing at the earth as if it had stolen her firstborn child.

Nell's sewing project sat discarded on the settee and, though she tried to focus on the important things, one thought shimmered and sparkled in her mind like a new bride flashing her diamond engagement ring. Michael Ashwood—no, not Michael, Mr. Ashwood. The girls weren't allowed to call him Michael.

Except Mr. Ashwood had kissed Nell, and he'd whispered in her ear, *Call me Michael,* and now she couldn't think of him as anyone other than Michael.

Like Archangel Michael, prince of the heavens, a healer and savior. Michael Ashwood with his hair the color of corn silk and eyes like the sky at dusk. He walked with purpose as he strode across the yard, his blue jeans clinging to his narrow waist, his shirt loose on his firm chest, or when he left the house during weekday mornings to do business things in his dark slacks and suitcoats. He was the protector of all the girls at the Ashwoods' house, but now he felt more like Nell's alone. He'd given her a piece of him and she'd given back.

Nell had always noticed Michael Ashwood. All girls of a certain age had, but she'd never considered him as a beau because he was a married man and one of her wardens.

Furthermore, Alice Ashwood was a beauty with dainty porcelain features, dazzling green eyes, and wispy blonde hair. They were a beautiful couple, the kind of couple that would be printed on the covers of magazines if they lived in Hollywood. Except they didn't live in Hollywood. They'd built their estate in the wilds of northern Michigan, tucked back in the woods. Still, it was not a rustic life. Horse stables, an in-ground pool, a beautiful house with lovely furniture, and then they'd opened it to others, to those less fortunate, to young women who needed guidance on their journey.

Nell was grateful for their generosity. She'd grown weak in the knees the first time she'd set foot on the Ashwoods' property, delivered there by her aunt and uncle, who perhaps wanted to keep her after Nell's mother's death, but simply couldn't afford to. Getting chosen by a couple like the Ashwoods was a gift from God himself. For over two years she'd lived there happily, peacefully, but now Nell's insides churned with desire and worry.

Michael Ashwood had kissed her, and she'd instantly fallen in love with him.

Nell picked at her needlework, but watched Alice, who'd stood, brushed the dirt from her apron, and gazed at the sky as if searching for some message in the feathery clouds. Her eyes sparkled in the sun and even in an old gardening dress, she dazzled.

As if sensing Nell's gaze, Alice swiveled and gazed at her. Nell blushed and looked quickly back at the wrap dress she'd been working on for weeks.

Nell, at seventeen, was beautiful too. She wasn't blind. She could see her shapely body, already formed, her thick lips and her deep-set brown eyes. Her hair was coffee-dark and brushed her waist. But the affections of men were alien to her. She'd never known her father. No close uncles or brothers. There'd been a distant grandfather she remembered vaguely from a visit when her mother needed money and they'd driven all night to Indiana and knocked at his door only to be turned away.

Nell remembered huddling there beneath her mother's flimsy spring jacket, rain pelting the tin roof of the man's house. He'd barely acknowledged his daughter, and he hadn't so much as glanced at the granddaughter he'd never met.

All her life men had been foreign. Until Nell turned thirteen and then, as if some internal machine switched on, her body had dramatically changed in a series of months. Breasts arrived, her period shortly thereafter. Her once-narrow waist grew thicker. She was still skinny by most standards, but now she had the shape of a woman. The baby fat on her face fell away and revealed cheekbones. It had been a startling transformation and one that was both welcome and disturbing.

Suddenly men noticed her, talked to her, went out of their way to open her door or engage her in conversation. She delighted in the attention, but at the same time found it hollow. None of the men cared for her. They flirted and wooed her, but they only half-listened when she spoke.

None of that mattered now, not since the kiss. A kiss that had happened so naturally, so divinely, as if it had been pre-ordained.

She'd been in the forest alone, writing in her diary.

"Nell." She'd heard his voice and paused, straightening up and turning to see Mr. Ashwood making his way through the high grass. He'd held a clump of daisies in his hand.

She had smiled shyly. "Hi, Mr. Ashwood." And she'd barely gotten the words out when he lifted her from the stump and pressed his mouth to hers.

"Call me Michael," he'd whispered as he let her go and then he'd run his hands through his hair as if shocked and ashamed at what he'd done. He'd apologized, said he didn't know what had come over him, but all the while she'd been standing on feet made of feathers. Her entire body had grown as buoyant as a balloon.

He'd confessed to her then that he'd wanted to kiss her for months, that he could think of no one but her. And as quickly as he'd arrived, he'd gone, disappearing back into the trees.

Nell's face burned at the memory and she looked up to see Alice hunched again in the garden, ripping and tearing at the weeds.

Giving up on the dress, Nell returned the sewing project to her room.

Cocoa lay stomach down on her bed, feet crossed at the ankle, reading a magazine.

"I'm going for a walk," Nell told her, sliding the unfinished dress into one of her bureau drawers.

Cocoa glanced up at her. "Sneaking off again, are we? Do you have some mysterious boyfriend you're meeting out in the woods? Some lumberjack?"

Nell's face flushed, and she reached back to push her hair behind her ears. "Very funny, Cocoa."

"Don't do anything I wouldn't do." Cocoa winked at her and returned to the glossy pages of her magazine.

Nell left the room and hurried down the hall.

It wasn't only the forbidden aspect that made Nell keep her lips tightly closed about the kiss. She also lived in terror that her joy would draw some karmic rebalancing. If she allowed herself to feel too happy about what had occurred, about the butterflies fluttering in her stomach, about the parade of daydreams that played across her vision each day, something, some force that had followed her since birth would steal in and rip it away.

Her mother had told Nell as much so many times it was as much a part of her as her brown hair or the circle of freckles on her left foot.

Bad luck follows you everywhere, Nell's mother had insisted at every tragedy both big and small. When they'd been rear-ended in her mother's new car, when their trailer burned, when men left; even stormy weather was blamed on Nell.

"You ain't comin'," Nell's mother had told her the last weekend of her life when she'd set off for the county fair to help with the cattle auction, "if the gods see you smilin' they'll unleash the rain and the whole day'll be ruined."

So Nell hadn't gone. She'd stayed home and counted the hours until her mother's return, refusing to eat the leftover casserole though her stomach grumbled, because her mother had promised to bring home a bag of cotton candy. Her mother had never arrived, and Nell had eventually fallen asleep on the rug in the living room, then been startled awake after midnight by two police officers. A stampede of cattle had crushed her mom. She'd died on the way to the hospital.

From that point forward, Nell knew her excitement and longing for the cotton candy had killed her mother just as sure as if she'd gone along to the fair.

She was misfortune waiting to happen, cursed perhaps, and bad galloped behind the good in her life as if it were its shadow.

Nell slipped out of the house through the back door, not wanting to encounter Alice in the garden. She moved first into the barn, inhaling the scent of the horses and the hay. It was a soothing smell, as was the sound of their snuffs as she walked along the stalls. She stopped at Spirit's door.

Out of the trio of horses the Ashwoods owned, Spirit was the Arabian. The other two were quarter horses. Spirit poked his bronze head over the door and Nell cradled it in her hands, rubbing his thick neck.

"Hi, Spirit," she murmured, resting her forehead against his.

He whinnied and she fed him an apple from a barrel. She gave the other horses, Barnie and Daisy, apples as well, and then continued out of the barn and into the woods.

Nell breathed the richness of the foliage at its peak. She returned to the place where Michael had kissed her and trailed her fingers through the fine tips of the yellow foxtail weeds. Her mother used to pick the stems when they'd taken walks during Nell's childhood. She'd tickle Nell's neck and ears. Nell picked one and closed her eyes, sliding the fuzzy tip down her forehead, over her nose and across her lips.

Something rustled, and she snapped her eyes open to find Michael approaching her.

He cupped Nell's face in his hands and kissed her. The kiss caused the world to tilt on its axis. She slipped sideways, and he grasped her, bracing one hand against the small of her back. Gently, he lowered her to the patch of soft grass. She lay back, confused, delighted, unsure of how to move, if she should stand up and run away.

"Mr. Ashwood," she murmured.

"Michael," he reminded her.

"Michael," she whispered, unable to speak his name at a normal volume.

He kissed her cheeks and forehead, moved down to her neck and collarbone.

"What about... Mrs. Ashwood?" She hated to say the woman's name, to break the spell, but fear of being discovered forced the words out.

"She's in the garden. After that she'll start dinner. It's just you and me out here, Nell."

"It's a sin, Michael," she whispered as his mouth moved lower, kissing her through her thin cotton dress.

He sat up, studying her with his thoughtful blue eyes. "Love is not a sin, Nell. It's the most beautiful thing. It's the only thing that matters. Has anyone ever loved you? Truly, deeply loved you?"

Her body was warm beneath him. She longed for him, for the weight of him. Tears spilled down her cheeks. "No," she whispered.

"Let me." He kissed her hard, crushing his mouth against her.

When he pulled away, he gazed at her, his eyes filled with something so extraordinary it took her breath away. For the moments that followed, seconds that spanned infinities, Nell felt seen for the first time in her life. Her heart expanded and bloomed and she thought it might burst inside of her.

He reached low and pulled her dress up over her head. She lay naked except for a pair of white cotton panties. Her flesh broke out in goosebumps and a voice in her mind urged her to cover her breasts with her arms, to curl into a ball and hide from his eyes. Surely, she did not compare to Mrs. Ashwood.

But when he lowered his mouth to hers, she forgot about her insecurities and gave in to the wants of her body.

Alice's grandmother Dahlia had believed people sensed the day of their death. Not in the specific, but in the larger wheel of time. Dahlia had insisted her son William, Alice's uncle, would die before his thirtieth birthday. And die he had at twenty-five years old one bleak February when he'd gotten disoriented in a snow storm and succumbed to the elements.

Dahlia would predict the year of her husband's death and finally her own, at sixty-eight from cancer. Hers was less otherworldly, as she'd been suffering from malignant tumors for years, but rumor in the family held that she would never die and when she did, much as she'd predicted, Alice had been as devastated as if the news had fallen out of a clear blue sky.

Dahlia had been Alice's port in the storm, the safe harbor. Alice's mother had been a distant, distracted woman so devoted to her abusive husband that she barely noticed her children. Alice's father was equally devoted, but to the bottle rather than his wife and children. And though Dahlia, too, had been a slave to her domineering, abusive husband, she'd never allowed him to steal her magic.

Alice had given only passing thought to her grandmother's premonitions over the years until the awareness of her own imminent death rose like a doomsday cloud, as ominous as the shadow of a great beast gliding beneath the surface of a tranquil sea. Just weeks earlier, Alice had seen this shadow and then it had slipped away, but it had left an impression.

Death has seen you, my dear, it seemed to say. *It has seen you and it is coming.*

Alice's eyes flicked to the porch where Nell had sat a short time before. The girl had gone, which suited Alice, who felt more and more that the girls in her care were not to be trusted. They pined for Alice's life, her home, her husband.

She gripped another handful of weeds and ripped them free. Alice imagined they were the adulterous threads tethered to her husband's heart or the covetous filaments crawling out from the bosoms of the girls. Alice tore them out and tossed them away.

Her hands ached, but she wouldn't stop. When she slowed down, the shadow pushed in, whispered in her ear.

I am coming.

~

Nell cried quietly into her pillow that night. She could not erase the memory of Michael in the meadow. The slick feel of his back beneath her hands. The things he'd whispered and then moaned into her ear. She wanted him despite the ache between her legs that came not from desire, but from the tearing when he'd entered her that day.

She was no longer a virgin, no longer pure, and the thought filled her with both dread and excitement.

Michael lay only rooms away, but it felt too far, desperately far, and she wanted to sneak into his room and climb into his bed and feel the warmth of his breath on her neck. It was an absurd fantasy. Michael slept next to Mrs. Ashwood. They were husband and wife.

Nell had committed an unforgiveable sin. She'd tempted him, caused him to stray, and for such a despicable act, she surely would be punished.

10

The Black Mountain Market was a small grocery store that catered to both the locals in the area and the tourists who came north to enjoy the Lakes in the summer. Adam parked and grabbed his wallet off the dashboard.

He rolled his head back and sighed when he stepped into the cool interior. Shopping cart in hand, he steered toward the produce, grabbing a watermelon, a bag of apples and two pre-packaged salad mixes.

Before the heart attack, Holly had always done the grocery shopping. She'd blamed this on his penchant to forget half the things on her list, but she'd also just enjoyed it. She regularly came home with strange items they'd never tried like pistachio halva or wasabi-flavored trail mix.

In the frozen aisle, he scanned the ice cream flavors before opening the door and leaning his entire head into the chilly enclosure.

"It's hotter than blue blazes out there," a southern voice boomed behind him.

Adam turned to see a tall man clad in jeans, cowboy boots and a Stetson hat. He looked like he'd just wandered in from a rodeo.

"Mind if I join ya?" the man asked, opening the freezer to Adam's right and leaning his lined face in. He closed his eyes and smiled. "I just about had a stroke gettin' from my truck to the store." He reached in and grabbed two pints of cherry chocolate ice cream.

Adam smiled. "Yeah, my dad likes to say it's so hot you could fry a pancake on the sidewalk."

The man laughed and slapped his leg. "I'm gonna remember that one." He extended a large tanned hand. "Ted Jackson."

"Adam Tate," Adam told him. "My wife and I just built a house up on Black Mountain Road. Do you live in the area?"

"Just off Ash Highway, 'bout three miles yonder." Ted pointed toward the front of the store.

"I guess we're neighbors then," Adam said. "Is that good? The cherry chocolate?" Adam gestured at the two pints in Ted's cart.

"So good, my wife and I each get our own container."

"That's an endorsement I'll trust." Adam took out a pint of the cherry chocolate ice cream.

The two men angled their carts toward the checkout.

"You're not a Michigan native, I presume? Accent and all," Adam said.

"Texan to my bones," Ted told him, popping the cowboy hat off his flop of graying hair. "We moved up here ten years ago, but I still think of San Antonio as my one true home."

"I've never been," Adam admitted. "Went to Dallas once on my way to Arizona to visit my dad, but that's as far south as I made it."

"Oh, you're missin' out, son. Put it on your bucket list. There's no place on earth like San Antonio. My wife would say I'm a bit biased, but I'm tellin' you true, it's one of a kind."

"I'll have to do that," Adam said.

He paid for his groceries and headed to his truck. As he started to get into the driver's seat, the Texan approached him again.

"It was a pleasure to meet you, Adam Tate. If you and the missus are looking for a new church, come on down to Touchstone Ministries. We've got a little Sunday service, all the coffee you can drink so long as you get there before Sal Moody, who hits the coffee maker a dozen times before the sermon starts."

"We're not really church-goers," Adam told him. "But I'll run it by Holly."

"That's a deal," Ted said. "And my wife would skin my hide if I didn't get your number so we can have you over for dinner."

Adam wrote down his number and handed it to the man, who folded it into his overstuffed wallet and then crammed the wallet into the back pocket of his Wrangler jeans.

"That'd be great," Adam told him. "Holly's a baker. She loves an opportunity to bring dessert."

"Well, that's a gal after my own heart. How's Friday night for ya? If it works, it will save me the call."

"Friday? Umm… I think so."

Ted chuckled. "I'll call tomorrow and confirm."

Adam climbed behind the wheel and pulled away. He thought of the man's invitation to join their church.

He hadn't wanted to tell the man that he no longer believed in God. That in the days after Holly's heart attack, he'd never believed in God so much in his life. Talked to him nightly, negotiated with him, begged him. Silence. He might as well have been pleading with a brick wall.

For a time, Adam had continued to pray and then it had dawned on him one afternoon as he watched Holly's body rejecting her first heart. They were all totally alone in this vast, uncaring world. If there'd once been a God, he'd abandoned them all long ago.

Adam had negotiated similarly as a child when his mother had died, but it had been different then. The ugliness of the world hadn't become fully visible. And then there were kind old ladies who told him tall tales like *God needed an angel* and *don't worry, she's always with you.*

Except she hadn't always been with him. She'd gone into the ground, and he'd never so much as heard her voice again.

Adam unloaded and put away groceries and then wandered through the rooms in search of Holly. She wasn't in the house. He found her in the side yard sitting on a stump a short way off from the hammock she'd been lying in that afternoon.

"How were the errands?" she asked.

"Good. I met someone."

"Not a buxom blonde, I hope."

"A tall Texan, actually. He invited us to dinner on Friday."

"New friends?"

"I think so."

Holly rubbed her fingers across the grooved wood in the stump. "The trees here are old," she told him, smiling. "Wrinkled and gray as if they've seen so much. They're watching over the saplings, imbuing their wisdom through a system of roots, like fingers holding each other's hands, growing old together. All their energies merging. The old giving nutrients to the young. Someday they'll collapse and their bodies will become the soil for the new life. The saplings will take root in their ancestors. It's so profound. Isn't it? The cycle of life?"

Adam smiled and rested a palm on a large beech tree, smooth in comparison to the oak, but still rough beneath his skin. "It is. Almost as marvelous as the way you describe it."

"Oh, no." She shook her head. "Words pale, they never do justice to the world."

"I wish I could see the world through your eyes," he told her, and then cringed. What a thing to say. "Hungry? I picked up some salad mixes. I could do some chicken on the grill?"

"Mm, yes, please."

Adam trailed behind Holly back into the house. He made chicken and salad and they ate on the back patio.

"What kind of ice cream did you get?" she asked after she'd popped the last bite of chicken into her mouth.

"Something the Texan recommended, chocolate cherry."

"Ooh, yum. Want some?"

"Nah, I'm good. I can get yours though."

She shook her head and stood. "Nope. I need to use the bathroom so it's a combined trip."

Adam propped his feet up on another chair.

A moment later, Holly stuck her head through the patio doorway. "Did you put the ice cream in the freezer?"

He grinned. "As opposed to the cupboard? You didn't see it? I put it right in the front." He stood and followed her back inside.

"Maybe I missed it," she said.

But when she opened the freezer door, there was no container of ice cream, though he was sure he'd set it right in the center where an empty space now stood.

"What the hell?" He opened the refrigerator and scanned the shelves. No ice cream there either.

"Adam..." Holly murmured.

"I swear I put it in the freezer," he said, shoving aside milk and yogurt in search of the little carton.

"I found it," Holly said.

Adam spun to see where Holly was pointing. The container of ice cream lay half in the pantry doorway on its side. Ice cream leaked from the lid onto the wood floor.

Holly grabbed a paper towel and started toward it.

"No… here, I've got it." Adam bent and scooped the container up, hurrying it to the sink. "Maybe it's not totally melted," he started, but when he pulled off the top, he recoiled. Dozens of black ants crawled through the melted ice cream.

"Oh, my God," Holly said, from behind him. "How on earth did those get in there? I mean, that ice cream's only been here for what, an hour?"

"I don't know." Adam dumped the ice cream and turned on the faucet, washing the ants and the ice cream into the food disposal. "I'm sorry, Holl. Want me to run back to the store?"

"Of course not," Holly said, rubbing his back. "It's only ice cream, babe. I'll have a handful of chocolate chips. Probably better not to eat a big bowl of ice cream, anyway." She kissed his shoulder and disappeared into the pantry, flicking the light on. It grew bright for a moment and then went dark. She flipped the switch several more times. "What in the world…?" she murmured. "We must be in a Mercury retrograde."

"A what?" He strode into the pantry and flipped the switch as well. Nothing. He reached up and unscrewed the lightbulb he'd just put in.

"Oh, you know, when the planet Mercury shifts direction. My mom used to tell me about it. Mercury goes retrograde and all the electronics malfunction. Really though, it's probably something with the wiring. Maybe we can get the electrician out here to fix it."

"Yeah…" Adam sighed.

Holly took a handful of chocolate chips from the bag and popped them in her mouth. "Don't sound so glum, my love. It's just a lightbulb." She squeezed his arm. "I, however, am in need of a nap. Care to join me?"

"No nap for me, but I'll tuck you in."

He followed her to the bedroom and Holly settled into bed.

"Did you turn up the air?" she asked.

"No, but I should. It's hotter than blue blazes out there."

She cocked an eyebrow. "Blue blazes, huh? Well, it's colder than a freezer in here."

Adam pulled the comforter to her chin and kissed her temple. "Are you feeling all right? No shortness of breath or anything?"

She shook her head. "I'm good. I promise. If anything feels off, you'll be the first to know."

"Okay. It's just... you've been sleeping a lot."

"Doctors' orders, remember? Lots of rest, naps, Marshmallow snuggles."

"Sweet dreams, honey."

"Are you going out?"

"Just for a walk."

"You're becoming quite a forest man, aren't you?"

He swallowed and scooted her over so he could sit beside her. "Not quite. I found an old house back there. It's been abandoned, and I've been poking around."

She frowned. "Well, don't step on a rusty nail. Those tetanus shots are a pain in the ass. Pun intended."

He grinned. "I promise I won't."

"Love you," she murmured, closing her eyes.

11

Adam stood at the edge of the yard and gazed at the house.

He had conflicting urges, a desire to go back in the house and an alternating desire to stay the hell away from it. He gave in to the former and hurried across the yard and up the steps before his nerve abandoned him.

The door swung in easily now, hinges groaning, the fight gone out of her. He stepped into the murky interior and drew in a breath of musty air that satiated him as if he'd been longing for it and the need had finally been fulfilled.

He stopped in the hall and looked at the wedding photograph. Surely this was Alice and Michael Ashwood. He imagined Alice, so petite, at the helm of a large sailboat. Adam touched the glass with his fingertip.

"What happened to you, Alice?" he murmured.

The mystery had gotten under his skin. He wanted to know more, not only about the sail, but about all of them, the Ashwoods and the girls who'd perished.

He went to the kitchen, opening the drawer where he'd previously seen a stack of letters. Adam plucked out the letters, three in all, addressed and sealed with little stamps in the upper corner. They hadn't been marked by the post office. They were ready to send but had never been mailed.

Chewing his lip, he contemplated what lay within the letters, and again, the oddness of them being left behind struck him. Moral code demanded he not open the letters. They belonged to someone else, but that someone else was long dead and he was here and now. He slid his finger beneath the flap of one envelope and pulled out a piece of pale pink stationery. It had a scent, something faded and floral. Adam thought whoever had written it had spritzed the letter with perfume before sliding it into the envelope.

August 9, 1956

Dearest David,

I am anxiously awaiting our rendezvous for Christmas in Detroit. The house has felt oppressive this summer, and it is not merely the heat. Angst and unrest fester amongst the girls as well as in our keepers, Michael and Alice Ashwood. It is a bit like living in a cage full of cats, hair raised, eyes glaring as they all parry and dodge around each other. Alice, in particular, has been out of sorts. The word 'hysterical' comes to mind.

I so long for the day when I can leave this place behind. It is odd to live in such a beautiful place with a grand home and property and still feel boxed in—trapped. I do so hope that Bill Haley and His Comets come back to Detroit next year for a show. I'd love to see him live at the Olympia Stadium.

I'll write again next week. I'm keeping this letter short because tonight we celebrate Nell's eighteenth birthday. I can't wait for you to meet her. I haven't convinced her to move with me to Detroit yet, but I'm close. She'd make a lovely match with your friend Marty.

Hugs and kisses. Can't wait to see you again.

Sincerely yours,

Cocoa

Adam re-read the letter and then set it aside. The next was not a letter at all, but a check payable to the electric company. The third was addressed to the Manistee County Sheriff's Office.

Dear Sheriff Boyd,

I have received your most recent letter and I am grateful that you continue to keep my girl in your prayers. I have recently come to the conclusion that my place in this world is closer to where she was last seen. Ten years have passed, and it is unlikely I will ever gaze upon her face again, but I believe my life would be better served walking in the places she last walked in. This house we built for her has lost its magic for me. I intend to relocate in the spring to Manistee, Michigan.

I look forward to becoming part of your small community.

Warm regards,

Alice Ashwood

Adam thought instantly of the article about the remains of twelve-year-old Marilyn Ashwood, discovered the year before in the Manistee National Forest. It seemed the Ashwoods had lost a daughter, and Alice had been planning to move closer to where the girl had disappeared. Oddly, the letter made no mention of Michael Ashwood joining her.

Curiosity piqued, Adam returned the letters to the drawer and headed for the stairs. He wanted to look at the photographs he'd noticed in the master bedroom, the bedroom that must have belonged to Alice and Michael Ashwood.

He started up the stairs, absent-mindedly gliding his hand along the banister. It came away coated in dust. He wiped it on his shirt.

Once in the bedroom, he returned to the dresser and opened the drawer he'd seen the photos in. A single piece of brown twine held the stack of pictures together. He untied it and studied the first image.

It included a group of girls, all teenagers, mostly pretty. A table covered in white linen and half-eaten chocolate birthday cake stood behind them.

He flipped it over and read. *Cocoa's eighteenth birthday. June 17, 1956. Cocoa (18), Nell (17), Mildred (16), Margie (15), Bitsy (17).* Adam assumed the numbers were the girls' ages. They had taken the photo two months before the sail.

Adam continued through the photos. The next showed the Ashwood couple in front of the house he now stood in, but the paint was still white and intact. A garden flourished at the side of the property.

Alice stood next to a dog, her hand buried in the scruff of its neck, face tilted down with a half-smile. Adam flipped it over and read *Alice and Michael Ashwood, summer 1954.*

More photos depicted younger versions of Michael and Alice Ashwood, but in these other photos a child accompanied them. Pretty, with blonde hair like her mother and blue eyes like her father. On the backs of the photos someone had written 'Michael, Alice and Marilyn,' along with accompanying dates. In 1939, Marilyn looked young, little more than six or seven years old. She sat on a lovely white mare, smiling brightly. Michael Ashwood stood beside her, one hand resting on the horse's flank.

Adam flipped through more photos of the little family, but there was not a single image of Marilyn after 1946, and Adam knew why. The girl had disappeared that year.

Adam returned to the drawer, a glimmer of shame crossing his thoughts as he moved aside panties and bras—the intimate things Alice Ashwood had once worn.

His finger caught on the corner of an envelope. He pulled out a letter which had previously been opened.

Dear Alice,

I am writing to inform you that sadly there have been no recent developments in the missing person's case of your daughter, Marilyn Ashwood. As you're aware, we have not conducted a formal search since 1946; however, I have taken it upon myself to organize a group annually for a volunteer search. We have created a grid of the Manistee National Forest and we search a new section each year.

My wife continues to light a candle for Marilyn at Mass every Sunday.

If there is any information relevant to Marilyn's disappearance, you have my word that you will be the first to know.

Sincerely,

Sheriff Boyd

Adam found no other documents in the drawer. He returned the photos and the letter and slid it closed.

He left the bedroom and stepped back into the hall. He'd gone in every room on the second floor except for the one at the end. He gazed at the closed door, his pulse quickening.

It was the knob that plagued him. Small and crystal with gold hinges.

A memory leapt to the forefront of his mind, one he hadn't thought of in years, had nearly forgotten. His aunt's door all those years ago, the door firmly closed and then he'd opened it...

"No," he blurted and shook his head to banish the memory. Children had a way of conjuring nightmares from nothing, and he wouldn't let those old phantoms distract him.

He put one foot in front of the other and took a quick breath as he grabbed the little knob and twisted. The door opened to a narrow set of stairs. An attic. As he ascended, fine streams of cobwebs caught in his hair and eyebrows. He pulled them away, keeping his lips closed, so they didn't get in his mouth.

Grainy sunlight streamed into the attic room from a small window at the opposite end. It wasn't a typical attic. Instead, it had been converted into a bedroom. A single twin bed sat wedged beneath the sharply sloping ceiling. A porcelain doll rested against a pillow embroidered with the name 'Mildred' at the head of the bed.

Adam shook his head, disturbed by the sight of the doll as he'd been disturbed by so many things in the house. The things that had once been precious to the girls who'd lived there, to the woman of the house, all left, discarded, rotting.

Adam's father had held onto his mother's belongings for years, only reluctantly giving them away to close friends and family after he married his second wife.

Adam surveyed a dresser that held novels and a small clock. The vanity was empty except for a hairbrush. He stepped toward it and shuddered. Strands of brown hair poked from the bristles of the brush.

He shifted back toward the bed, noticing the corner of a book poked from beneath the mildewed mattress. He lifted the mattress up and saw a copy of *Plants of Michigan* resting on the box springs.

Adam flipped through it. The pages were thick and warped, as if dampness had seeped into it. A single page had been earmarked. He studied the image there.

Atropa Belladonna stated the headline at the top. Drawings of a plant with green leaves and small purple black berries dotted the page.

Common names: deadly nightshade, belladonna

Warning: Poisonous! Both berries and foliage are toxic when consumed. If ingested this plant may cause delirium, hallucinations and even death.

Adam frowned at the description and then dropped the book on the mattress.

He started deeper into the attic and smacked his head on a beam in the low ceiling. Dark spots danced in his vision. He grunted and cupped a palm over the throbbing flesh that would likely be a big goose egg he'd have to explain to Holly.

As he turned back toward the door, he froze. A woman stood there. Dark liquid oozed from the corners of her mouth and dribbled down the front of her faded dress.

Her mouth opened and black liquid spewed onto the wood floor.

12

Adam gasped and leapt back, hitting the back of his head against the same beam he'd struck with his forehead. He winced and ducked, still shuffling backwards as his eyes blurred with fresh pain.

He expected to see the woman advancing toward him. But the narrow room stood empty. There was no woman, no black bile on the floor.

He sank slowly onto his knees, sitting back on his heels and putting a hand on his chest. His heart struck against his ribcage like a trapped bird trying to flee. He leaned forward and tried to catch his breath, closing his eyes against the ache reverberating through his head.

No woman had been there. He'd imagined her. The first smack to the head had called forth the fear he'd been harboring about the hallway in his aunt's house, the closed door at the end.

He shook his head, wincing at the flare of pain that accompanied the movement.

Gingerly, he climbed back to his feet. Gripping the banisters and walls for support, Adam descended first the attic stairs and then the main stairs, wondering vaguely if he'd hit his head hard enough to sustain a concussion. He'd had one once in high school when he'd slammed head on into another player during a soccer game. He'd gotten a concussion and the other guy had gotten a broken nose.

Adam stepped from the house, woozy, and walked on jelly legs down the steps. His head buzzed faintly. He moved around the exterior of the house, his eyes registering the shapes and shadows in the growing gloom. His gaze drifted past the pool, sludgy and stagnant, but then he whipped back, staring. Something large and pale floated in the murky water.

He couldn't make sense of it, but then as he stepped closer it took shape. White fur fanned out in the dingy water.

"No," he moaned. "Marshmallow."

Adam took a stumbling step and then ran, jumping into the stinking water. It was deeper than he'd expected, and he went under, head beneath the surface, nose and mouth filled with the sludge. He swam frantically, gulped air and pushed toward Marshmallow, Holly's beloved pup.

Adam reached for the dog, but his hands came down on something hard. A white birch branch had fallen into the pool. Its bark was rough beneath his fingers. He shoved it away, clawed through slimy weeds, searching for Marshmallow's large soft body, but didn't find him. He swam in circles until, exhausted, he dragged himself onto the pool's ledge.

Adam knelt and searched the water for any signs of the dog.

Marshmallow was not in the pool.

Adam's head throbbed as he trudged away from the house and back into the woods. His clothes were sodden, his boots heavy, and a headache the size of Mount Rushmore expanded behind his eyes.

At the edge of his yard, he paused and stared at their new house, their dream home. Tears pricked the backs of his eyes. He thought of Holly tucked inside, body fighting desperately to accept her new heart, and he thought too of the house he'd just left, once occupied by a group of girls with their whole lives ahead of them, all snuffed out in a single day. The unfairness of the world pressed down on Adam, and he wanted to drop to his knees and cry.

He might have, if not for the scream that suddenly ripped through the thick summer air. It was high and hysterical, a scream of absolute terror, and it had come from his house.

Adam broke into a run, leaped onto the front porch and crashed through the door.

The kitchen was empty.

"Holly?" he shouted, pounding down the hallway into their bedroom.

She lay in the bed, eyes closed as if deep in sleep, the covers pulled up to her chest. She didn't stir and as he gazed at her, he noticed another shape beneath the covers beside her. A clearly human shape. Someone else was in the bed.

Adam grabbed the corner of the comforter and jerked it off, flinging stinky water onto Holly, the bedding, and the floor.

She startled awake, blinking up at him.

"Adam? What is it?" She looked confused, eyes dropping from his face to the comforter gripped in his white knuckles. She saw the dark droplets on her arm and stared at them.

"I... did you scream, Holly?" Adam demanded, but he knew the answer. She'd been asleep. She was only half awake now.

"In my sleep?" she asked.

He touched his forehead, wondering again if he'd hit his head harder than he thought, if he was seeing things and hearing things. "I must have imagined it."

"Adam, why are you wet? And"—she wrinkled her nose—"you smell terrible."

Adam closed his eyes. "I fell in a pool."

"A pool?"

"At the old house I told you about. There's a pool." He pressed a finger to the tender spot on the back of his head. "I'm sorry. I've gotten muck everywhere. I'll clean it up after I shower."

Holly sat up, shaking her head at the splatters on the bed and floor. "Goodness, it smells like somebody died in that pool."

Adam backed out of the room. "I'll wash it as soon as I shower. Why don't you go to the couch or out to the porch?"

She yawned. "Yeah, maybe the porch. See if I can catch the last of the sunset."

"I'd kiss ya, but..." He pointed at his soaked clothes.

"Air kiss," she said, blowing him one.

He caught it. "Any idea where the ibuprofen is? I've got a headache."

"Darn, that's not fun," she said. "A fall in a gross pool and a headache, to boot. I put it in the pantry. Maybe you should lie down for a bit."

"Painkillers and a shower and I'll be okay."

Adam walked to the pantry and flicked on the light. The bulb burst above him and he shouted and jumped back as bits of fine glass rained onto the wood floor.

"What the hell is wrong with this thing?" he grumbled. Enough light filtered in to find the ibuprofen. He grabbed the bottle and shook out two pills, then on second thought added two more. He swallowed them with a gulp of water and trudged to the shower.

13

1956

8 Days before the Sail

The girls picked through the forest, each carrying a basket. Primarily, they picked blackberries, but Alice added other things to her basket and she explained the various plants they came upon. Their days in the woods were part of Alice's more unconventional teachings, but Mildred enjoyed them and though Cocoa sometimes snickered when Alice explained the uses of various weeds, she too seemed to like wandering amongst the trees and fields.

Mildred paused at a large elderberry shrub and plucked several of the shining black berries from a branch, lifting them to her lips. Alice's hand flashed toward her, palm connecting with Mildred's cheek and sending the berries flinging to the grass.

"Those are poisonous," Alice snapped.

Mildred's cheek stung. Her eyes welled less from pain than embarrassment. She caught Nell's stare for only an instant, and then the older girl looked quickly away.

Mildred unfurled her hand and allowed the rest of the berries to drop and disappear. A purple-black smudge remained on her palm and she unconsciously wiped it on her slacks, horrified when it instantly stained the fabric.

After several minutes where Mildred was sure the other girls were laughing at her, Alice moved to her side. Her fingers brushed along Mildred's back, perhaps in a gesture meant to be comforting, though it might have been to swipe away a burr for all the warmth it brought.

"I'm sorry," Alice murmured, not looking at Mildred but blinking down at the high grass. "But you must never, never-ever, eat things in the forest that you're not absolutely sure of."

"I thought it was elderberry," Mildred mumbled, wanting to put a hand to her cheek, but wanting more for everyone to forget it had happened.

"What are they?" Cocoa asked, studying the plant.

"Belladonna—deadly nightshade," Alice told her, face pale.

Nell stood next to Cocoa, also considering the purple-black berries.

"That's why I do this with you girls," Alice explained. "The abundance of the forest can sustain life, but it can also take it away. Even the most deadly plants have their place and it's important that we are aware of them all."

Mildred saw Cocoa and Nell exchange a look. It had sounded more like Alice envisioned the belladonna as a tool to use against enemies rather than a berry they needed to be aware of so they didn't poison themselves.

"What can we do with belladonna?" Nell asked. "Does it have any positive uses?"

"It does. Every part of the plant is poisonous, but diluted properly we can use it as a sedative and to treat other ailments. I strongly urge against it though. Only a person who understands plant medicine can safely use it to heal. Even the picking of this plant can have adverse effects. For instance, if Mildred had a cut on one of the fingers she used to pick the berries, the poison could be travelling through her bloodstream as we speak."

Mildred lifted her hand and searched for cuts or scrapes. There were none.

"Let's start back," Alice said. "I believe we've done enough today."

When they returned home, the girls took the baskets of berries into the house, but Mildred offered to assist Alice in the barn with the other plants she'd picked. Alice had turned one room into an apothecary of sorts. There was straw and sawdust on the floor, but the wooden shelves were lined with jars of powders, roots and dried herbs.

"What's this one?" Mildred asked, touching a glass jar filled with a cinnamon-colored powder.

"It's willow bark powder," Alice explained, removing several clumps of milkweed from her basket. "My grandmother Dahlia taught me many years ago the plants for healing and those for not... In our modern world, it's so easy to pop down to the store and buy a bottle of aspirin, but I find it soothing, collecting the bark, grinding it down. It's a useful skill despite what Michael says."

Mildred glanced up, surprised. Mrs. Ashwood never called her husband Michael in front of the girls. He was always Mr. Ashwood.

"He doesn't want you to do it?" Mildred asked.

Alice shook her head. "It's not that. He thinks it's nonsense, a waste of time. Men are driven by urges foreign to *most* women." She enunciated the word most. "Lust and greed primarily. Women seek to understand, to heal, to give life rather than take it. We're the superior gender in most ways, but it's the nature of our world that those who are willing to dominate others will nearly always get what they want because they simply take it."

The declaration surprised Mildred. She had always seen Alice as a devoted wife. The woman who oversaw their schooling and training at the Ashwoods' house rarely spoke of any personal matters.

"Are you happy here?" Mildred asked, unsure why she'd posed the question. A long silence lapsed, and she wished she could take it back.

"When Michael and I envisioned this house and then constructed it from our dreams, I could not imagine ever loving a place more. It was a place that held me in a way my mother never did. When Marilyn and I ran barefoot in the yard or swam in the pool or sat rocking in the swing, I might have been cradled in the arms of a great mother. As if this house and land had been imbued with a maternal spirit. I could never have imagined that one day this place would fill me with dread. That one day I would look upon the glittering pool and want to fill it with dirt, bury it, and burn this house to the ground."

Mildred gazed at her, startled, but also filled with exhilaration. Alice was confiding in her. She was telling her, Mildred, things she'd probably never spoken to another living being. Mildred committed the words to memory as if they were gold coins she was slipping into a safe.

"Who was Marilyn?" Mildred asked quietly, sensing that Alice had forgotten her there, had begun to tell a story that had been festering within her for a very long time.

"Marilyn," Alice breathed, "was my beautiful daughter."

Mildred had never heard the Ashwoods had a daughter. She doubted the other girls knew either. The sailboat they took out for a weekend every month in the summer was named *Darling Marilyn*. Mildred had never thought to ask where the name had come from.

"What happened to her?"

Alice fingered the lace on her collar. Her chest appeared blotchy.

"What happened to her?" Alice repeated Mildred's words. "I don't know. That's the worst part of all. I do not know what happened to Marilyn. We went on a day trip to Lake Michigan. Michael had family over that way. Marilyn and her cousin wandered off into the Manistee National Forest and only Wilma returned. She'd lost track of Marilyn. They'd been racing about gathering up wildflowers and then…"

Mildred waited, breath held, but Alice didn't go on.

"You never found her?"

"We never found her. No one did. She'd had on this little charm bracelet with bells. Someone heard the bells. We searched and searched. I had blisters for weeks. I stayed there at Michael's brother's house. I walked for hours every day, calling out for her. But she was gone."

"Mr. Ashwood didn't stay?" Mildred kept her tone quiet, unobtrusive. She feared Alice would suddenly remember who she spoke to and end their conversation.

"Oh, no, not Michael. He had business things to tend to. Life goes on, he told me." She snorted and pulled so hard at her collar that the lace ripped. "She'd be twenty-two now. She'd be married or…" Alice shook her head hard. "No, she'd be doing something greater than that, something grander. She wouldn't rely on a man for her happiness."

14

Adam woke to the sound of music. He reached beside him but found Holly's half of the bed empty.

Groggily, he stood and padded to the dresser where he'd plugged in his cell phone the night before. The screen was black. He pressed the on button, but it did nothing.

Irritably, he dropped it back on the dresser and walked into the hallway, squinting at Holly's clock made from a hunk of driftwood. It was three a.m. He yawned and stretched, recognizing the song coming from the kitchen.

Joan Osborne crooned from the speakers. Adam had heard Holly play the CD so many times he knew the songs by heart. He paused at the kitchen doorway.

Holly had lit her tobacco-scented candle. It sat flickering near the open window above the sink. She wore her old tie-dye apron, the one her mother had made her, and whisked around the kitchen, adding spices to three separate bowls in a line on the counter. She sang the words to the album beneath her breath, nodding along with the tune.

It was a familiar scene, the early-morning routine she'd performed when baking at the café for over five years. He hadn't seen her do it since they'd closed their shop. He'd forgotten about it. He smiled and rested his head against the doorframe, flooded with gratitude that she was well enough to be spinning about the kitchen like a character in a Disney movie.

She looked up and spotted him. "Oh, no, did I wake you up?"

He smiled. "If you did, I'm happy for it. I haven't seen you doing this in a long time."

She grated fresh ginger over one bowl. "I woke up an hour ago and this old ritual was calling to me. I dug my CD out of a box in the study, found this candle, and set to work. God only knows what we're going to do with the forty-plus muffins when they're finished baking, but I also made a pie for dinner tonight and figured some muffins can come too."

The CD caught, and the started skipping.

"Poison, poison, poison, poison," Joan sang in a clipped electronic voice.

"Oh, no…" Holly hit stop on the CD player and opened it, lifted the disc out and turned it over.

"Is it scratched?" Adam asked.

She shook her head. "No, not that I can see. Darn it. I love this CD."

"Maybe you can buy it and put it on your phone? Step into the twenty-first century a bit."

She smirked at him. "I don't think a man who doesn't even have an email address should lecture me on stepping into the twenty-first century."

"I had an email at the coffee shop."

"*We* had an email at the coffee shop," she corrected. "And I'm the only one who ever read it."

He moved behind her and wrapped his arms around her waist, wishing he could ignore the bones jutting from her hips, the feel of her ribs beneath the back of her t-shirt. He rested his chin on her shoulder. "The only person I want to talk to is standing right here."

She sighed and leaned into him. "Don't start getting frisky now. I haven't even gotten these things in the oven."

He kissed the back of her neck. "I better help you then."

She laughed. "Call Marshmallow in first. I let him out a little bit ago."

Adam opened the kitchen door and leaned into the dark of early morning. The outdoors smelled rich and damp. Light spilled from the kitchen windows and revealed dew sparkling on the grass.

"Marshmallow!" he called. "Come on, boy, time to come in."

He gazed across the yard toward the woods. In the dark he could barely make out the tree line except for a craggy ripple against the navy sky. He thought of the Ashwoods' house standing in the thicket of trees, slumbering, or perhaps like a wolf it came alive at night, watching and waiting.

He shuddered and closed the door.

As he turned back to the counter, he heard a rustle behind him. Marshmallow coming back—maybe he'd use the doggie door for once. Adam had lured him through it by offering sausage treats, but Marshmallow refused to use it without an incentive.

Marshmallow's fluffy white head did not appear through the little door. Instead, a slimy white hand snaked through the plastic flap. Dirt-caked fingernails clawed against the floor.

Adam gasped and stumbled back, crashing into Holly, who held a batter-filled muffin tin. She yelped and dropped it. The tin hit the floor with a thwack and batter splattered across both of their legs.

Adam spun and grabbed Holly's waist, afraid she'd fall, but she'd managed to clutch the counter. He looked back at the door, but the hand was gone. The doggie door sat still as if nothing at all had come through it.

"Damn, those were the ginger-carrot ones," Holly murmured.

She took a rag from the counter and crouched, wiping batter. She glanced up at him. "What happened? Lost your footing?"

He blinked at her, his mouth dry, and tried to find words. Instead, he nodded. "Here, let me do this." He pulled her to her feet. "I'm sorry I killed the ginger muffins."

She shook her head. "No big deal. I guess the universe was trying to tell me I'd made too many."

He smiled and took the rag, returning to the floor. As he wiped, he heard the rustle of the doggie door again. He whipped around, nearly slipping forward into the batter.

Marshmallow poked his head into the kitchen. He spotted Adam on the floor and shuffled through, lapped at the batter.

"Oh, no, you don't," Holly scolded, taking Marshmallow by the collar and leading him out of the room. "We're not visiting the vet because you ate a bellyful of flour, sugar and ginger."

She returned a few minutes later and Adam looked up to see a clipboard in her hand. "We're both awake. Why don't we get this done?" She waved the paper.

Adam frowned and pinched the bridge of his nose. "I actually have a bit of a headache. I might try to catch a few more hours' sleep."

Holly sighed. "Adam, not completing this won't prevent the inevitable. Someday I'm going to die. It would be better if we had this filled out."

"And we will, I promise." He kissed the tip of her nose and made for the bedroom. He didn't know why exactly he so abhorred that little piece of paper. It didn't change anything and yet he felt by delaying it, they were buying more time.

Denial, Holly called it.

So be it. If denial could get him out of bed every morning, he'd hang on to it as long as he could.

~

"Ready for this?" Adam asked, parking the van in the Jacksons' driveway.

"Heck, yeah. It's been quite the shock going from the coffee shop to a quiet house in the woods. I didn't realize how much I'd miss the chitter-chatter."

Adam retrieved the pie and muffins from the back seat and followed Holly to the door.

She'd barely knocked when Ted greeted them wearing his same Stetson and cowboy boots, but now paired with an embroidered country and western shirt.

He grinned and grabbed Adam's hand, giving it a firm shake. "Adam, howdy. And this must be Mrs. Tate."

"Holly," she offered, reaching out to shake his hand.

Through the doorway a woman appeared in a motorized wheelchair. Her red-brown hair was twisted on top of her head. She wore a full face of makeup and layered silver and turquoise jewelry.

"Hi, y'all," she said. "I'm Cheryl, Ted's old ball and chain." She stood shakily to her feet. Ted grabbed her elbow to steady her.

"I'm Adam and this is my wife, Holly."

"A pleasure to meet you both, and my goodness, look at that pie. Darlin', did you make that all by yourself?"

"I did, at about three this morning in fact." Holly laughed.

"Good grief, was the rooster crowin' that early? I haven't seen three a.m. since I was twenty-five." Cheryl laughed and settled back into her chair.

"We used to own a bakery and coffee shop, so I got in the habit of waking up early to bake. I haven't done it in months, but for some reason I woke up with the urge this morning."

Cheryl reversed and directed her chair into a large kitchen where sun filtered through skylights in the slanted roof. "I made brisket tacos, and I left Ted in charge of the beer and wine."

Holly held up a glass plate. "This is blackberry pie. I picked the blackberries behind our house."

"You did?" Adam asked, surprised.

Holly smiled. "Yes, during one of your meandering hikes."

"Well, it looks divine," Cheryl exclaimed.

A parrot squawked from a tall cage in the corner.

"Hello, hello," he shouted, ruffling his red and green feathers.

"Oh, he's beautiful," Holly said, setting the pie on the counter and walking toward the bird.

"That's Razzle Dazzle," Cheryl told her. "My baby bird. Course, he's not a baby anymore."

"And he's not dazzling either," Ted said, giving the parrot a peeved look.

As if on cue the parrot quipped, "Drop dead, Ted. Drop dead, Ted."

Holly's mouth fell open, and she looked at Adam, who was unable to contain his laughter.

Ted grimaced and waved his cowboy hat at the cage. "Damned thing picked that up last year when the grandkids a-came to visit and watched that movie."

"*Drop Dead Fred,*" Cheryl added.

Ted put a gray cover over the cage and the bird went quiet.

"He'll talk our ears off otherwise," Cheryl explained. "Shall we sit on the veranda?"

15

"Sounds lovely," Holly said.

"You ladies head out there. Adam and I can handle the food."

"Do you want a glass of wine, Holl?" Adam asked.

"Sure, that'd be great."

"Can you make that two?" Cheryl asked.

"Absolutely, coming right up."

Cheryl stood and braced a hand against one wall, sliding the glass door open with the other. Just beyond the door, she stepped to a walker, which she pushed toward the patio table. Holly followed her out.

"Multiple sclerosis," Ted explained. "She's still very mobile, takes care to keep up and moving around. It doesn't hurt that she's stubborn as all git-out."

"When was she diagnosed?" Adam asked, opening a bottle of red wine and pouring two glasses half full.

"Going on seven years now. She started using the scooter about a year ago, but she tries to do it sparingly, wants to keep her legs strong."

"That's understandable."

Ted pulled open the refrigerator. "Want a beer? Or are you a wine man?"

"Nothing for me. I'll take these to the ladies and come back to help with the food."

Adam stepped onto the back patio. Torches burned at either end, releasing a strong lemony aroma. He handed Holly and Cheryl their wine.

"Are those citronella?" he asked, gesturing at the torches.

"They sure are," Cheryl exclaimed. "Gotta keep 'em lit once the sun sets or the skeeters are on us like vampires."

Holly laughed. "We better put those on the list for the next hardware store run."

"Good idea," Adam agreed.

He stepped back inside. Ted handed Adam the plates stacked with silverware and he carried out the tacos.

"How did you end up in Michigan?" Adam asked Cheryl and Ted after they'd finished eating dinner.

"On account of our kids," Ted explained. "Our son got his degree at U of M, met a girl from Michigan and wanted to put down some roots. Our daughter followed him not long after. Then the two of them conspired to get us out here by having babies and only bringing our grandkids back to Texas twice a year."

"Do your kids live nearby?" Holly asked.

"Jamie does. She lives on Black Lake with her husband and two daughters. Gabriel's in Petoskey, he's a surgeon at the hospital up there. He's got three young ones and his wife Tia stays home with them. They all come over for dinner every other Sunday."

"That's wonderful," Holly said. "My brother only lives an hour away now, which is nice. He hasn't come over yet, he's giving us time to settle in, but we're excited to be close to family."

"Where'd y'all move from?" Cheryl asked.

"Grand Rapids," Adam said. "Holly's brother used to live there too, but he moved north a few years ago. We've been coming up to see him every couple of months, and Holly and I just fell in love with it up here. We always wanted to retire up north, and we landed on the Black Lake area when we had a weekend at a cottage on the lake."

"We both knew this would be eventually be home," Holly agreed, resting a hand on Adam's arm.

"How did y'all meet?" Ted asked.

"We met on a plane flying to Arizona," Holly explained. "We weren't originally seated next to each other, but some newlyweds wanted to change seats. She was by Adam and I was by the husband. We agreed to the switch, and I ended up in the seat next to Adam. He was a nervous flyer."

"Planes give me the creeps and I made the mistake of watching that movie *Final Destination* a week before I flew out to visit my dad in Sedona. That's where he lives with his second wife."

"His foot was tapping so fast it shook half the plane." Holly leaned into Adam, smiling. "The woman across the aisle kept giving him nasty looks. I finally started telling him some vulgar jokes to get his mind off his nerves. Within ten minutes we were both laughing so hard the dirty looks were coming from every direction."

Adam grinned. "Mind you, we were on a red-eye flight. We stopped laughing at one point and it was dead silent on the plane and we realized how loud we'd been."

"Which only made us laugh harder," Holly said.

Cheryl and Ted laughed.

"That is a great story," Ted exclaimed. He held up the wine bottle.

"More wine?"

"Just a smidge," Holly said. "Thank you."

"And why were you headed to Arizona?" Cheryl asked.

"I was going to a retreat out there in Sedona," Holly offered. "My mother had just died, and I'd been feeling out of sorts. My mother was an artist and a poet, a bit of a wanderer. My dad always said I got my zest for life from her, my heart…" She touched her breastbone and laughed sadly.

"How did she die if you don't mind my asking?" Cheryl asked.

"She had a heart attack when I was twenty-two," Holly said. "She'd hardly been sick a day in her life and then she was standing at her easel one day and collapsed. My dad had died two years before in a car accident. That left my brother Duke and me. When I stepped on that plane for Arizona, I was searching for… some remedy for the pain, I guess. Adam and I laughing was salve on this open wound. I thought I was helping him, but really he was helping me."

"That's lovely," Cheryl said. "And then you stayed in touch and just hit it off?"

"We did," Adam said, thinking back to that long-ago night and how he couldn't believe his luck in ending up on a plane next to this funny, warm, beautiful woman. "We talked the entire flight and then Holly asked if I wanted to meet for a hike. She could have asked if I wanted to join a cult, and I would have agreed. We spent most of the week together." Adam chuckled. "My stepmother was pissed because she'd planned all these activities and I blew most of them off, though I dragged Holly along for a few."

"We changed our flights so we could fly back to Grand Rapids together," Holly explained, "and that was that. We moved in together a month after we got home."

"That is such a beautiful story," Cheryl said wistfully.

Adam squeezed Holly's hand. "We think so. How about you guys? How did you meet?"

Ted's eyes sparkled as he leaned forward. "In a truly Texan way. I was injured at a rodeo and she was my savior."

Cheryl laughed and shook her head. "When you put it that way, it does sound romantic. But"—she winked at Ted—"my Ted here was a rodeo clown and I was selling popcorn and gave him a band-aid for a cut on his cheek." She laughed. "But I'll tell you, when he wiped off his clown make-up, I was smitten."

"Enough about us, I want to hear about this bakery you sold. Did you make pecan rolls at this bakery?" Ted asked, licking his lips.

Holly smiled and sipped her wine. "I most definitely did. Do you like those?"

"Oh!" He groaned and clapped a hand on his chest. "Do I like them? I have dreams about them."

"You think he's jokin'." Cheryl laughed. "But at least once a month he comes into the kitchen all grumpy because he dreamed about these pecan rolls we used to get in Texas that he can't find up here."

"I'll tell you what," Holly told Ted. "You get the recipe and I'll make you a full pan."

Ted's eyes widened. "There is an angel in our midst, Cheryl."

Cheryl tweaked his ear. "I coulda told ya that, darlin'. So, tell me, are y'all gonna open another bakery up here? We sure could use one."

Adam rubbed the back of his neck, glancing at Holly, who he could tell was about to reveal her illness.

"I'm sick," Holly admitted. "I had a heart attack two years ago and I've had two heart transplants, but my body hasn't taken well to them."

Ted's face paled and Cheryl put a hand to her mouth. "Oh, darlin', oh, goodness, that's just not fair." She reached for Holly and rubbed her arm.

Ted too reached a comforting hand to Holly's shoulder, giving first hers a squeeze and then Adam's. "That is a cryin' shame, just terrible," he said.

"That went into the decision to sell the café," Adam explained, swallowing the lump in his throat that lodged there whenever they talked about Holly's heart problems. "Our big dream had always been to build our house up here. In the beginning, the plan was to open a café up here, maybe even consider franchises, but when she had the heart attack, we let that go. Between selling the business, selling our house, and an inheritance from Holly's mother, we figured we could float for five years if we didn't go overboard. A bit like early and probably temporary retirement."

"But it's highly unlikely I have five years," Holly said.

Cheryl's eyes widened. "Oh, don't say that, honey. God works in mysterious ways."

Holly took Adam's hand and kissed it. "I won't argue with that, but… I've made peace with it, with whatever comes. It's this guy that I worry about because he's made it his life's mission to take care of me and I want to make sure he keeps on living."

"Holly…" Adam started. He didn't want to go there, not tonight. He couldn't think about that bleak future, not right now.

"It's okay, honey." She leaned over in her chair and kissed his cheek. "We don't have to talk about this. Our new friends know and we can leave it at that."

Adam blinked back tears, standing quickly. "How about I clear some plates and bring out the pie?"

"I'll help. Give these ladies a few minutes to talk," Ted agreed.

Ted followed Adam into the kitchen.

"I'm mighty sorry to hear about all yer troubles," Ted told him. "If there's ever anything at all that Cheryl and I can do, you just say the word."

"Thanks," Adam sighed, stacking the dinner dishes by the sink. "I do have a question about something though, not about Holly, but have you ever heard of the Ashwoods?" Adam dropped his voice so Holly and Cheryl wouldn't hear them through the screen door.

Ted nodded as he rinsed a plate and loaded it into the dishwasher. "Sure, yeah. Their story is local lore around here. Sailboat full of girls goes missing. Stories like that survive."

"Have you ever heard anything about it? About what might have happened?"

"It came up once during a prayer group I led," Ted admitted. "Hand me those plates there, will ya? I'll just get these rinsed and loaded before the food dries on them."

Adam handed him the other plates.

"One woman in our group knew the Ashwoods as a girl. She was friends with the woman of the house, Alice Ashwood. She wanted to say a prayer for the departed, may they rest in peace. Afterwards we all got to discussing it over coffee. The whole thing quite disturbed the woman, Emily."

"Did she know the husband as well?"

"The sole survivor? Maybe that's not what you'd call him since he wasn't on the boat. Yes, she knew him, though when I tried to add his name to the prayer, she hollered right out that he wasn't to be part of the prayer." Ted smiled and raised both eyebrows. "Christian or no, people can hold a grudge. After all, that accident occurred fifty-odd years ago. The man has probably long since gone to the grave himself."

"Did she say why she didn't want him added?"

"No, but after the group had ended, I was still at the ministry with two parishioners, both long-time locals. Apparently, there'd been whispers about the man. I won't speak 'em here. It's not my place to soil the name of a man based on speculation and gossip, but I sense Emily might have known such things and never forgiven him for his indiscretions."

"Did she think the accident was his fault?"

Ted closed the dishwasher and picked up a stack of dessert plates. "I can't imagine how she'd make that connection, but she had fire in her eyes, so it's possible."

Adam picked up the pie and followed Ted back out to the porch.

"I had a Mustang," Holly was telling Cheryl dreamily. "Cobalt blue with tan leather seats. I loved that car, but…" She shrugged. "The van was the practical choice after I got sick."

Cheryl nodded. "Oh, I hear ya, doll. Before Gertrude, that's what we call our van, I drove a Land Rover. That thing was a beast, but I loved it. In the winter when other people were stuck in the ditch, I was climbin' right over the snow banks."

Ted laughed. "She was a menace in that thing."

Adam cut slices of pie and handed them out.

"My dream car has always been a Corvette Stingray," Holly said, sliding her pie closer. "You know those ones with the big haunches and the sleek nose. Gosh, I remember my brother borrowed one from one of his buddies in high school to take his girlfriend to the senior prom. I just swooned over that thing. I even had dreams about it."

"Those are pretty cars," Cheryl agreed. "And you'd look just like a movie star riding around in one of those."

"This here pie is as good as all git-out," Ted exclaimed, shoveling a large bite in his mouth.

"It is. You've outdone yourself with this one, honey," Adam told Holly.

"Holly," Cheryl said, pointing her fork at Holly. "You have to join us for a ladies' club tomorrow. I swear to you it's not a bunch of old biddies sharing the town gossip—well, not entirely anyway." She winked at Holly. "Lulu brings mimosas and Fannie brings all the left-overs from the nursery. We do plant swaps, eat cookies. Norma Anne Frisk makes these cookies with dried cherries and walnuts that will make your heart sing. What do you say? Tomorrow at noon. We meet at a different lady's house each week, but tomorrow we're having it here."

Holly glanced at Adam. "Do you mind?"

"Of course not."

"Be careful, Adam," Ted cut in. "This one's so busy you'd think she was twins. Holly signs on with her gang and you're not like to see her again until Christmas."

Cheryl shook her head. "Don't you listen to him, you two. This one's busy as a hound in flea season. He puts on like he's a man enjoying retirement, but there's barely a wrinkle in his sittin' chair."

"On that note," Ted said to Adam, "I don't want you to be left out. Best if you join me for some fishin'? I've got a little boat we can take out. What do you say about that?"

Adam imagined the Ashwoods' house. He wanted back in, wanted to continue searching, but he could feel Holly's eyes on him.

"Sure, why not? If I'm calling myself retired, I probably should act the part now and then."

16

"I'm off to luncheon with the ladies," Holly told Adam the next day, wrapping her arms around his waist.

He kissed her and inhaled the scent of freshly washed hair, still wet and draped over her shoulders.

"I need to savor this smell because soon my nostrils will be filled with the scent of fish guts," he told her.

Holly laughed and pulled away. "Maybe you'll get lucky and the fish won't be biting."

Adam grinned and held up two crossed fingers.

He'd never been a fisherman. His father had dragged him out a time or two during his childhood, but sitting still for hours had never appealed to Adam. Likewise, he didn't enjoy the cleaning or the eating of anything they caught.

He walked to his truck and paused, gazing toward the woods that led to the Ashwoods' house. He considered calling Ted and cancelling, but sensed Holly would feel guilty if he spent the day home alone while she was out.

Adam arrived at the lake to find Ted launching a small metal fishing boat.

"I brought a six-pack of beer. I doubt we'll make much of a dent, but I got in the habit years ago and never seemed to break it," Ted offered.

"I'm not really a drinker anymore," Adam admitted. "After Holly had the first heart attack, I didn't want to risk it."

Ted grabbed poles and a tackle box from his truck and loaded them into the boat. "Yeah, I hear ya. I haven't tied one on in ages myself. Partially due to my prostate, but more so because of Cheryl's condition."

They climbed into the boat, and Ted motored them to a deeper spot in the lake.

"How did it happen? The heart attack," Ted said.

Adam gazed over the side and watched the sands slope down and give way to dark water.

"I wasn't in the coffee shop that day because I had a meeting with a new coffee roaster in town. Fifteen minutes into the meeting, I had this terrible feeling. I can't even describe it. I stood up and ran out the door, didn't say a word to the guy. I'd left my cell phone in my truck. I grabbed it and saw I'd had ten calls from the café.

"That's when I found out she'd collapsed and been rushed to the hospital. She was in complete heart failure and ended up getting an emergency transplant. She was lucky, really lucky, in that department. Then her body started rejecting the heart. They got her on the list for another transplant and she got that one a little over a year ago. For a first transplant, the survival rate is around six years, that drops with a second transplant and there have already been signs that her body isn't completely taking to this transplant either."

"Can she get a third?"

"Three is very rare. I don't know if four exists at all. It's felt like a death sentence. Holly still lives full-throttle, but ever since it started, I've sensed… our time is limited. And the doctor made it pretty clear that was true. Get your affairs in order, wills, end-of-life wishes because in a situation like this she might have years or only months.

"She might drift away in her sleep some night. That might be my greatest fear of all, which is selfish because that's what would be best for her, but for me, well, I just can't imagine waking up to find her still and cold in the bed beside me. No, actually I can imagine it. I have imagined it and it makes me break out in a cold sweat."

Adam had told no one of the fears he'd had since Holly's first heart attack, but as he sat in the boat, it poured out of him.

"Since the first attack we've been operating on a level ten, me especially—doctors' appointments, research, surgeries, two transplants, the selling of the café, the selling of the house, buying the land up here, the permits, excavating, building the house. I've been like a robot with the details. Holly's the one who keeps me human, reminds me to slow down and actually be here. Whatever happens, barring a miracle, my days with Holly are numbered, and that fact runs like a freight train through my head every waking moment. The only thing that keeps me sane is the busyness and suddenly it's all been stripped away. It was like our life got cut in half. The life before the diagnosis and the life after. Everything changed. In an instant the sky opened and this huge hand reached down and erased our future."

Ted stopped the boat and leaned forward, grabbed the anchor and heaved it over the side.

"It's an awful burden to bear," Ted agreed. "When Cheryl got sick, I went mad tryin' to help, then I went absent. Started working later and comin' up with reasons to stay away. I feel terrible about it now, but at the time, I just couldn't handle the helplessness. I'd always been a doer, getting' it done. Nothin' I could do about the MS. Our son Gabriel helped. He was the one who understood the medical thing.

"But then I came around. Our pastor helped me to recognize there was a lot I could do. I could get the house ready. Wheelchair ramps, bars in the shower. We'd need a master bedroom on the ground floor, so we converted our study into a bedroom. Most of all I could be with her, just be, no advice, no fixin'. That was the hardest hurdle for me to jump over, shuttin' this big mouth of mine and just existing beside her, puttin' an arm around her when it got to be too much and she wanted to cry, and givin' her the space to push back against it, to walk even when it hurt."

"I try to do that," Adam sighed. "But... when I slow down, when everything gets quiet..." He swallowed thickly. "The fears paralyze me. Sometimes I'm okay. I have this refrain. 'We're all heading there. Some of us just take an earlier train.' When I think of it that way, I'm okay. I can breathe.

"But... when I imagine all the mornings I'll have to wake up without her, when I think of all the things I would have shared with her that she would have loved, that she'll never laugh about or cry about again, that's when I freeze up, when I think I can't possibly do it." Adam took the pole Ted handed him. "Do you think it takes a toll on you mentally? Keeping it all together for Cheryl, always trying to stay on top of her illness?"

Ted threaded his worm on the hook and looked out at the water thoughtfully. "I've become accustomed to it. It was harder in the beginning. The first year was a tough one. It takes a village, as they say, and our community, the ministry, our children, our friends... they helped us through."

"Yeah," Adam murmured, wondering not for the first time if it had been a mistake uprooting and moving north. They'd left friends behind, their customers, staff, trusted doctors.

"We're here for you, Adam. Cheryl and I and our whole community. Not to kick a dead horse, but talk with Holly about coming down to the church if for nothing else than to greet some friendly faces each week."

Adam nodded and gazed out at the horizon, growing still. A sailboat floated out there, the sail gray and tattered. Black stains streaked down the canvas like dark veins filled with black blood. Adam searched the deck, but it was empty. No captain at the wheel, no family sitting on the deck. The wheel spun like an abandoned Ferris wheel with a ghost operator.

"Got a bite," Ted announced, jerking Adam out of his reverie.

He watched Ted reeling in the line, and then it went slack.

"Lost it." Ted shrugged.

Adam's eyes flicked back to the distant spot on the lake, but the sailboat in the distance looked perfectly normal. A tall white mast hung slack. People moved around the deck.

A long silence lapsed as Adam considered the question rolling around in his head. He didn't really want to ask it, feared he might alienate his and Holly's first friends by putting it out there, but... he needed to. He needed to address it with someone and oddly, Ted Jackson seemed like the man.

"Ted, have you ever seen a ghost?"

Ted didn't startle. His line held steady as he glanced over his shoulder at Adam. "Sure. At least that's what my gran called 'em. Grew up in one of those Civil War houses and now and then I'd look out the window and see a man in uniform passin' through the yard. Looked like he'd stumbled out of a Civil War reenactment. Gun over his shoulder and everything. It became commonplace around our house. I must'a glimpsed him four or five times. Have you?"

Adam studied Ted's expression, half-expecting the man to crack a smile and admit he was pulling his chain. He didn't, just kept his eyes on the line.

"I saw something years ago," Adam said. "My father's sister had died. I was young, only six, and didn't know how she'd died. Nobody talked about it. There was a lunch at her house after the funeral. I remember everyone wearing black, my dad sitting stone-faced, my mom consoling my grandma, who was crying. I had to use the bathroom, but the one downstairs was occupied so I went upstairs. There was a bathroom at the end of the hall. I walked toward it. The door was closed and… I had a strange feeling. A scared feeling, I guess, but everything that was happening was so foreign. The house felt like an extension of the funeral, claustrophobic and sad. I remember putting my hand on the knob and sort of thinking I shouldn't open it, but I had to pee so bad I was afraid I'd wet my pants. I turned that knob, one of those old-fashioned faux-crystal ones.

"I opened the door, and it was dim in there, lit by a lamp with a maroon shade. I started in and then stopped. My aunt was lying in the bathtub naked. The water was dark-colored and her breasts were exposed. Her mouth was open and one of her arms had flopped across the rim of the tub and there was a huge gash in her wrist. It was red and her skin was"—Adam grimaced at the memory—"kind of peeling open. I noticed then how her eyes looked more like jawbreakers than real eyes. That's what I thought, which I know sounds morbid, but remember, I was only six. Her tongue hung from her mouth. I started screaming and ran back down the hall. I tripped going down the stairs and tumbled down the last five, landed on my arm and fractured it."

"Good golly, that's a harrowing tale."

"Yeah," Adam agreed. "I never went in that bathroom again, never, but I dreamed about it almost every night for years. My grandma and aunt had lived together, so we still went over there pretty regularly, but I rarely went upstairs at all. After graduating from high school, I finally mustered the courage to talk to my dad about his sister. I didn't tell him what I saw in the bathroom, but I knew she must have killed herself. The family never spoke of it, though.

"After she was gone, it was like… she'd never existed, like her suicide meant we couldn't even remember the good stuff. He told me that yes, she'd killed herself. She'd battled depression most of her life and that winter had been an especially dark one for her. My grandma found her. Years later, after my mom died, that scene was burned in my memory. I couldn't walk into my mom's bedroom. I was terrified I'd see her there, dead, skin turned black. I avoided the room. I didn't go to my mom's funeral. I haven't been to a funeral since my aunt's."

Adam tugged on his pole, watching the bobber bounce and

wondering why he'd spilled that long-ago story to this man he barely knew.

"That would be pretty traumatic," Ted said, slowly reeling in his line. He cast it back out. "Did you ever tell anyone about it?"

Adam watched his bobber drifting on the surface of the dark lake and shook his head. "Not until right now."

"And what has it knockin' around in your head after all these years?"

Adam stared into the water and imagined the things he'd seen at Ashwood House.

"I'm not sure, but I think… it has something to do with trying to make sense of it. Was my aunt still there in that tub? Or had I imagined her in the worst possible way because the experience was so upsetting? What does it mean for what comes after that I saw her there…?"

Ted cocked his head to the side. "Those are some heavy questions you're contemplating. I don't pretend to know the answers to such profound contemplations, but I think we go on. Is there a piece of us left behind?" Ted nodded. "I think there may just be."

17

1956

7 Days Before the Sail

Mildred peeked out the window and double-checked that all the girls were at the pool. Mrs. Ashwood was on one of her walks.

Margie did a cannonball into the water and Cocoa gave her an exasperated look, shaking her magazine.

Mildred hurried down the hall and up the stairs. She started in the Ashwoods' bedroom, stepping gingerly across the floor and keeping her ears perked for any sounds below. She slid open the top drawer of Mrs. Ashwood's dresser.

A framed photograph lay face-down in the drawer. She stared at it. Already she was committing a sin by snooping in the Ashwoods' bedroom. What difference did one more make?

She grabbed the picture and turned it over.

Mr. and Mrs. Ashwood stood on a beach with a child between them. Mrs. Ashwood wore a high-waisted polka-dot bikini. Her blonde hair, long then, flowed over her slender shoulders. Mr. Ashwood looked handsome in black-and-white striped swim shorts. The girl between them wore a white one-piece swimsuit. One hand held Mrs. Ashwood's and the other was extended, showing off a large pink shell. This must have been Marilyn, the long-lost daughter.

Mildred traced one nail-bitten finger over Marilyn's golden hair. She wanted to keep the photo, to spirit it off to her room in the attic and tuck it beneath her mattress, but didn't dare. She returned it to the drawer and peeked into the hallway.

When she heard nothing, she crept from the Ashwoods' room into Cocoa and Nell's bedroom, easing the door closed behind her. Mildred stood for a moment and gazed around the room, eyes lighting on Nell's single bottle of Miss Dior perfume, the pale blue cashmere sweater draped over her desk chair, and the framed photograph on her bedside table. She walked to the photograph and picked it up. She knew it was Nell's mother. She'd overheard Nell telling Cocoa once that her mother had died in an accident.

The woman was pretty, though nothing like the beauty exhibited by her daughter. She had a worn look about her. Mildred's mother would have called it rawboned. Her cheekbones stuck sharply from her face and the concaves of her eyes were too pronounced. She had a vicious look about her, despite her polka-dot dress and smile. The smile was false. There was fury in her eyes.

Of all the girls at the Ashwoods' house, Nell was the secret-keeper. She shared little about her life before coming to the house and if any of the girls confided in her, her lips were sealed. Mildred knew this because she'd eavesdropped on more than a few of those shared secrets and never once had she heard Nell pass on the information to one of the other girls. Mildred herself had spilled a few of those secrets, desperate to win favor with Cocoa or Bitsy, but it nearly always backfired because the girls would later comment on how Mildred couldn't keep her mouth shut.

She could, though. There were secrets she'd never told, many of them. She kept them tucked in the back of her mind like tiny jewels hidden in a drawer. They were valuable, those secrets. The kind that she might someday draw out and use—for what, she did not know.

The secrets she wanted most of all were the ones hidden inside Nell's diary. What confessions did she make as she sat scribbling night after night?

Mildred kneeled by the bed and ran both hands beneath the mattress, but found no diary. She stood and started toward Nell's dresser. A door slammed on the first floor. Mildred straightened up as the footsteps started up the stairs.

She lurched across the room and into the closet. The door stood open a crack, and Mildred tucked herself into the shadows, praying silently that it was Bitsy or Margie who'd entered the house.

The door to the bedroom opened and Nell stepped inside. She wore her navy-blue one-piece swimsuit with a towel tied around her waist. Her long hair was wet and draped over one shoulder.

Mildred held her breath as Nell moved around the room. She opened her nightstand drawer and took out her copy of Virginia Woolf's *To the Lighthouse*, the book they'd been reading and discussing in lessons that week with Mrs. Ashwood.

Beyond the bedroom, more footsteps clomped up the stairs.

Mildred shrank further into the closet.

Nell had heard the footsteps as well, and she watched her bedroom doorway. Mildred could not see who passed by, but the steps stopped outside Nell's bedroom. Mr. Ashwood slid into view. "Hi, Nell. How are you?"

Nell smiled and fiddled with the ends of her hair. "I'm good, Mr. Ashwood."

"Michael," he told her.

Mildred frowned. She'd never heard him tell any of the girls to call him by his first name.

"I passed Alice on the road," Mr. Ashwood said. "She won't be back for an hour. Meet me at the stables?"

Nell nodded, and when she spoke, she sounded breathless. "Yes. Okay."

Mr. Ashwood left the room. After his footsteps faded, Mildred watched as Nell quickly stripped naked and hung her bathing suit on the hook by the door. Heart quickening, Mildred tucked herself behind the hanging clothes, but Nell didn't peer into the closet. She grabbed a dress from her dresser and pulled it over her head.

Mildred waited until she heard Nell walk from the bedroom and down the stairs. She pushed out of the closet, pulse thrumming in her ears. This was the time to hunt for the diary. Nell had gone to the stables, but why? Mildred wanted that information more than she wanted the diary.

She crept from the room and ran down the stairs, bursting into the bright day. Behind the house, the laughter and chatter of the girls at the pool rang out. Keeping to the trees, Mildred snuck around the opposite side of the house toward the stables. She wormed through the barn door and waited for her eyes to adjust to the gloom.

Mildred crept through the door, peering into the gloom. As she moved further in, careful to walk lightly, she heard a human sound.

She peeked through a crack in the tack-room door. There was movement and in the dim light, she at first thought one of the horses had somehow gotten in, but then the forms took shape. Michael Ashwood lay on the floor, but no, not on the floor, on top of Nell.

Nell's pale, strained face was there beneath him. He was moving back and forth and though he wore his shirt and trousers, Mildred saw his bare bottom. She clenched her teeth together to muffle the gasp that nearly slipped out.

Mr. Ashwood moved faster now, grunting. Mildred stared at Nell's face, unsure if she enjoyed what Mr. Ashwood did to her or if it hurt. Perhaps it was something in the middle, and though Mildred had never so much as kissed a boy, she knew full well what was happening between Nell and Michael Ashwood.

"Yes," he rasped, and then his movements slowed and stopped.

Nell clutched his shoulders, and Mildred saw she was smiling.

Alice couldn't quite recall when she'd started taking the walks. Long walks around the property, following deer trails through the woods, sometimes out to the road, walking the shoulder, dust coating the hem of her skirt.

Mostly she thought of Marilyn on her walks. She left Black Mountain Road and slipped back in time to the years when she'd had a living, breathing daughter. A vivacious daughter with golden hair and inquisitive eyes and a thousand questions.

Marilyn had wanted to know why it rained, where the snow came from, who painted the rainbows. On and on she'd talk, and Alice had loved to listen to her and to watch her transition to infant, then toddler, little girl and eventually young woman. In the last summer of Marilyn's life, Alice had noticed boys gazing in admiration at her child. She'd known then it was only a matter of time before Marilyn would slip away and it had terrified her.

Perhaps Marilyn had felt that terror and run off. Michael had implied as much now and then, that his wife was a little off-kilter, that she'd smothered their beautiful daughter, that perhaps Marilyn had escaped so she could breathe.

Alice turned back into the driveway, legs scissoring in her skirt as she walked. A fine sweat beaded her brow, but she didn't wipe it away. She rather liked it, the proof of her exertion, a bit of relief in a body and a brain that lately had felt like a coiled snake shrinking into itself as danger lurked ever closer. The house had grown stifling as the summer lurched on. Outside, Alice could breathe.

It had been on her walks that she'd decided to return to the west side of the state, to abandon her home, the girls in her care, her husband. Return to the last places Marilyn had walked. Oh, but she hadn't walked. Marilyn had run and skipped and danced. She'd brought a lightness to Alice's life and the years since her disappearance piled on Alice like layers of heavy coats. She felt their weight now as she moved sluggishly up the driveway. The closer she grew to her house, the heavier the burden became.

18

The fish weren't biting, and Adam was grateful when Ted suggested they call it a day. They drove back to the shore and loaded the boat onto the trailer.

"Gonna be a toad-choker this afternoon. Make sure your windows are closed up tight," Ted told him as Adam started toward his truck.

"A toad-choker?"

Ted gestured at the sky. Dark clouds blotted the southern horizon. "Rainstorm, a doozy according to the weatherman this morning. Course he's wrong more than he's right, but them clouds have me thinkin' he's right."

Holly wasn't home when Adam returned. He took out his cell phone, fearing it had died. The battery showed fifty percent power. It seemed to work if he charged it in his truck rather than the house.

"Hi, honey," she answered.

"Hey, just checking on ya. Everything good?"

"Yeah, great. We've had so much fun we decided to drive up to Cheboygan. I'll be home for dinner though. I could stop for takeout."

Adam almost told her not to, he'd cook something, but then thought of the Ashwoods' house. He wanted more time inside it. "That'd be great. Whatever sounds good to you."

"According to Cheryl the only takeout in these parts is pizza." Holly laughed. "Pepperoni and mushroom?"

"Perfect. See you in a few hours."

He started down the hall to their bedroom and stopped. The muddy reddish footprints again spotted the rug. Had Holly tracked the dirty prints in? Or had they been there all along and some trick of the light rendered them less visible. He'd clean them after he returned from Ashwood's house.

Adam changed out of his sandals and pulled on long hiking pants and boots. It was hot in the clothes, but he'd found a few itchy red bumps on his ankle the day before and didn't know if he was wading through poison ivy every time he went to the Ashwoods' house.

~

Adam strode across the property into the old house. The impulse to go inside had annihilated any consideration for the trespassing issue.

His fervor wavered at the base of the stairs. A trickle of cold sweat slid between his shoulder blades and beneath the waistband of his pants. Was she up there, the woman who'd stood in the attic doorway, or had she merely been an invention in the moments after slamming his head into a rafter?

Squashing his doubts, he took the steps quickly. The door at the end of the hall stood closed and he couldn't recall if he'd left it that way, but of course he had. No one else had been in this house except him in years, probably decades. Maybe no one had stepped inside since Michael Ashwood himself had fled more than fifty years before.

He slipped down the hall to the master bedroom. From the top drawer of the dresser, he took the photos wrapped in twine and slid loose the image of the five girls. He flipped it over and read their names again. Cocoa and Nell were the first two girls in the image. Cocoa looked the oldest, with dark blonde hair pinned on her head. Her lips were painted red, a shade which he suspected matched her figure-hugging dress. The second girl, Nell, had a much more innocent face. Where Cocoa cast a sultry gaze at the camera, Nell's chin was tilted down, her eyes glancing up to catch the photo perhaps seconds before the shot was taken. Her skin was powder-white, her hair long and glossy. Unlike Cocoa, Nell wore a plain dress that went nearly to her ankles. She was naturally beautiful and, Adam suspected from her body language in the picture, she was shy as well.

He carried the picture back to the first bedroom. This room, if the embroidered pillows were to be trusted, had belonged to Cocoa and Nell. He didn't know why he wanted faces to go with the belongings, why he felt compelled to know them, but the urge existed just the same. He moved to the bed with Nell's pillow and sat on the edge. It protested his weight and released a puff of dust into the room.

He considered her picture. She'd slept on this bed, head on the pillow beside him. What had that last day been like for all the girls? Had they eaten breakfast together? Had petty squabbles as most teen girls do in the morning? Had they been excited for the sail that weekend, greeting the morning with anticipation?

Thinking of the book he'd found beneath the attic bed, Adam stood and lifted Nell's mattress. Nothing lay beneath it. He did the same to Cocoa's mattress and again found nothing. He moved on to Nell's dresser, opening drawers and gently moving aside her clothes. In the lowest drawer, which held half-mended things, the bottom of the drawer wriggled as if there was space beneath it. He prised at the edge of the wood and lifted the false bottom. A diary lay in the dusty cavity.

He lifted the book out. It was soft with a yellow vinyl cover splotched with blue-black mold. Bright cartoonish flowers decorated the front. A small gold lock held the diary closed. He tried to open it and the clasp held. He sat on the bed and fiddled with it until it popped open. It was a flimsy lock, more for show than actual protection. A lock that said 'keep out, this is secret.'

The cover page stated, *This Diary Belongs to Nellie Madden.*

Outside a crack of thunder split the quiet, and Adam twitched, turning to the window. A streak of lightning flashed and with it came scattered raindrops that escalated into a downpour. The world beyond the window blurred.

Adam turned back to the diary. The first entry was dated January 1st, 1956.

'*Dear Diary,*' it began.

Above him, Adam heard a creak as if someone had taken a step.

He paused, listening. Another creak did not follow the first. It was likely the rain causing the old house to complain, but Adam imagined the woman in the attic doorway.

He stood and walked across the room, pushed the door closed. He'd barely turned away when something shuffled outside the door.

Adam froze, listening. Though he heard no discernible sounds beneath the rain, he sensed a presence beyond the door. Something shifting, pacing even, as if trying to make sense of this block, this closed door that had been open for decades.

Adam stared at the doorknob, teeth on edge. Had it moved?

Beyond the windows the rain beat down.

The thing in the hall stirred restlessly. It was angry, Adam thought. Angry that he'd invaded the house and that he'd closed the bedroom door.

Ridiculous, his mind shouted. Adam jerked the door open, flinching away.

Nothing lunged at him.

He peeked out, relieved to find the hall empty, and slipped from the room. The closed attic door loomed opposite him, the crystal knob oddly bright in the gloomy hall. Adam turned and hurried down the stairs.

He wanted to take the diary home, get the hell out of the Ashwoods' house. At home he could make a pot of coffee and read the diary from the comfort of their couch while rain soaked the yard, but he had no interest in venturing into the deluge. The den had the most intact furniture of all the rooms in the Ashwoods' house and it felt... safer.

Adam closed the study door and settled onto one of the loveseats. He opened the diary, fanning the pages, and a folded sheet of paper slipped out. He bent and picked it up.

It wasn't dated, but the handwriting was different from that in the diary.

Dearest Nell,

I pine for you. These last two nights have been eternities stretching endlessly. I long for your soft skin beneath my hands, your lips beneath my mouth, your melodious laughter in my ear. I know that you are afraid, my love. Afraid of this passion, afraid of this affection, but I beg that you stare that fear in the face and rush with me into the flames. I will be by your side every step of the way. We both know I think that there is only one way. If we are to leave this place and be together, we must do whatever it takes.

Meet me tonight at midnight at our place in the woods.

Until then.

All my love,

M

Adam folded the paper and set it on the couch beside him. He opened the diary and scanned the pages. Many entries detailed the minutiae of Nell's days—lessons with Alice Ashwood, winter activities the girls had enjoyed such as sledding and making snow angels. Nell had made lists of sewing projects and tallied chess matches between her and Bitsy. On some pages, Nell had written about her mother, who Adam thought must have died before the diary was written, as Nell wrote of her in the past tense.

He flipped toward the end and found the first log dated in August of 1956.

August 1, 1956

He kissed me. He kissed me and had my eyes been closed I would have believed an angel had descended from heaven and pressed his lips to mine. He kissed me and my body turned to fire and danced and sparked and I have been unable to eat a bite since. Cocoa has commented that I seem strange and I long to tell her about the kiss, to share the joy that is bubbling inside of me, but I cannot.

Whatever he says, it is wrong. It is wrong in the eyes of God and yet I do not think I can stop. I do not think I want to.

The next entry was dated five days later.

August 6th, 1956

Today M gave me the remedy. That's what he calls it, the remedy to end Alice's suffering. He whisked me away to a beautiful hotel on the rocky shoreline of Lake Huron and we made love and drank champagne. When he handed me the small paper bag, I thought it was a ring—foolish girl. It was rat poison.

I lay in bed last night feeling the tin pressed beneath my mattress. It seemed to burn below me like the Princess and the Pea, except my fairytale feels as if it cannot have a happy ending. M is a married man. If all goes to plan, he will be a widower and I will be... what? His future wife? His young concubine? I cannot share my fears with anyone. This is the only place I feel safe to utter the dark thoughts plaguing me constantly. If I do this, I will be a murderess. Can I ever truly be redeemed for such an act? Even if she does want to die, even if she is suffering. How can I force the hand of God?

Adam's stomach churned. Michael Ashwood had given Nell rat poison to kill his wife.

"Holy crap," Adam murmured.

He turned the page to the next entry.

August 7th, 1956

Tomorrow is my eighteenth birthday and I am in love. Yet I have never wanted so much to disappear, be gone, cease to exist. I want to write about M, all the details of his hands and his words, but I find tonight that my hand is shaking so fiercely I can barely focus this pen. I'm sure it is my own imaginings, but I felt Alice Ashwood's eyes on me at dinner as if I had a scarlet A sewn onto my blouse. We read that book this winter, all of us girls together reading aloud by the fire in the den and now... now I am as guilty as Hester. I cannot look Alice in the eye. And even in the depths of my guilt, I long for him.

19

Adam's palms grew slick as he read. He stood and paced away from the couch, flipping to the next entry.

August 9th, 1956

Today I turned eighteen, and Alice handed me a choice. A train ticket to accompany Cocoa to Detroit leaving Monday, an apartment, a new life, an opportunity to flee from the terrible thing beneath my mattress, but in that choice, I would also be fleeing from Michael, my love, my heart and soul.

I can't think about it now. I am too conflicted, too frightened. My birthday party was lovely, but strange. Bitsy cried when her gift for me, the gold peacock given to her by her grandmother, vanished. Mildred went out of her way to tell me that the dress Alice had given to me once belonged to her missing daughter. I feel in the previous weeks as if I've stepped into someone else's life. I am never at peace.

The final entry was dated August 10, 1956—the day of the sail.

M said we must do it this weekend during the sail. On the boat when we are far out in the lake, far away from anyone who might intervene. He says 'we,' but it is I and I alone, for he will not be on the boat. I alone must slip the powder into her tonic before bed.

I love him so much. It makes me ill to think of life without him, but there's another illness growing, the illness of fear, of terror at what happens when I wake up the morning after on the boat and I hear the girls saying Mrs. Ashwood has not yet risen. How will I speak? I fear I will run to the deck and throw myself over the side.

And what of all that comes after? When we sail back to shore and we must watch the men carry her empty body in that long walk along the deck?

M will gather us girls around and say it's not our fault. And then the real terror will begin, because surely there will be questions, perhaps not an interrogation, but can I stand on sturdy legs if a policeman so much as asks me my name? Or will I crumple to the floor sobbing and screaming, 'It was me, it was me?' He says I am so strong. That I need only to remind myself again and again that it is a merciful act, that it is right.

But is it right?

Adam closed the diary and released the breath he'd been holding. One of the girls in the Ashwoods' house had been conspiring to kill Alice Ashwood, conspiring with Michael Ashwood. Not only to kill her, but to do it during the sail.

The rain ratcheted up another level, pounding the roof of the house.

He reclined on the couch and opened the diary again, flipping back to earlier entries. There was no mention of M before August 1956. Nell had mentioned Michael here and there, but she'd called him Mr. Ashwood and their exchanges had been insignificant.

~

Adam didn't know when he'd dozed off. His chin rested on his chest and the diary lay open in his lap. The rain had stopped, though it still dripped from the eaves.

He heard another sound and sat up quickly, the room slanting as a wave of dizziness washed over him.

From the second floor came the distinct pounding of footsteps. They stopped and then started again, but now coupled with the sound of dragging. A person was dragging something heavy across the floor. The footsteps started down the stairs, and the thing being dragged knocked a loud thunk on each step. It sounded like… like a body. A head smacking the steps one after another.

Adam pushed to his feet and crept toward the door. He pressed his ear against the wood and listened.

Nothing.

Adam snuck his cell phone from his pocket. The screen was black, the battery dead again.

He waited and listened. Whoever had been moving must be

standing just down the hall in the foyer. Did they know he was in the house?

His fear of opening the door agitated him. He was not a man prone to irrational fears and yet for the second time that day he found himself hunched behind a door, as if that provided some kind of protection—and from what…?

"From nothing," he muttered. "Because there's nothing there."

He opened the door, legs squared and ready if someone stood on the other side.

The hall and the foyer beneath the stairs yawned empty.

Adam hurried through the damp forest toward home. He didn't have a clue what time it was, and hoped Holly hadn't been trying to reach him.

As he stepped from the trees into the clearing behind his house, he spotted Holly in her garden. The grass and leaves sparkled from the rain. She'd changed into a faded dress with garden tools sticking from the sagging pockets and red mud boots. A smear of dirt marred her forehead. She studied the ground as if perplexed.

As he walked toward the house, she lifted her hand, shielding her eyes from the glare. The ring glinted in the sun, and Adam froze, staring at it.

"Hey there, handsome, out dancing in the rain?"

"Not quite, got caught in the downpour and took refuge in that old house."

"I stuck the pizza in the oven. Cheryl's friends gave me some beautiful mums, and I wanted to get them planted."

"I'm going to take a quick shower and then I'll join you."

She laughed. "Doesn't that seem counterintuitive? Showering before you play in the garden?"

He laughed, but the sound rang hollow. "If you smelled me, you'd be thankful I'm hitting the shower first."

"Not swimming in the sludge pool again, I hope."

He shook his head. "I've learned my lesson on that one."

Adam kicked off his boots inside the front door and walked to the study, pausing in the doorway. Holly must have cleaned the footprint from the rug. He closed the door behind him. He slid the photo of the girls from his back pocket and sat it on his desk, rifling through the drawers for a magnifying glass. He found it and held it over the image, zeroing in on Cocoa, specifically on her right hand dangling at her side. She wore a ring on that hand, a ring with a pale stone and an ornate setting. He shoved the glass and the photo in the drawer and moved back to the bathroom, stripped naked and turned on the shower.

Adam stood beneath the warm spray of the water, gradually turning it cooler. Bowing his head, he let the water run down his chest.

A girl in the Ashwoods' house had worn the ring. A ring that he'd found on one of several skeletons buried in an unmarked grave. Holly now wore the ring. A ring that belonged to a woman who'd disappeared during a sail in Lake Huron.

He closed his eyes and tried to piece it together, and the answer loomed big and ugly in his mind. The girl with the ring had been one of the bodies. If she'd been in the unmarked grave she couldn't have disappeared during a sail.

Maybe she'd given the ring to someone, to a person who'd died and been buried on the property where they now lived.

Then where were the coffins?

Where were the gravestones?

He hadn't asked those questions in the spring when he'd found the skeletons. He'd written it off as a family burial plot and yet... hadn't people been burying their dead in boxes for thousands of years?

Adam imagined the photo of the five girls of the Ashwoods' house and for an instant their flesh fell away and they were five skeletons gazing at him from black sightless holes.

20

After Adam helped Holly plant her mums, they ate their now lukewarm pizza on the porch. Holly sat on the swing and Adam in one of the rocking chairs he and Holly had bought from an Amish furniture store. As he ate, his eyes trailed to the ring on Holly's middle finger. His skin crawled each time he looked at it and he was tempted to insist she take it off, but he bit back the words, knowing the flood of questions that would come with such a demand.

"I invited Cheryl and Ted to our housewarming party," Holly said, tossing a piece of pepperoni to Marshmallow, who'd been watching anxiously each time Holly lifted the pizza to her lips.

"Oh, wow, yeah. I forgot about the party."

She raised an eyebrow. "You remember the party was your idea? And that it's tomorrow?"

"Yes, and I'm looking forward to it. It just slipped my mind."

"You've been off in the weeds a bit," Holly said, tapping on her temple. "What's going on up there?"

Adam took another bite, chewed and swallowed while he considered an answer that might satisfy her. "All the change, I guess. I didn't realize how accustomed I'd become to the routine of our old life. Still trying to figure out how this new one works."

"Pizza and naps mostly," she said.

~

Adam opened his eyes. The gossamer curtains billowed into the room, revealing Holly standing at the window, gazing at the sky where textured clouds moved quickly across.

"Honey," he murmured, scooting over and pulling back the blankets. "Come lie down."

She didn't turn.

"Holly."

The curtains continued to blow, but Holly did not stand within them.

He sat up and looked around the room, gazing again at the window. The curtain rippled, but no one stood within it.

Optical illusion, his brain lied, and Adam ate the lie because today was the housewarming party, and he couldn't start the day off by diving into that abyss.

Holly had already been awake for a while. Her empty oatmeal bowl sat in the sink beside her French press, which held only an inch of coffee in the bottom. Adam made his own French press, skipping the oatmeal. He found Holly on the porch swing, rocking and reading. Marshmallow lay curled beside her.

"Good morning beautiful." He kissed her.

"Mmm... you taste like coffee. Good morning to you."

"I'm going to run up to Cheboygan and pick up the food," he said, setting his coffee mug on the porch rail so he could stretch his arms overhead.

"Already?" She looked at her watch. "It's not even eight-thirty."

"Yeah, I'd like to get it early so we have time to assemble it on decent plates. I'm sure it will be in those aluminum pans."

"You're hoping to pawn it off as homemade?" She laughed.

He grinned. "None of our friends are that gullible. Now if we said *you* made it, they might believe me."

"Okay. Come here," she said.

He knelt in front of her and she cradled his head for a moment before kissing him on the lips. "I love you," she murmured.

He pulled away and his eyes caught on the ring on Holly's finger. He stood up quickly, averting his eyes from her hand. "I love you most," he told her, giving Marshmallow a rub on the head. "Need anything else while I'm gone?" he called out as he headed for his truck.

"Nope. Drive safe."

~

As Adam turned off of Black Mountain Road, he passed a little diner and his stomach rumbled. He braked and, checking that traffic was clear, made a u-turn and drove back to the café.

The No Lake View Diner was only a few degrees cooler than the already warm day and smelled of frying bacon. Adam's stomach gave another shout as he headed toward the counter.

In the front right corner sat a table of old men talking loudly. Half-eaten donuts, a few plates of eggs and coffee mugs surrounded by a scattering of plastic creamers lay strewn across the table.

Adam sat at the bar. "Can I have a cup of coffee and two eggs over easy with toast, please?" he asked the waitress, who slid a plastic laminated menu in front of him.

"Cream or sugar?" she asked.

"Nope, black is fine. Thank you."

"That was not in 1965!" one of the men exclaimed from the corner table. "Bill Marsh fell in the lake in 1956. You're reversing the years."

"Inverting," another man corrected.

"Inverting what?" the original guy who'd been talking shouted, tipping his head sideways as if hard of hearing.

All the men looked to be well into their eighties with age-spotted faces and white tufts of hair, if any hair at all.

"The years," a man wearing a shirt that read 'Professional Grandpa' in large green letters announced. "You switched '65 with '56." He hooked his fingers together as if that somehow clarified his point.

"Anyway," the original story-teller began. "Bill fell in the lake in his damned tuxedo. Wanda had steam coming out of her ears when he showed up at the church in that wrinkled tux. It had shrunk right up to his knees and elbows on account of him taking it to Sudsomatic, the laundromat down by the old bowling alley, and tossin' it in one of them big drying machines."

"He didn't wash it!" another man bellowed, laughing and slapping the table. "Just dried it. He stood up there in the church next to Wanda reekin' of pond scum and fish guts."

All the men laughed now, sending their table quaking.

Adam ate his eggs and listened to the stories of the old-timers. After he finished, he pulled ten dollars from his wallet and left it on the counter before making his way to the men's table.

"Hi," he said. "Sorry to interrupt."

The men turned to look up at him.

One of them squinted his way and then felt along the table for a pair of spectacles. "Is that my grandson, Charlie?"

"No, it ain't Charlie," another man snapped. "Charlie's barely five foot seven, and this fella is well over six feet tall."

"My name's Adam Tate. My wife and I just built a house out on Black Mountain Road. I wondered if I could join you? It seems you guys have been around for a while and I wanted to get a little history on this place."

Several of them seemed surprised by his question, but one nodded. "Sure you can. Pull up a chair. I'm Jerry. This joker beside me is Doug, or Dougie, as we call him. That one there with the hearing aids that don't hardly work is Bruce. Next to him is Ray and that last old coot wearing the grandpa shirt is Bill. We don't get much young blood at this table. Our wives shoo us out the door every morning like a gaggle of naughty schoolboys they're tryin' to get rid of."

"They are tryin' to get rid of us," Ray announced. "Last night Rita fed me a bowl a' chili that had me runnin' to the john all night. Tryin' to kill me is what she was doin'."

"Last I was at yer place, you had yer socks dryin' by the kitchen oven," Bill told Ray. "I don't blame her a bit fer tryin' to snuff you out early."

"Not a lot of young folks move up here to stay," the man called Dougie cut in. "Is this a summer-type house you've built?"

Adam shook his head. "No, it's permanent. We sold our business and… retired, I guess."

This struck the men as funny, and a peal of laughter rang out.

"Retired? What are you, son? Thirty years old?" Ray demanded.

"Thirty-seven."

"And you're retired!" Bill's eyes went wide. "What on God's earth are you gonna do with yourself for the next fifty years? Jesus and Mary. If my wife said we were retiring fifty years ago, I would have swum out to sea and let the tide take me away."

"Pearl would not have let you retire even if you had so much money you were wipin' your ass with it," Ray said.

Adam smiled. "My wife is sick, so we're… this was her dream. To live up here and we wanted the time together."

"Cancer?" Bruce asked. "That's what took my Nancy in '92."

"Heart failure," Adam said. "She's had two transplants and there's just no knowing, but the doctors said to prepare for the worst."

"Damn doctors and their no-good, rotten opinions," Ray insisted. "High and mighty, that's what they are. Thinkin' God gave them the right to pass judgment. You don't believe it, son, understand? It ain't over til it's over."

"Well, we're all dyin', Ray," Dougie reminded him. "Sooner or later we're all going into the ground."

"Not my Rita," Ray broke in. "She's gettin' cremated, already got an urn picked out and everything. Right now, she uses it for flowers. I said, 'Rita, I'm not spending the rest of eternity sittin' on some mantel above a fireplace, thinkin' I missed a turn and ended up in Hell.'"

"All right, all right," Jerry cut in. "What's on your mind, young man? I don't think you sat down to hear about our troubles."

"I overheard you talking and realized most of you have lived in the area for a while."

"I'd say!" Bill announced.

"The house we built is on Black Mountain Road up near the former Ashwood place."

A hush fell over the group, and they gazed at him thoughtfully.

"Must be deep in the woods to be up there. Gosh, is that house still standin'?" Dougie murmured.

"Yeah, it is," Adam continued. "And I've gotten an itch to find out more about what happened to the women who vanished during their sail."

"You and all the county," Ray said, lifting his coffee cup from the table and moving it shakily to his lips. "These drugs I've been takin' for the tremors don't do a damn thing," he muttered as coffee slopped onto his plate.

"Nothin' we know that everyone doesn't know," Jerry explained. "Alice and her girls went out for a weekend sail and never came home."

"The rumor mill was churning on the daily for a while there," Bill offered. "Not that you can put much stock in those, but one of the more insidious bits of gossip was that Alice Ashwood had done it all on purpose, killed herself and all the girls."

"No way, no how," Dougie said, shaking his head vehemently. "I knew Alice Ashwood. She used to come into the auto shop for an oil change and that woman was a saint. Always cartin' those girls, who weren't her own kin, mind you, into town for treats and pretty dresses.

She wasn't real social, but she donated to every charity at the church. That woman had a heart of gold."

"Maybe she did," Bill said, "but I have it on good authority she lost her marbles a bit after her daughter went missin'. My Pearlie found her swimmin' naked as a jay bird in the bay one time. The woman barely blinked an eye. Just got out, put a dress on without dryin' off and went walkin' down the road back toward home though she was a good five miles away from her house."

"Might be my son can help ya," Jerry offered. "He was a deputy for twenty-odd years. Retired now."

"That would be great. Thank you."

Jerry scrawled his son's name, Rob Donahue, and a phone number on a napkin stained with coffee. Adam slid it into his wallet and thanked the men before making for the door.

As Adam climbed into his truck, Bruce with the bad hearing aids came hobbling from the diner faster than it seemed his spindly legs could carry him. He waved at Adam to stop.

Adam rolled down his window.

"I gotta tip for ya, son. Man by the name of Leroy Dieter. Lives on Black Mountain Road. Can't see the house from the street. Four twenty-two is the address. He's got a big ole stone mailbox. That's his family's place, and he's lived there since he came into the world seventy-some odd years ago. He's got a phone, but don't ever answer it. He's not odd per se, but he don't leave much, so showin' up is the best way to pin him down."

"You think he'd have some information about the Ashwoods?"

"I sure do."

21

6 Days before the Sail

Mildred paused in the doorway, watching Cocoa applying makeup to Nell's upturned face.

"Everyone has one spectacular feature," Cocoa said, popping the top off a tube of lipstick. "You have great lips. Nice eyes too, but it's the lips that men will see." She rubbed the dark red lipstick over Nell's already pouty lips.

Mildred walked down the hall and slipped up the stairs into her own room, sitting at a chair in front of the vanity mirror. She studied her reflection with her square face, wide-sloping forehead that ended at her greasy brown hair.

"Beady eyes, thin lips…" she murmured, searching her face for that one spectacular feature and not finding it. "Bulbous nose, oily skin, thick eyebrows." She'd tried to pluck her eyebrows once after watching Cocoa do it, but it had stung so badly that tears rolled down her cheeks.

There was no special feature in Mildred's face. The only thing going for her was tucked behind all the flesh and bone. Her brain. How did someone make a brain beautiful?

Mildred had a thousand visions for her future. A famous novelist like Charlotte Brontë, a quirky artist living in New York, a traveler back-packing through Europe, a female pilot like Amelia Earhart, a renowned scientist like Marie Curie or perhaps something much simpler, a wife and a mother tending to a garden and rocking her babies to sleep each night.

Oddly, the wife and mother felt the most out of reach of those dreams. It was not merely the stuff of hard work. To become a wife and mother, one had to fall in love, gain the favor of a man, be proposed to, get pregnant. She could imagine stepping off a train in Nepal, bag heavy on her shoulders, a wrinkled map clutched in her hands, but she could not envision a man who might make her a wife. He had no face, no shape. He was merely a shadowy blur.

Or he had been, but now… now she could picture someone there. Since seeing Michael Ashwood and Nell tangled in the tack room, Mildred had begun to fantasize about him as the face in those visions. He was much older than her, far too old for Mildred or for Nell, but many women chose older, more experienced men. Mildred knew from the expression on Nell's face that she was no more practiced in the ways of lovemaking than Mildred herself was.

"Mildred and Michael sitting in a tree, K-I-S-S-I-N-G," Mildred sang, feeling around in her vanity drawer for the bits of makeup she'd stolen from the other girls. There wasn't much. A tube of lipstick nearly rubbed to its base, a compact with rouge, another compact with eyeshadow that had a cracked mirror.

Mildred puckered her lips. The red looked strange, as if she'd been sucking a cherry lollipop.

"Oh, Michael," she crooned. "Meet you in the barn? What will we do if your wife finds out?"

Over Mildred's shoulder, she caught movement in the mirror. Bitsy stood in her doorway, eyes narrowed on Mildred's face.

"What are you doing?" Bitsy asked, wrinkling her nose as if disgusted by the sight of Mildred.

Mildred glared at her in the glass, her face growing hot. She said nothing and after several awkward moments, Bitsy turned and disappeared down the stairs.

Mildred grabbed a tissue and rubbed the lipstick from her mouth. It smeared across her cheek and left her looking clownish and even uglier than usual.

"I hate you!" she snapped at her own reflection.

~

Cocoa put the final touches on Nell's makeup and lifted the handheld mirror. "What do you think?"

Nell considered her reflection. Her eyes looked larger, her full lips shiny. She almost resembled the girls in Cocoa's magazines.

"I like it," Nell said.

Cocoa studied her, cocking her head askew. "I know that love-struck look. Who is it? Leroy from the farm down the road?" Cocoa grinned and pinched Nell playfully on the arm.

Nell blushed and looked away.

Cocoa sighed and gazed wistfully toward the window. "Love is like a drug, isn't it? Like your first shot of whisky that burns all the way down and leaves you feeling fuzzy and breathless."

Nell's face grew hotter, and she pushed her dark hair off her forehead. "I've never tried whiskey."

"What?" Cocoa feigned shock. "Love's better, but whiskey's easier to come by. I'll bring a bottle home with me tonight. Tommy can buy it. You and I can sneak off to the woods and get a little tipsy."

Nell gazed again at her reflection and swallowed the lump in her throat, wondering what Michael would think of her face.

Cocoa took the mirror from Nell's hand and propped it against her pillow. "You could come with me to Detroit, you know?" Cocoa told Nell, twisting her hair up and securing it with bobby pins. "David has several very handsome friends. We could get an apartment in the city."

Nell stood and moved back to her own bed, sitting on the edge and watching Cocoa as she pulled on her slip and then drew her red velvet dress over her head.

"Why are you going out with Tommy Miller if you have a beau waiting for you in Detroit?" Nell asked.

Cocoa twiddled her fingers at Nell. Her mother-of-pearl ring caught the sun and shone. "This ring is pretty, but it's not an engagement ring, not even a promise ring. Until David makes a promise, I'm a free woman to do as I please."

"Do you want David to propose?"

Cocoa picked up her pearl necklace, securing it around her neck. "Not yet. I'm having too much fun."

~

After Cocoa left, Nell watched Tommy Miller's pick-up truck blowing up dirt as it twisted along the driveway and disappeared into the forest. They were driving to Cheboygan for dinner reservations. Nell tried to imagine what they'd have for dinner, maybe something fancy like duck or veal. Afterwards, they were going to the picture show.

The idea of a date seemed so lovely and ephemeral. She'd never been on a date. She wanted Michael to take her on a date, but of course he couldn't. He was a married man. They couldn't be seen out on the town with him opening doors and buying her dinners. They couldn't stroll along the beach holding hands or share an ice cream soda.

All those impossibilities made her heart hurt. She loved Michael. She loved him so intensely she wanted him to be hers and hers alone, but she hated to imagine she would never go on a date, never get dressed up the way Cocoa had tonight—electric with excitement, the night filled with possibility.

~

A chilly breeze had rolled up the hill from Lake Huron that morning, leaving the clothes stiff and dry as Alice took them off the line and carried them into the laundry room.

She frowned at a pair of Nell's panties. They had a slight discoloration, as if the girl had bled. Alice tilted the underwear. She knew Nell's monthly cycle. It happened during the new moon and currently the moon was approaching full. Nell might have tucked them into a drawer and forgotten to have them washed. There were simple explanations, but a disturbing truth tugged deep in her belly. Brief glances that had passed between Nell and Michael. A handful of moments when they'd both been unaccounted for.

Alice had assumed it would be Cocoa he chose with her flirtatious smile and her constantly swiveling hips, but it made sense now that it was Nell. Easy prey. A girl who—unlike Cocoa—had been ignored by everyone who was supposed to love her. She was the kind of girl who would worship him, see him the way he saw himself.

Alice closed her eyes and slowed her breath, sensing that looming shadow creeping ever closer.

Had God abandoned her?

Or had Alice abandoned God?

Her exit from the church had been swift and undramatic after Marilyn had vanished. Alice had been devoted. Hadn't she? Or maybe it had only been routine. Had it been reverence that led her to worship or simply the need for sameness? She'd gone every Sunday, perhaps in part so she could dress Marilyn in pretty dresses and show her off to the congregation.

Vanity, one of the seven deadly sins. And how many more had she committed?

And then there was Michael. He'd surely committed them all. Perhaps Marilyn had been taken as punishment for Michael's sins rather than Alice's own.

She picked up one of his shirts, a favorite of his—navy blue and white. She jerked a button off and dropped it. It rolled across the floor. She snatched a second button and third and squeezed them so tight in her fist her trimmed fingernails dug into her flesh.

Gathering her wits, she folded the shirt and added it to Michael's stack of clothes.

22

After Adam picked up the party food, he drove toward home, but bypassed his own house, heading to the address given to him by Bruce from the diner. He spotted the stone mailbox and turned onto the dirt driveway. It ended at a stone house that looked similar to the mailbox.

As Adam climbed from his truck, the front door swung open and a man moving with the help of a cane walked out and down the steps.

"Help ya?" he called.

"Hi, are you Leroy?" Adam asked.

"Yes."

"I'm Adam Tate. I live about a mile up the road."

The man nodded. "The new place up there?"

"Yeah. My wife and I built it. I'm sorry to just drop in on you like this."

The man smiled. "Not a problem. It's nice to see a neighbor being neighborly."

"Yeah..." Adam said, flooded with guilt that his intention was not to be neighborly, but to grill the man for information. "In fact, we're having a little housewarming party this afternoon if you'd like to come by."

"A party?" The man scrunched his already lined face.

"Just a little get-together. Eat some food, talk."

"Ah, I see. Well, I don't get out much. What time is this party happening?"

"Five o'clock."

The man shook his head. "Nope, no can do. My shows come on around then and I like to be tucked up tight by seven sharp. I appreciate the invitation though."

"You're welcome. Maybe some other time."

"Sure, sure." The man started back toward his house.

"While I've got you out here, can I ask you a few questions about the Ashwoods' house?"

Leroy turned back, squinting at him. "The Ashwoods? What in heavens for?"

"I stumbled on the house after we moved in and I've been curious. I haven't been able to find anyone who knows much about what happened."

"Well, that's 'cause everybody who knows is sitting at the bottom of Lake Huron."

"Were you in the area when it happened? The sailboat going down?"

"I was in this area, right here at my house."

"Do you remember anything strange that weekend? Anything that might have been related to the Ashwoods?"

The man leaned heavily on his cane, his face thoughtful. "Yeah, sometime that weekend, before we knew they'd gone missin', I remember my mom commenting on smoke in the sky comin' from the Ashwoods' house. It looked like they had quite a blaze going on."

"Did they often do bonfires?"

"Sure, sure—burning brush and twigs, and fires for the girls to sit around—but this looked like a helluva fire. I remember my ma being a little worried. 'What if it's the house?' she said, but then she dropped it, figuring she was being paranoid about the whole thing. Being a young lad myself, I would'a gone to check it out, but I had a touch of the flu that weekend."

"You're saying that after the women would have gone sailing, but before they were reported missing, there was a big fire, so... the fire didn't come from them?"

"Hard to say. I'm not sure where it came from. Might'a been Michael Ashwood was home by then and doing some burning. Could also have been smoke blowing from somewhere else."

"Huh, that's odd, isn't it? Were there many other houses in the area that might have been burning something? I mean even today it's pretty isolated."

"If the wind was just right that smoke could'a blown from miles away. Might not have been the Ashwoods' place at all."

"Is there anything else at all that seemed peculiar around that time? Before or after the sail."

The man shifted around on his feet, wincing as if his legs ached.

"Another strange thing… I went up by the house a time or two after the tragedy. I always took walks in the woods, and before Alice passed, I'd come across Alice once in a while and she'd offer me a lemonade and we'd sit on her porch and chat. I was right sad about what had gone on. I've never been much of a sleepin' man, an affliction my daddy suffered from and his daddy before him. In the evening, I'd walk to get the jitters out.

"One night I was out that way by the Ashwoods' place. I saw a light on in the window and glanced at it a few times, not thinking much, until I noticed not one but two shadows behind the curtain. The man, I'm sure, was Michael Ashwood, tall and square-shouldered, but the other was smaller, more like a woman, not so very unlike Alice Ashwood, who barely came up to Michael's shoulder."

"Could it have been family visiting? Someone who came to support him after the tragedy?"

"Could'a been, but I never saw anyone who matched that. No newcomers in town who said they were there helping Michael. There were only two cars in the driveway that night—Michael's pick-up truck and Alice Ashwood's Newport."

"Did you think it was Alice? Is it possible Alice survived the sail and faked her own death?"

Leroy smiled. "Sounds like the plot of them shows my wife used to watch. Before she died, she liked something called *NCIS* with all kinds of far-fetched crime stories."

"A lot of the cases they cover on that show are actually real, fictionalized, but coming from real cases."

Leroy shook his head in wonderment. "The world just gets stranger and stranger. To tell you the truth, sometimes I don't think it's bad that my wick has just about burned out. I'm not sure I want to see what's comin'."

Adam nodded. "I know what you mean."

Leroy wagged his finger back and forth. "Oh, no, you don't. You're a young buck. You've got a lot of road still to cover. No point gettin' cynical until the arthritis keeps you from doing much about it. Right now, you've got the world by the balls, pardon my French. Don't let 'em go."

Adam laughed. "Sometimes it feels like the other way around."

Leroy guffawed and pounded his cane on the ground. "Don't I know it. You just hold yer wife tight and wake up every morning like it might be your last, that'll keep the world at bay for a while. Anyhow, do I think it might'a been Alice up there?" He shook his head. "Not likely. Alice was a good woman, a simple woman, not the kind to hatch any murderous schemes. If anyone was like to do something like that, it was Michael Ashwood."

"Why do you say that?"

"There was something not quite right about him. My ma used to call him a flimflammer. He was real good at charmin' people, but if you looked hard, you could see dark thoughts swirlin' behind those fancy blue eyes a' his. He was a womanizer, no doubt about it. Most of the townsfolk knew. I'd be surprised if Alice herself didn't know.

"And I'd be lyin' if I said that wandering started after their daughter went missing. It had been going on for years. Probably going on before they even got married, but I believe Alice turned a blind eye and as long as she had her daughter, that was fine, but I think there came a point after Marilyn vanished when it wasn't fine anymore. I heard of 'em fighting a few times, pretty nasty fights.

"I overheard my ma and pop talking about it one night. She told my pop that Michael Ashwood hauled off and smacked Alice right across the face. I'm sure he didn't think anyone was lookin', but they were. My ma and her sister had just come walking around the side of the grocery store when it happened. Alice looked embarrassed and got right into their car. Michael didn't even have the decency to look ashamed. In fact, I remember my ma saying that he looked murderous, like he'd intended to do more than slap her, and she was sort of grateful they'd come along because who knows."

"He hit her? Was that a regular thing?"

"Hard to say what happens on the regular behind closed doors."

"Was Alice close to anyone? Anyone who might know more about what went in the house?"

"All in all, the Ashwoods kept to themselves. In a town like this, that was seen as bein' uppity, thinkin' the regular folk was below 'em. A few ladies thought they were charitable havin' the girls' home, but other folks saw it different. More than a few whispered they had all them girls to keep Michael at home. Others said them girls put on airs too.

"I'll tell you, though, I knew from a young age that Alice had a loving heart. I remember the first time I met her. I was just eight years old. I'd gotten an ice cream in town after workin' five days on the farm pitchforkin' the cattle stalls. I biked all the way into town for an ice cream cone. I'd only ever had ice cream once in my life and I dreamed about it. I bought that ice cream cone, chocolate-flavored, got one lick and tripped on the curb. Ice cream right into the street." His face paled. "I can still remember how my stomach just plunged right outta me, and I was tryin' not to cry because there were some other boys from school there. They were laughin' at me. I started off down the block, lookin' for somewhere to bawl my eyes out, and all of a sudden, I felt this hand on my shoulder, a soft hand, like a little bird had landed there. I turned to see Alice Ashwood. I was blinkin' back tears, and she said, 'This is for you.' And she handed me a bonafide banana split. I'd never had one of those. Those were expensive. I stood there, struck dumb, and she put that bowl in my hands, patted my head, and just walked off down the street."

~

Adam returned home to find Holly, Cheryl, Ted, and several older women he didn't know in the backyard. They'd erected a large white tent, and two women were stringing party lights along the edges.

"Look what Ted and Cheryl brought us," Holly called.

"I tried to call and warn ya, but your cell went straight to voicemail." Ted laughed.

Adam pulled out his cell phone and frowned at his phone's blank screen, shaking his head irritably. "Something's been off with my phone. Thanks though. That looks great. I hadn't even thought about a tent."

"There's my favorite brother-in-law," a voice shouted. Holly's brother Duke walked around the side of the house carrying a stack of folding chairs.

"Duke! Hey, man. How are ya?" Adam grabbed him in a half hug and took several of the chairs, walked back into the tent and set them up.

"I'm good. Feeling guilty I haven't made it up here before now to see the new house. It's brilliant. I can't believe how fast you got it built."

"Yeah, the contractor did a great job."

"You did too, Adam," Holly called. "I'm pretty sure you worked longer hours on this house than any of the crew."

Adam shrugged. "I had to make sure it was done the way we wanted it."

"If I ever stop working sixty hours a week," Duke said, "I might contact them. I keep looking at property. I'd love to build, but damn if it doesn't seem like a massive undertaking."

"It was that," Adam agreed.

Holly walked over and put an arm around Adam's waist. "Everything went good picking up the food?"

"Yep, easy-peasy."

The party was a success. Everyone raved about the food, which Adam admitted they'd ordered from a restaurant further north. Adam and Holly's friends from Grand Rapids had joined them along with Duke, Ted and Cheryl and several of the ladies in Cheryl's group.

Adam popped the top on a bottle of craft beer and opened two more for Fiona's husband Carl and Diane's husband Lonny. Holly had gone to high school with both the women and Adam had become close with their husbands after he and Holly started dating.

The men sat on deck chairs on the front porch talking about the latest PGA tour. Most of the women were still in the backyard beneath the tent.

Adam handed the men their beer and sat down. He only half-listened, enjoying the first beer buzz he'd had in over a year.

Marshmallow emerged from the woods. The dog's muzzle and front legs were dirty, as if he'd been digging. As he trotted toward the house, Adam realized Marshmallow held a bone clutched in his jaws.

Nearly knocking over his beer, Adam jumped up and leapt off the porch, grabbed Marshmallow's collar and directed him back into the trees.

"Uh-oh. Did he get ahold of some carrion out there?" Duke called. "Better not let him in the house or your new couch will be reeking of dead animal for weeks."

Adam, sweating, offered a thumbs up, half dragging Marshmallow toward the woods. The dog resisted, planting his feet.

"Come on, Marshmallow. Come on."

As Adam had feared, Marshmallow had dug a gaping hole beside the pudding stone. Marshmallow had dug deep, flinging dirt across the large boulder and burying the grass surrounding it.

"Drop it... drop it!" he commanded Marshmallow, who held the bone tight for another moment and then reluctantly released his jaws. "Shit... shit... shit," Adam muttered, tossing the bone, a femur, into the hole and kicking at the dirt to cover it back up. He ripped handfuls of weeds and grass and added it to the hole.

Adam tried to push the pudding stone over the hole, but it was enormous and didn't budge. He opted for armfuls of sticks and brush, throwing them into the hole and snapping at Marshmallow each time he crept closer. After he'd covered the hole, he put Marshmallow in the house.

"Deer or something dead out there?" Lonny asked.

Adam sat and picked up his beer, taking a big swig. "Something," he muttered.

23

Hungover from the previous night's libations, Adam downed a few aspirins with a glass of orange juice.

Through the window, he saw Holly sitting outside in the hammock. A puff of white nestled beside her, which meant she'd managed to get Marshmallow into the hammock.

Something scratched at the wood floor beneath him. He hadn't checked the animal trap he'd put in the crawlspace and wondered if something had gotten caught inside it.

Adam grabbed a flashlight and shuffled into the pantry, opening the crawlspace door. He dropped into the hole and crawled on hands and knees toward the trap. Despite the sound he'd heard, he couldn't see anything inside the metal cage. The cavity beneath the house smelled dank and earthy. It wasn't an unpleasant smell. He liked the scent of dirt, but something mingled with it, something flowery, almost like perfume.

Adam peered into the murky corners, but he couldn't see much beyond a few feet away. The scratching had stopped as soon as he climbed into the crawlspace. No glowing eyes peered at him from the shadows.

As he started back toward the opening, something shifted in the dirt beneath him. Before he could peer closer, arms reached from the ground and wrapped around his back, yanking him hard onto his belly.

He shrieked and grabbed hold of one arm, but the flesh slid away and left only slick bone beneath his palm. Screaming, Adam tried to wrench the bone free, but it held him pinned to the dirt floor. His flashlight rolled out of reach.

The skeleton arms squeezed tighter, forcing the air from Adam's lungs, cutting off his shouts. He couldn't breathe. His lungs felt like they'd explode. He clawed at the dirt, trying to scramble forward, but the grip around his torso was too strong.

A blast of light poured into the crawlspace.

"Adam? Is that you?" Duke called.

"Help," Adam croaked.

Duke jumped into the crawlspace, squatting with surprising agility for the large man. "What is it? Are you stuck? Throw your back out?"

The bony arms released him. Adam pushed onto hands and knees and fled toward Duke, who hoisted himself back out of the hole. Adam followed, lunging away from the opening, grabbing the cover and slamming it back into place. Dirt clung to his t-shirt and face.

"Whoa, take a breath. You okay, man?" Duke asked. "You're so white you look purple."

Adam rubbed his face, pushing his fingers into the corners of his eyes. His headache had gone from a three to an eight in the previous thirty seconds. "Yeah. I'm fine. Too much beer last night."

"I'd say it was probably the tequila, not the beer that's giving you trouble."

"Tequila?" A fuzzy memory accompanied the word. Carl had pulled out a bottle of tequila and insisted they go shot for shot. "Ugh, shit. I forgot about that. God, I haven't had a drink in months. I thoroughly overdid it."

Duke chuckled. "You got to rambling about some pretty strange stuff, I'll give you that."

"I did?"

"Yeah, corpses in the ground and something about a sinking ship. At one point, you tried to run off into the woods. Lonny tackled you to the ground. We half considered tying you to the chair."

Adam stared at him in surprise. "Where was Holly?"

"She'd already gone to bed. She was tuckered out."

"I should have gone to bed with her, made sure she was fine."

"She was fine and she insisted we keep you up and get you drunk. Holly said you never relax anymore, and it was our duty to get you good and sloshed so you couldn't stress for a night."

"Well, I should have known better."

"What's going on, Adam? Why'd you just come flying out of that hole like a demon was snapping at your heels?"

"I'm… feeling strange, a little obsessed, maybe. I can't seem to get a grip on things."

"Hold up," Duke said. "What do you mean, you're obsessed? Obsessed with what? Holly's heart? She mentioned you've been a little off."

"It's more than that. Something happened…" He almost spilled it. Told Duke the whole story from the first bone he'd seen in the ground. Instead, he bypassed the mass grave and skipped forward. "I found this old house in the woods not far from here. Turns out it belonged to a couple who used to care for teenage girls. A bunch of them went missing after a sailboat ride in Lake Huron."

"Damn, that's rough."

"Yeah."

"I'm not making the connection though with your… being obsessed or whatever."

"It started with curiosity. Just going out to the house to poke around. The place is strange. It's like they all walked out the door one day for a picnic and never returned."

"Or for a sail."

"Yeah, but they didn't all sail. The husband was out of town. Why didn't he take any of their things when he moved away?"

"Grief."

Adam sighed. "After my mother died, my dad couldn't even part with her old medicine, with her little notebooks of to-do lists. It took him years to get rid of that stuff. I was almost as bad. I carried around boxes of her stuff for years. Finally, Holly got me to part with all of it except a few mementos. I'm just saying it strikes me funny."

"So that's the obsession? Digging around some old abandoned house?"

"No, not exactly, not the house itself, but… the girls. With what happened to them."

"Their boat sank, and they drowned."

"You're probably right. I mean, that's the logical thing. I guess I'm just floundering here," Adam admitted.

"How so?"

"I've always worked, had a purpose that got me out of bed every morning. Holly's been my purpose for a long time, but work was like the glue that held it all together. We had the coffee shop, and that was a seven-day-a-week kind of gig. After that I was working on this place and I was hands-on at every level. If I wasn't here, I was at doctors' appointments with Holly. Then we finished this place and… I don't know. I've felt detached, like the gravity of my life has been removed and I'm floating away.

"Holly wants me to be present, to sit and listen to the crickets and watch the moon rise, and sometimes I can, but… the idle time makes me think, and what I think about is her heart and life without her and what I'm going to do on the other side. When I start going down that road, I want to rage and smash things and throw my hands up at this whole fucking charade."

"And this other situation gives you something else to focus on."

"Yeah. Holly's been telling me for years I need a hobby. Maybe this is it."

"Picking around an old farmhouse? Imagining what happened to the people who lived there?"

Adam shuddered, feeling the phantom touch of the skeleton that had reached up from the ground and taken hold of him.

Duke chuckled. "Have you considered taking up golf instead?"

That afternoon, Holly and Duke left to visit an old friend from their childhood days. Adam begged off, citing his hangover. Though they both gave him skeptical looks, they left him behind.

Adam waited until the van disappeared down the driveway and then he stuffed his feet into his boots and started for the Ashwoods' house.

As Adam jumped onto the porch, his breath, which he hadn't realized he'd been holding, shook loose. Stepping through the door felt like walking into the house of an old friend and yet… an old friend didn't live here. No one did and no one had for a very long time.

Adam passed the wall of photos in the foyer and paused to look at an image of Alice and Michael Ashwood.

"What happened to you?" he whispered, focusing on Alice's face—young and bright beneath her wedding veil, clueless to the horrors lying in wait.

He half expected a response, but she stared back unspeaking, her lips frozen in a smile.

Adam had explored every room in the house except the basement and when he opened the door, a cold, musty air drifted out. He was instantly transported back to the crawlspace in his own home and the arms reaching up to drag him down. He didn't want to go down there, had no intention of going down there.

Narrow steep stairs led into the black. He couldn't see the floor at the bottom. The stairway might have plunged into a hole a thousand feet deep. Even as his better sense demanded he shut the door and walk away, Adam knew he needed to see what lay at the bottom of those stairs.

He didn't have a flashlight, so he retreated to the kitchen and shuffled through drawers, remembering one had contained candlesticks and matches. When he found it, he took out two long white candles, slid one into his back pocket. He drew a match from the box, swiped the red tip along the side. It lit and went out. He tried a second one. The wooden match broke. He dropped it on the counter and grabbed a third. This one he managed to light long enough to get the head of the match to the wick of the candle. It lit, bloomed orange, and shrank back to a tiny flame.

He shoved the box of matches into his pocket, cupped one palm around the flame, and returned to the top of the cellar stairs. Walking slowly, his feet far too big for the narrow planks, he started down. Cobwebs prickled over his face and arms. Little strands burst into flame and fizzled out.

It was an old Michigan basement. Uneven walls constructed from stone and concrete lay beneath the house. He saw a set of wooden shelves. Glass jars and cans lined the shelves. They'd been labeled with masking tape. Cherries, apples, zucchini, cucumbers. On the next shelf, large bags of grain and flour were stacked. Adam caught two glowing eyes staring out from between the bags. When he moved his candle closer, a small rat scurried away and disappeared behind the shelf.

A photo, scattered with rat poop, lay behind the jars. Adam pulled it out, shaking off the small black pellets. It was a duplicate of the picture he'd found in the upstairs bedroom that depicted the five girls, but in this copy two of the girls' faces had been slashed and scratched as if someone had taken a black pen and not merely scribbled but stabbed at their eyes. The two obliterated faces belonged to Cocoa and Nell. The image troubled him, and he shoved it back onto the shelf.

Something shifted to his right and Adam turned, blinking into the darkness.

He sensed that someone stood tucked into the corner, watching him. His skin crawled and a voice in his head urged him to run. Race back up the stairs and into the daylight. Instead, he inched closer, holding the candle a full arm's length away to see what lay in that inky space. He took a step and another. A breath blew at him, warm and rancid-smelling. His candle puffed out.

24

Adam halted. The darkness so startled him he could not remember which way the stairs lay. He took a faltering step back. Something darted toward him. He threw up his hands and bellowed as a strong wind blew him backwards, rushing through his hair and clothes. Behind him, something banged.

Adam turned and groped for the stairs, finding them only when his shin slammed against the bottom step. He cursed under his breath.

Where was the trickle of light from the first floor?

Even as his mind posed the question, he knew the answer. The sound he'd heard had been the door above him slamming shut. Leaning forward to grab the planks with his hands, Adam fumbled up the stairs. At the top he searched the darkness for the door handle and when his fingers closed upon it, the vision of his aunt in the bathtub, blood dripping from her wrists, seared across his mind.

The door would be locked. He would be trapped.

But it wasn't. The handle turned, and he burst into the hallway, where the heavenly wash of daylight brought the world back into focus. He lurched away from the basement door, shoving it closed, and made for the living room. He slumped onto a rodent-eaten chair, which protested, but didn't collapse.

"It's fine, you're fine," he murmured.

The candle he'd shoved into his back pocket had broken when he sat down. He yanked it out and tossed it on the floor. The fractured candle rolled and stopped. A dark stain peeked from beneath the woven fabric.

He contemplated the stain and then stood and grabbed the edge of the rug. He dragged it to the corner and folded it in half. A dozen or more of the discolorations mottled the hardwood. He leaned closer, thinking they were burns, but no, they looked like spilled red wine that had left a blackish residue in its wake.

One spot appeared crusted over. When Adam got close, the scent of blood and vomit washed over him. He recoiled. The smear had likely been dried for decades. It made little sense that it smelled, and when he sniffed at it again, no trace of the odor remained.

He left the house troubled by the besmirched floor. The stains could have come from an accident long before the women went missing, but… why did one area contain a texture as if no one had cleaned it up? Rather than clean it up, someone had pulled a rug over top of it.

If Alice Ashwood had been such a shoddy housekeeper, surely the rest of the house would reveal similar disarray. Then again, she'd shared the house with five teenage girls. It wasn't out of the question to think one of them had concealed the spill to hide it from the Ashwoods.

But it wasn't a spill, it was vomit. The odor was unmistakable. Surely not even a young girl would hide vomit beneath a rug.

He trudged through the woods and his boot caught on something hard. He pitched forward and landed on his hands and knees. A stick jabbed into his palm and Adam winced, pulling it free.

Adam sifted through the grass for the object that had tripped him. His fingers closed on a long metal pole. He tried to lift it, but it was heavy and embedded in the dirt. He walked the length of it, clearing soil away. The metal pole was at least thirty feet long and streaked in black.

Adam moved in a circle around the pole, kicking at the dirt. His foot struck something hard, and he dug it from the ground. It was round with spokes, but also burned black. He held it up, studying it.

As he gazed through the spokes that revealed the forest beyond, Adam understood what he held. The wheel of a ship.

"Of a sailboat…" he whispered.

~

At home, Adam grabbed the photo of the girl from the Ashwoods' house. He laid it on his desk and stared at it, considering first Cocoa's ring and then studying her features. He thought she most resembled the woman he'd encountered in the attic.

"The ghost," he said, and then a laugh bubbled out of him.

What was he saying? That the house was haunted, that Cocoa had visited him there. What other explanation could there be?

They hadn't drowned in Lake Huron; their boat hadn't capsized. They'd died in the Ashwoods' house, and Adam felt certain those ominous dark stains were evidence of whatever crime had been committed there. His stomach churned at the thought because he, Adam Tate, had helped to cover up that crime more than fifty years later.

He pushed the photo back into the drawer and walked to the bathroom. He needed a shower. Whatever had rushed through him at the house seemed to have left a residue. He wanted to scrub it away.

Adam stood beneath the spray turning the handle until the water practically scalded him. As he thought of the Ashwoods' fate, the water turned icy.

"Whoa," he gasped.

He fiddled with the handle, but he'd cranked it all the way to hot. Frustrated, he turned it off and stepped, shivering, from the shower.

A dizzy spell swirled through him and he grabbed the sink with one hand, swiping the fogged mirror with the other. His eyes looked bloodshot.

Something flickered behind him and he spun around, losing his balance.

"Adam!" Holly exclaimed, catching him before he crashed into the wall. She breathed heavily, her thin arms snaked around his waist.

Adam grabbed the doorframe with his hand, easing his weight off Holly.

She looked at him, eyes shifting back and forth between his own. "Are you drunk?"

He blinked at her, rubbed the bridge of his nose with his thumb and forefinger and shook his head. "No. Still suffering from last night's poor choices."

Holly smiled and handed him a towel.

"Where's Duke?" Adam asked.

"He got a call from one of his staff and had to head home. He's going to come back next weekend for a visit though."

"Oh, okay. Did you guys have fun today?"

"Yeah, it was nice to catch up." Holly took his hand and led him down the hallway to the living room. "Have a seat and I'll get you a glass of water."

"I can get it," he told her, but she shook her head and gave him a little shove toward the couch.

He sat heavily. Marshmallow padded in from the kitchen and put his head in Adam's lap.

"Hey, buddy, how's the floof boy doing today?"

Marshmallow licked his hand and then flopped onto the floor.

The television set turned on, releasing a screech of sound as a movie appeared with a couple shrieking on a rollercoaster ride. Both Marshmallow and Adam jumped to their feet.

Holly appeared in the doorway. "What are you watching? My gosh, it's loud."

Adam snatched the remote off the coffee table and turned it off. He took the glass from Holly and sat down slowly, trying to steady his hands to take a drink.

"I think I'd like to go to Cheryl and Ted's church tomorrow morning. Touchstone Ministries," Holly told him.

He looked up, surprised. "Really?"

She shrugged and smiled as if shy about the proclamation, which was unlike her. "I know it's never been your thing. It's never been my thing, but… I'd like to go. I keep having this daydream of sitting in the quiet of a church watching the sun filter through the stained-glass windows. It seems really peaceful."

He took her hand. "Okay, but I'm not wearing a tie."

She laughed. "You don't even own a tie."

"Exactly."

In the morning, Adam made coffee, groggily moving around the kitchen. He'd woken several times in the night, eyes shooting open and ears perked for a sound. Once he'd heard a door slam loudly and when he sat up, he'd found their bedroom door closed tight, though he knew he'd left it open. He'd discovered Marshmallow in the hallway, whimpering, and let the dog back into the bedroom. He'd returned to bed, but his sleep had been restless.

Adam poured boiling water over the grounds and leaned heavily against the counter, gazing out the window at the light steadily creeping across the lawn.

He heard Holly coming down the hall.

"Good morning, sunshine." He smiled.

But Holly did not stand behind him. Silhouetted in the doorway was the same woman he'd seen in the Ashwoods' house. Her eyes were sunken in her head and black dribbled from the corner of her mouth. A large, dark vein stood out against her pale forehead. Her dress was dirt-caked, her fingernails black.

"Can I…" The words stalled. No. He could not help her. She was dead. She was dead and standing in his doorway, watching him as if she'd only just stepped off a path in the woods to say hello.

The front door opened and Holly started in.

"No, don't come in here," Adam shouted, spinning toward the door, ready to block her entrance.

On she came, holding a handful of flowers from her garden.

"Holly, no!" he commanded.

She stopped. "What's wrong? Did you drop something?"

The muscles in his face were frozen in place. Surely, she could see the terror there, but apparently not as she peered beyond him. He expected her own face to go ashen, her eyes to widen as she spotted the girl in the doorway. Holly stepped closer, searching over his shoulder and down at the floor as if looking for a broken glass.

Adam turned, though he already knew the girl would be gone.

25

1956

5 Days Before the Sail

"Girls?" Michael looked sternly from Cocoa to Nell. Nell, who still held the whiskey bottle clutched in both hands, shook as she lowered it, face blazing.

Cocoa grinned and shrugged, stubbing out her cigarette and tucking it back into the silver case embossed with little stars. She stood from the log and wiped off the seat of her pants. "Just girls being girls, Mr. Ashwood." She laughed.

"Please go back to the house, Cocoa. We'll talk about this later."

Cocoa held a hand out for Nell, who stood shakily to her feet.

"Not you, Nell," he said. "I'd like to speak to you now."

Cocoa lifted an eyebrow. Nell nodded.

"I'll see you back there," she murmured.

Cocoa started away and then turned back. "Take it easy on her, Mr. Ashwood. I supplied the bottle."

"I'm sure you did," he said curtly.

When they were alone. Michael took the bottle from the log and sniffed it before raising it to his lips and tilting it up. Amber liquid poured from the opening into his mouth. He closed his eyes and swallowed.

"How was it, Nell?" he asked, handing the bottle back to her. "Did you like it?"

She blinked, unsure of how to answer. Was it a test? Was she supposed to say no?

"I'm not sure," she admitted. "I feel a little… funny."

He stepped forward and leaned close, inhaling her. "I smell it on you."

She fidgeted, playing with the buttons on her shirt.

Michael lifted his fingers to her hand, brushing hers away as he tugged the button from the fabric. He squared off in front of her, taking both hands to her shirt now and deftly pulling each button free. She stood before him, her shirt open to reveal her white lace bra. He lifted a finger to her throat and slid it down, tracing a line between her breasts.

"I haven't been able to stop thinking about you," he whispered, kissing her collarbone.

She swallowed, the warmth in her face travelling down. She felt the pulsing between her legs, that now familiar craving.

"Me too…" she murmured, moaning when he reached one hand beneath her skirt and sought the warmth there. She leaned into him.

He kissed her neck and shoulders. He didn't take his pants off, only unbuttoned them and let them fall to his knees. He lifted her up and pressed her back against a wide birch tree. She wrapped her legs around him. As he closed against her, she closed her eyes and buried her face in his neck.

Mildred stood as still as a great oak. She barely breathed as she watched them, the nakedness of Nell with her skirt up and Michael with his pants slipping down. It was wrong what they were doing, and Mildred's whole body prickled with the knowledge of what she'd witnessed now, not once but twice. The power of it made her fingertips tingle, her heart race.

Nell had begun to moan, Michael to grunt. How brazen of them to commit such an act in the open forest for anyone to stumble upon them. Alice Ashwood had stayed in bed most of the day with a headache, but still she haunted the property like a ghost, slipping amongst the trees, along the roads. What if she decided to get up, take in the fresh air?

The thought of it both excited and terrified Mildred. What would become of them if Alice Ashwood discovered Michael's infidelities? Surely Nell would be sent away, but would they all be?

~

When Michael finished, he lowered Nell into the soft grass onto her back. She sat up and clutched him.

"I feel guilty, Michael," she murmured against his chest.

He sighed and nodded. "I understand, I do. I feel guilty too, Nell, but I want you to understand, Alice and I haven't lived as a husband and wife in years. Alice turned cold toward me a long time ago."

"You don't love Alice anymore?"

He looked at her squarely. "No, I don't. Alice is unwell. She has been for many years. Mental things. She's getting worse. She's talked about killing herself and… well, I think I might help her."

Nell's eyes widened. "But… that's a mortal sin."

"She's living in hell. This world for her is pure hell. She wants to leave, but she can't do it on her own because of what you said. It's a mortal sin."

Nell pulled her knees beneath her. Michael moved her hair aside and kissed the back of her neck.

"I won't pretend that I don't feel what I feel, Nell. I love you. I love you so much it hurts."

She looked up at him, eyes widening. No man had ever told her he loved her. Her own mother had barely spoken the words. It took her breath away.

"I can't live without you, Nell. I can't. If they take Alice away, they'll take all of you as well. It wouldn't be appropriate, a grown man living with you girls."

Her stomach clenched painfully at the thought. In that instant, she thought she'd die if she lost Michael.

"Nell… would you help me? Help me set Alice free?"

"Set her free? What do you mean?"

He tipped her chin up. "Free her from this life. Let her pass on in peace."

Nell stared at him, unblinking. Her mouth quivered.

"It's not murder if the person wants to die, Nell. And then we could be together. Don't you see? It's the only way. We're on a track right now that ends with Alice in a mental institution trapped for the rest of her life. I couldn't keep the girls here. It wouldn't be appropriate."

"But if she died… how could we possibly be together?"

"We'd start over. Sell the house and move anywhere we want. Florida or California. Somewhere without winters, somewhere with beaches as white as cream and water the color of gemstones. Can you imagine? I could give that to you, Nell. Anything you've ever dreamed of."

~

"Did he flip his lid?" Cocoa asked, when Nell returned from the woods. Cocoa sat at the vanity table, rolling her hair into curlers.

Nell wrapped her arms across her chest. "No, not really. He just said not to do it again and not to let Mrs. Ashwood find out."

"No kidding. That wet rag would probably send us both packing. Can you say hypocrite? She's married to a guy who puts away three snifters a night, not to mention I've seen her throw back a few."

Nell swallowed, shame at the mention of Alice Ashwood making her squirm. "Yeah. I'm going to get into bed. I'm pretty tired."

"Are you sure? Bitsy and Margie are making popcorn to watch *Alfred Hitchcock Presents*."

"I'm not up for it tonight."

~

Nell lay in bed. Her skin vibrated where Michael had kissed her. Her panties were still damp, her inner thighs sticky. She should have showered, but didn't want to wipe the sensation away. She wouldn't sleep, not for a while. She'd relive it again and again.

Nell tried to imagine him. He was somewhere in the house. Maybe settling into his chair to watch *Alfred Hitchcock Presents*. Maybe he'd even gone to bed with Alice. Did he still make love to his wife? Did he kiss her the way he kissed Nell? The thought made her burn. Made her want to kick off her covers and run from the house.

Michael was not hers. He was married to another woman, a woman who had cared for Nell, taken her in, and shown her kindness. They'd given Nell things she wouldn't have had if she'd gone into an orphanage or been moved into a foster family.

Nell hadn't said yes to his proposition, not exactly, and yet Michael acted as if she had. He talked about ways that would be easiest, insisting again and again on one—poison. No one would look too deeply. Alice had a lifetime of health issues. She'd simply fall asleep and never wake up. It was kind, merciful even.

A pinch of poison and Alice Ashwood would be gone.

26

Adam put on a falsely cheery smile as he and Holly got ready for church.

Holly wore pale gray slacks and a sleeveless white blouse. She arranged her hair in a French braid. Adam opted for khaki shorts—the heat was simply too oppressive for pants—and a red golf shirt.

"I feel like a doofus in this shirt," he told her, smirking.

His father had bought him the shirt as a gift when he and his wife had visited Holly and Adam for Christmas the year before. He'd never worn it and never intended to.

"You could just wear one of your normal shirts. The plain gray one would be good."

"Nah, it's okay. Now if my dad asks about the shirt, I can tell him I wore it at least once."

As they headed for the door, Adam grabbed his phone off the charger. The screen was black.

"God dammit!" he shouted, shaking his phone as if that would somehow spark it back to life.

"Honey, it's okay. It's just a phone."

"It's not okay, Holly. It's not okay because if I'm away from the house and something happens, you have no way to call me and it hasn't been working and I haven't taken the time to get a new one."

"Adam..." She put a hand on his arm.

He dropped his eyes, ashamed at his outburst. "I'm sorry... really. I don't know what's gotten into me lately."

"Well, I am dragging you off to church this morning. Maybe you need a little outburst so you don't start laughing hysterically during the service."

He grinned and slipped the dead phone into his side pocket. "Better laughing than screaming."

~

They arrived at Touchstone Ministries fifteen minutes before the service was scheduled to begin.

Ted greeted them at the door. He beamed and grabbed Holly in a hug before giving Adam a vigorous handshake.

"Cheryl's at the end of the row if you want to sit with us," he said. "Coffee over there."

Adam and Holly took their seats. Holly chatted with Cheryl and Adam watched the rest of the congregation file in and sit, many greeting each other like old friends. Holly glowed as she chatted with Cheryl, waving and calling out hellos to several other women.

"That's Georgette from the gardening group," she told Adam. "And that's Meryl. That one over there in the big cream-colored hat is Kittie."

Adam smiled at the women and nodded in their direction when they waved.

The pastor walked to the front and started his sermon.

Adam tried to concentrate on the man's words, but found his mind wandering to the Ashwoods'. The bodies in the ground, the ring, Nell's diary, the presence of something in the house, and now the discovery of the sailboat. A sailboat burned to nothing but scrap, resting in the woods just yards away from the Ashwoods' house.

Around him, people began to stir.

"Is it over?" he whispered to Holly.

She grinned and wrapped an arm around his back, giving him a squeeze. "And you actually survived," she murmured in his ear, kissing it.

Ted waved him over, and Adam stood and made his way to the back of the church, where Ted stood next to the minister.

"This is Pastor Brian," Ted told him.

Adam offered his hand. "Adam Tate. Great to meet you."

"The pleasure is mine, Adam. Did you enjoy the service today?" the pastor asked.

Adam nodded, watching Holly sitting at the end of the pew talking to Cheryl. "Yes, it was great, thanks."

"I see Troy Lutz," Ted told them. "I'm just going to pop over and see if he wants to volunteer for the October hiking trip."

Ted wandered away, and Adam turned back to the pastor. "Could I ask you something unrelated to the service?" Adam asked.

"Of course."

Adam untucked his shirt, fiddling with the hem. "I'm curious what the Methodist faith says about ghosts."

"Ghosts?"

"Yeah, like the spirits of the dead."

"Well, the Methodist belief system is heavily influenced by an eighteenth-century priest named John Wesley. John was a deeply spiritual man who not only believed in the existence of spirits, he'd had a childhood encounter with one known in his family as Old Jeffrey, a spirit or perhaps poltergeist who haunted the rectory where John and his family lived as a child. It was a brief haunting, lasting for only about two months, but it was an impactful event that affected not only John, but his entire family. They told accounts of slamming doors, footsteps, groaning, the rattling of chains and other phenomena. Though I've never experienced such things myself, I have little doubt they exist."

Adam stared at the pastor, mouth slack.

The pastor smiled. "Not the answer you were expecting?" He chuckled. "Tell me, Adam, have you yourself encountered such a phenomenon?"

From the pew, Holly stood and started toward them.

"I... umm... I'm not sure, but I'd rather not talk about it in front of Holly. She has a heart condition and I don't want to upset her. Do you think we could meet and discuss it?"

"By all means."

"Thanks, yeah, that'd be really helpful."

"Hi," Holly said brightly, extending her hand to Pastor Brian. "That was a beautiful sermon today. Thank you."

"The pleasure is all mine, Mrs. Tate. I do so hope we'll see you again."

"You will. In fact, you might be seeing me pretty regularly. Cheryl and her gang have just recruited me to help in the kids' program. It starts in just a few minutes. Do you mind, Adam?"

"No, of course not. I think that's great."

"Maybe you'll join me for a walk?" the pastor asked Adam. "It's my usual Sunday ritual before counsel in the afternoon."

"Sure, yeah. I'll come find you after?" Adam asked Holly, giving her a quick kiss.

"I'll be downstairs," she told him.

"You won't be able to miss it," the pastor explained. "Follow the smell of cookies and the sounds of giggling."

Adam followed the pastor out of the church along a cobblestone pathway that led to a paved trail in the woods.

"This is a great path," the pastor said. "Especially if you like to ride a bike. I'm only a leisurely rider myself, but avoid most of the roads these days. Too many distracted drivers, I'm afraid."

"Yeah, I've never been a bike rider myself. Holly always forces me to rent one of those tandem bikes when we go to Mackinac Island, but otherwise I prefer to stay firmly on two feet or four wheels."

"To each their own, I say. Would you like to speak now that we have a bit of privacy?"

"I don't even know where to begin," Adam admitted. "I found an old house in the woods near our property out on Black Mountain Road. The Ashwoods' place. Have you heard of it?"

"I have."

"Have you ever heard anything… weird about it?"

"I can't say I've heard strange things about the house, but I've heard the story of the Ashwood family many times over the years. Such a tragedy is remembered in a community as small as this."

"I've gone into the house several times and… stuff has happened. I've seen things."

"Would you like to tell me about them?"

"Not really." Adam chuckled. "Now that I'm saying it out loud, it sounds even more far-fetched."

"I've devoted my life to a system of belief that relies on faith, Adam. Faith calls upon us to believe in what we cannot see, what we often cannot explain."

Adam stuffed in his hands in his shorts pockets. "I've seen a woman, or women. Sometimes it seems like the same person, other times she looks different as if she's… sort of a merging of several women."

"And you suspect this entity is one of or multiple of the girls who once lived at the Ashwoods' house?"

"I think so, and they're dead. The person I see is clearly dead and seems to be trying to tell me something or she seems angry. The… entity is just a tiny piece of the puzzle. Lightbulbs exploding, sounds under the floor, stuff going missing." Adam raked both hands through his hair. He imagined the remnants of the sailboat but could not confess to this last revelation because he knew what it meant. It meant he had unearthed the Ashwood girls, and he'd reburied them.

"I understand why this would disturb you. Have you asked the spirits what they want?"

Adam shot him a surprised look. "Tried to have a conversation with her? Well, no. I mean, she hasn't spoken. I don't think she can… talk to me."

"Maybe not in the usual ways, but something is being communicated, wouldn't you say?"

"Sometimes that's what it feels like, and other times I wonder if I've made it all up," Adam sighed. "As some reaction to what's happening with Holly, you know? I've heard of stuff like that. People creating delusions to avoid the much darker truth of what's coming."

"Because Holly has a heart condition?"

"Yes, it's more than that. She had a major heart attack two years ago, followed by a heart transplant. Her body rejected the first heart, and she's had a second transplant, but… she may reject that one too."

"Do you feel at peace about Holly's condition? Or are you conflicted?"

"Shit, I'm conflicted about all of our conditions, the human condition." He realized he'd sworn. "Sorry for the profanity."

The pastor smiled. "Sometimes that's the word that most sums up the way we feel. But tell me a little about that, the conflict."

Adam tugged at the collar of the stiff polo shirt and wished he'd gone with a t-shirt after all. The fabric was too thick for the humidity. "I've wondered"—he paused, stuck on his next words—"about being an atheist. If maybe that's what I am, an atheist."

"A person who doesn't believe in God."

"Yes."

"It's a curious thing to wonder about. Most everyone wavers in their faith at times. Tell me when the thought of being an atheist first arose for you."

"After Holly's first heart attack. Initially I prayed. Night after night, I prayed so hard. It was the first time I'd ever felt almost like… I don't know, a devout person." He chuckled and tugged again at his collar. "But then… one night I started wondering, *Who am I praying to?* And that question amplified each day as she struggled and then her body rejected the heart.

"I started devouring the news. Articles about murdered children, drunk drivers wiping out whole families, mosques getting bombed, and I… started to feel like… there's nothing out there. There's no one running the show. It's just us. Mass chaos, cause and effect. And no thought has ever so terrified me because now… now I'm afraid that the moment Holly goes, dies, I'll know she's just descended into darkness. At that moment, she'll cease to exist and I'll still be here waiting for my own moment. My turn to… disappear and all those 'we'll meet agains' won't matter, because there is no 'again,' no life beyond that last breath."

"That is a terrifying contemplation."

"Which is why I wonder if I'm making the"—he fluttered his fingers—"encounters up. As if I'm searching for proof that there is life after death and so I'm hallucinating it into being."

"Have you ever experienced that before? Anxiety or fear causing you to create false realities?"

"No."

"Perhaps your rational mind can't offer the answers you seek, Adam. You're pondering questions that cannot be answered in this life. That being said, for many people, faith arrives through extraordinary albeit sometimes strange encounters. If it gives you peace to believe the encounters are real, why not allow for that?"

"Peace? Oh, they're not giving me peace, they're… haunting me. Literally." He laughed dryly.

The pastor nodded. "A calm sea does not make a skilled sailor. And so do the trials of our lives shape us into beings of strength and courage."

Adam tried not to release the frustrated sigh that bubbled in his chest. "What would you do, Pastor? If you were me?"

A little smile played on the pastor's lips as he glanced at Adam. "I would pray and I would look upon whatever arises as an answer to the questions I seek."

"That's it? Pray?"

Pastor Brian looked at him sidelong. "Perhaps I can give you something more tangible, or shall I say someone? Her name is Hattie Porter. Follow me back to the rectory and I'll write down her phone number."

"Who is she?"

"She is a woman who helps in matters such as these."

"Like an exorcist?"

The pastor shook his head. "In our faith, we don't work with exorcists, but you're not the first parishioner to come to me with troubling experiences. I like to be able to offer more than guidance. Hattie is a bridge of sorts."

"A bridge to what?"

"To the spirits who remain."

27

Adam stepped from the car and started toward the house, but paused when Holly didn't follow him. He walked to her side of the van and pulled open the door.

"What is it, honey? Are you short of breath?"

"I'm great, really, I am. Just tired. Can you pour me onto the porch swing?" Holly yawned and stretched her long legs out of the car, kicking off her red flats. She pointed and wiggled her toes.

"Feet aren't hurting, are they? They don't look swollen." He cupped one of her bare feet in his hands.

She giggled and pulled her knee back. "Quit that, you're tickling me. Now pour me onto the porch swing, husband."

He grinned. "Pour you?"

"Yes, I've melted into this seat. Go get the kitchen ladle, the big silver one, and scoop me up."

"No ladle needed," he announced, reaching beneath Holly's knees and back. He swung her out of the car.

She squealed.

"You're so hot," he told her, the wetness of her shirt and pants damp against his skin.

"That's why I told you to get the ladle."

As he carried her, he leaned his cheek down and pressed it against her forehead, but he didn't detect a fever.

"Feeling okay?" he asked.

"Like melted ice cream," she murmured.

"Is that good?"

"It's grand."

Adam laid Holly on the swing and she curled on her side. From the garden, Marshmallow appeared and trotted over to the porch, licking Holly's face. She laughed and rubbed his head.

"Glass of water?" Adam asked.

"Yes, please, and my book. It's sitting on the coffee table."

Adam filled a glass of water and started toward the living room, then paused and stared into the pantry. The trap door that led into the crawlspace stood open. He gazed at it, knowing he hadn't left it open and doubting that Holly would have. He walked to the pantry and stared into the dark hole. Cool air leaked from the space beneath the house. He nudged the door closed with his foot and it dropped back into place with a thud.

Adam started back out with the water and book and then turned on his heel and went to the bathroom, retrieving the thermometer.

"Humor me," he told her, handing her the thermometer.

She smiled and stuck it beneath her tongue. When it beeped, she pulled it out and looked at it and offered it to him. "98.8—perfectly normal."

He studied the numbers. "Okay, good." He kissed her forehead. "Want me to make some lunch?"

She shook her head and waved her book, *In The Woods* by Tana French. "Nope. I ate a few too many cookies at church this morning and spoiled any hope for lunch. I want nothing more than to find out who killed Katy."

"Sounds significantly more fascinating than *Gatsby*."

She grinned. "I dare say it is."

"I think I'll take a walk." He stretched. "After I change out of these godforsaken clothes." He clamped his mouth shut. "Goshforsaken."

She laughed. "Off to break into that old house again?"

"It's been abandoned for ages. I'd hardly call it breaking in."

"Uh-huh. Well, don't get attacked by a rabid opossum holed up in the chimney."

"I haven't encountered any wildlife yet, but if I do, I'll run the other way."

"Unless they're babies, then take a picture with your phone so I can see them."

"Deal."

~

Adam trudged to the house, following the trail of trampled grass he'd worn into the weeds in the previous days. He had a singular focus. He was going to follow the pastor's advice and ask the spirit what she wanted.

At the edge of the property, he spotted movement and paused.

A doe stood near the gnarled apple tree. She craned her neck up to capture an apple.

Adam slipped his cell phone from his back pocket. The screen was black. The phone was dead, and he'd forgotten to charge it on their way to church.

"Idiot," he muttered, chastising himself for not having gotten a new battery.

Adam shoved the phone into his pocket and gave the deer a wide berth as he made for the front door.

Once inside, he stood in the hallway and considered what to do next. He'd encountered the spirit in the attic and the basement. Neither space seemed welcoming. He wanted to pose the question, but he didn't want to return to the places he'd encountered the entity.

"Hello?" he called, feeling first trepidation, but then, when no one answered, foolishness. Had he actually expected a voice to respond?

Reluctantly, he ascended the stairs to the second floor and squared off against the doorway at the opposite end.

"Just do it," he muttered.

On stilted legs, he marched down the hall and grabbed the knob, turned it and pulled the door open.

Nothing happened.

He started up the stairs, stopped, and returned to the second floor. He grabbed a chair from the master bedroom and propped the door open.

The attic looked as it had before. He didn't feel a sense of being watched, but he still turned in a full circle twice before moving into the room.

"What do you want?" he demanded.

Nothing shifted in the house.

He'd discarded the plant book on the bed when he'd been in the room before, but he hadn't explored the room as thoroughly as the others. Adam lifted the mattress. Other things had been tucked beneath it—scraps of cloth, bits of jewelry, make-up, two additional books and a gold pen. He lowered the mattress and moved to the dresser, opening and rifling through the drawers, pushing aside clothes. He didn't find anything that seemed important.

He trudged back out of the house and through the forest, disappointed, but also slightly relieved. Perhaps he and Holly could drive up north and go out to dinner. He could use a break from thinking about the Ashwoods' house.

As he started across his yard, Marshmallow greeted him, whining and jumping up, planting his paws on Adam's chest. A tremor coursed through Adam and he searched the porch for Holly. She was no longer on the swing.

"Where is she, boy?" Adam asked, running across the lawn to the house. He started up the steps, but Marshmallow veered sideways toward the garden.

Adam saw her then. Holly lay crumpled just outside the gate into her garden.

"Oh, God, oh, Jesus..." He ran to her. Her skin was hot, her face translucent and shiny.

He fumbled out his cell phone, remembered it was dead and chucked it, furious, into the grass.

Holly's phone lay beside her curled hand. He grabbed it, clamped his teeth together when he saw his own name on the screen. She'd been trying to call him.

He dialed 911.

28

Holly lay in the hospital bed, the pulse of her heart etching across the black screen. Adam clutched her hand, unable to quell the guilt that had consumed him since the moment he spotted her on the ground.

The ambulance had arrived within fifteen minutes. She hadn't had a heart attack, but had contracted the flu, which, if left untreated, could have led to a heart attack or stroke.

Though the doctor had assured both Holly and Adam that she was responding well to the antiviral medicine, Adam sat perched on the edge of his chair, fearing at any moment she'd go into convulsions.

"It's okay," she murmured, squeezing his hand.

"It's not. I shouldn't have left you. I knew you were feverish. In my gut, I knew."

"Adam… please. Please stop putting it all on yourself."

"I'm going to buy a new phone and I'm getting one of those emergency call buttons that alerts me and emergency services."

"I'm here for a few days and you are not going to haunt my bedside twenty-four seven. Okay? Duke is coming up in a few hours. Cheryl and some of the garden ladies are coming tomorrow. I want you to go home and chill out. Make sure Marshmallow is okay. Watch some movies. Call Ted and go fishing. Just enjoy your time a bit, okay? You're getting a reprieve. You don't have to worry about me for a few days."

"It's not like that, Holly. I want to worry about you. I want to be here with you."

She shook her head. "I won't let you. I'm going to sleep and read. You can come visit, but you're not staying around the clock."

Adam, despite Holly's urging, refused to leave until Duke arrived. His brother-in-law gave him a hug and told him much the same thing Holly had: *go home, put your feet up, Holly's in good hands.*

~

Adam left the hospital and drove to the cell phone store. As usual, his cell phone charged fine in his truck. He struggled to explain to the salesperson why he needed a new one. Only after he raised his voice did the young man agree to credit him partially for the phone and issue him a new one.

As he left the store, he spotted a strange little shop called The Divine Messenger. The display window held tall clear crystals, spinning rainbow-colored chimes, and stacks of antique-looking books. A Ouija board stood front and center in the display.

As he stared at it, the door opened with a tinkle of bells and a tall, thin woman emerged, carrying a sparkly purple bag. Impulsively, Adam caught the door before it closed and stepped inside.

Flutes played from the speakers and a water fountain trickled from a table in the center of the store. Scented mist rose from the fountain and wafted toward him.

"Hi," a woman called from behind the glass counter. "Welcome to The Divine Messenger. Can I help you find anything?"

Adam pointed toward the window display. "One of those, a Ouija board."

The woman, clothed in a red dress tied with a leather rope, stepped from behind the counter. She wore a wreath of twine, leaves and flowers on her head. She saw him looking at it and reached a hand up to touch the wreath.

"We celebrate Lughnasadh the entire month of August here at The Divine Messenger."

"Lughnasadh?"

"The pagan harvest festival. You're welcome to take some apples home." She gestured toward a stand next to the counter that held a wicker basket overflowing with apples.

"Thanks."

She stopped at a wall and took a plastic-wrapped Ouija board from a shelf. "Here you go."

He stared at the front of the box. Beneath an image of the board with two hands on it were the words 'Mystifying Oracle.'

"Do these things actually work?" he asked.

The woman tilted her head and studied him. "Work? That's an interesting word, don't you think? Exertion, labor. I dare say it's not meant to work. But does it connect? Does it offer a gateway, be that into our own consciousness or into the realms of spirit? I would answer yes, it has served many in that capacity for well over a century."

"Have you used it?"

"Yes."

"And you… got answers?"

"Yes."

"Like what?" he asked, unable to hide his irritation at her vague responses.

She stepped behind the counter and scanned the barcode on the box. "That information isn't for you. What you are meant to know, you will know, but if you plug your ears and close your eyes, you'll never see or hear anything at all."

"Thanks," he grumbled. "That was really helpful." He started toward the door.

"Before you go," she called out, "a warning, if I may."

He turned back.

"It's not a game. Respect it."

He nodded and stepped from the store. Tucking the board under one arm, he climbed into his truck and headed for home.

It was dusk by the time Adam reached his house. Marshmallow whined and pushed against him when he walked into the kitchen.

"Hey, buddy." Adam knelt and scratched the dog's head. "She's okay. No need to worry. Mom will be just fine."

Marshmallow licked his face and then trotted to the door and barked.

"Gotta go potty?" Adam asked. "You know you have a doggy door, right?" He opened the door and Marshmallow ran into the yard.

Adam heated a can of bean and ham soup and slathered a slice of bread with butter, eating standing up as he watched Marshmallow criss-cross the yard, marking the trees and chasing a crow that landed by Holly's garden. He rinsed his dishes and then called the dog back into the house. After Marshmallow was fed and had settled into a pile of fluff in the living room, Adam eyed the Ouija board.

He ripped off the plastic and dropped it in the trash, carried the board to the coffee table in the living room. He lifted the lid.

A triangular piece of plastic labeled 'the planchette' sat in a cardboard base next to an instruction sheet.

He glanced through a list, which included instructions such as 'never use the Ouija board in a graveyard,' and 'never use the Ouija board if you think it's a game.' An additional sheet explained how to ask the board questions.

Adam removed the cardboard and stared at the board beneath it. It had been designed to look aged, though clearly it was cheap cardboard. At the top stood a sun with the word 'yes' printed beneath it and on the opposite side a moon above the word 'no.' Below that an alphabet and the numbers one through ten.

Adam set the board on the table and situated the planchette in the center. He placed his fingers lightly on the plastic and glanced at Marshmallow, whose head rested on his paws. He watched Adam with mild curiosity.

"Why am I even doing this?" he muttered, embarrassed to even have his dog in the room.

Adam tilted his head back and tried to think of a question.

"Is there anyone here?" he asked.

Marshmallow's ears perked up, but the planchette did nothing.

Adam tapped his fingers on the plastic guide.

"Umm... are you here?" He tried a second time. Again, no movement on the board. Adam counted to sixty and then lifted his hands up. "What a waste of twenty bucks."

He stood and went to the kitchen, grabbing one of Holly's muffins from a Tupperware and his new phone. He dialed the hospital and asked for Holly's room.

"Hello?" she answered.

"Hey, honey, how ya feeling?"

"Pretty good. Sleepy even though I haven't done anything but sleep all day. Duke's still here. Apparently, the cafeteria has some kind of chocolate pudding he can't get enough of. He's been down there twice already."

Adam laughed. "Sounds tasty. I just ate one of your muffins. I doubt the pudding holds a candle to those."

"Eat 'em up. A few more days and they'll start to get gross. The humidity turns baked goods into mold factories."

"I miss you, Holl. The house is so quiet without you." Adam didn't want to admit how lonely he suddenly felt, not to mention his lingering shame at having left her earlier that day. He crushed the thought, refusing to allow for the possibilities of what would have happened if he hadn't come back when he had.

"I miss you too. Stick one of my t-shirts on Marshmallow tonight and let him sleep in the bed. It'll be like I never left."

"Very funny. Marshmallow will end up sleeping on my head and I'll wake up choking on his fur in the middle of the night."

Holly laughed. "Well, at least you'll be thinking about that instead of me."

"I'm always thinking of you, Holly."

"Then think of me getting a little R&R. I'm fine, more than fine. Duke just walked in with two more containers of chocolate pudding. Try to relax tonight. Okay?"

"Okay," he sighed.

"I love you."

"I love you most."

He hung up the phone and started back toward the living room glancing down the hallway. Footprints again marred the grey rug. Footprints he knew hadn't been there earlier in the day. Adam stalked back to the kitchen and grabbed a dishrag. He returned to the hall and froze. The footprints were gone.

Clenching his jaw, he snatched the rug from the floor, marched it to the kitchen and shoved it into the wastebasket. He returned to the living room and flipped on the TV, flipped through channels in search of a movie. He needed something action-packed to tune out the thoughts wreaking havoc in his brain.

Adam selected a film with Samuel L. Jackson. As he watched, he heard a knock on the door.

He glanced at his cell phone. It was almost nine p.m. Adam stood, Marshmallow trailing him, and walked to the door, pulling it open, but no one waited on the porch. Adam leaned out and looked each direction.

The driveway lay empty and the woods were little more than black silhouettes against the darkening sky.

"Hello? Anybody out here?"

No one answered.

He returned to the couch, slumped down, and turned up the volume. Not two minutes later, the knock came again.

He didn't want to get up and check, but the knocking grew more insistent.

"Damn it…" he muttered, stood and stomped to the door. This time Marshmallow hung back, growling from the living room arch. Adam yanked open the door.

No one. The only sound was Holly's wind chimes tinkling from the far end of the porch.

He slammed the door harder than necessary and returned to the couch. When he sat back down, he turned the volume to its maximum level.

Several minutes passed when the knock came again. He ignored it. He would not open it, would not give whatever it was the satisfaction.

As the pounding increased, the cream-colored planchette on the Ouija board shifted slightly. Adam stared at it. It moved again. Marshmallow barked and lunged at the board.

"Marshmallow, no!" Adam snapped, holding the dog back. "Come on," he demanded to the board. "Come on, what do you want?"

The planchette slid towards a letter: M. It started away, paused.

The knocking grew louder.

"What? M-what?" he shouted.

The knocking came again like a drill bit into Adam's skull.

"Go the fuck away!" he shouted at the door. "Go away, go away!" He stared at the board and his blood boiled behind his eyes and it was everything he could do not to throw the planchette against the wall and snap the Ouija board in half. He was terrified, but the terror made him so furious he could barely breathe.

As if channeling Adam's rage, the planchette streaked off the board and hit the wall.

Another knock came, but this one wasn't from the door. It was the living room window. Adam looked at the window and found Ted there staring in, face creased in worry.

29

1956

4 Days Before the Sail

"I have some business with the bank across the street," Michael told Nell after she'd settled onto a stool at the gleaming counter. "Why don't you get yourself an ice cream soda." He handed her a crisp one-dollar bill and then slipped out the glass door.

The man behind the counter, who'd been drying tall clear glasses with a white cloth, followed Michael with his eyes. When he shifted his gaze back to Nell, he had a mischievous gleam in his eyes. It reminded her of the fox in the storybooks at the Ashwoods' house where the fox tricked the hen into his cave and ate her.

"So, you're one of Ashwood's girls, huh?" He winked.

"I live at the Ashwoods' house," she told him, though she sensed he hadn't meant it that way. He was referring to Michael. *You're one of Michael's girls.*

The man grinned, revealing yellow teeth. "Lot of pretty girls around that man," he continued, eyes sliding slowly over Nell. He leaned forward as if he intended to get a closer look, check out her legs beneath the bar, but she jumped up and ran out of the shop.

She fled down the block and then slowed, looking behind her, afraid the man had followed her. He hadn't.

Breathing hard, she searched for a spot to sit where she could still see the entrance to the bank, but was out of view of the soda shop. She found a bench and collapsed onto it. Pressing her knees together, she sat and folded and re-folded the dollar Michael had given her.

He walked out ten minutes later and, as he started across the street, she stood and waved at him.

"Mich—Mr. Ashwood," she called out. She limped down the side-walk. Her left calf ached as if she'd strained something during her flight from the soda shop.

Michael tilted his head. "What are you doing down there? No soda?"

She shook her head.

"Okay, well, one more quick stop."

She followed him to his truck and winced as she hoisted herself inside. Her calf throbbed dully.

He drove to the opposite side of town and parked in front of the hardware store.

"Back in two shakes," he told her.

Nell watched Michael disappear into the store. She massaged her calf and tried not to think about the way the soda shop man had looked at her. Like she was food he wanted to eat. She shivered despite the warm day and pulled Michael's coat from the backseat, draping it over her shoulders.

He emerged from the store carrying a small paper bag, which he tucked into the leather case propped behind the driver's seat.

"Where are we going?" she asked as he guided the truck out of town, taking US 23 north along the Lake Huron shoreline.

"Somewhere very special, but it's a surprise." He winked at her.

Nell watched the forests pass by. Sometimes she caught glimpses of beachgoers or boats floating in the dark Lake Huron waters.

When he turned onto a rocky peninsula, Nell leaned forward and studied the structure looming before them.

"What is it?" she asked.

"The Misty Point Inn. I rented us a room. We can't stay the night, but we can spend a couple of hours. I set it up so Alice thinks you're helping Harold Dupont with book-keeping and I'm running errands."

"But… what if someone sees us?" Nell studied the two-story white hotel. The paint was chipped and faded, perhaps from the strong Lake Huron winds.

"Like who? Look around, darling, there isn't a soul in sight. Mo Peters has owned this place for twenty years and it's not exactly a hotspot. Put that little scarf over your head. I brought champagne."

Nell draped her blue silk scarf over her head and tied it beneath her chin, tucking in her hair. She followed him into the hotel room, cupping a hand over her face for fear someone might see them, but as Michael had said, there wasn't a soul in sight. The parking lot stood empty, the road beyond likewise. Not a single boat floated on the still surface of the lake.

Michael closed the door and pulled the scarf from Nell's head, sinking his hands into her hair and kissing her. He walked her backwards to the bed. She barely had time to gasp as she fell back and he climbed on top of her.

~

After they made love, Michael lay beside her, tracing his fingers down her throat and over her pale breasts. She shivered and goose flesh broke out along her neck and arms.

"I can't wait for us to be together, Nell. We'll drink champagne every evening. We'll watch the sunrise every morning and the moonrise every night."

Nell buried her face in his chest. "Oh, Michael. I want that so much."

"And so you shall have it. Champagne?"

"Yes, please."

Nell had never tasted champagne. The green bottle perspired on the little wooden table in the corner of the room. Michael took two glass cups from the bathroom and filled them each halfway. He returned to the bed and handed her a glass.

"To us," he said, clinking his glass against hers and taking a sip.

Nell lifted the glass to her lips. The champagne was sweet. It tickled her nose and fizzed cool down her throat.

After she finished her champagne, Nell stood, slightly dizzy. She wrapped a sheet around her body and walked onto the balcony. A breeze blew in off the lake, swirling her hair on her shoulders. Michael walked up behind her, pulling her back against him and kissing her shoulder.

"I have something for you."

He led her back into the room. Nell sat on the edge of the bed and watched Michael reach into his leather case. Her stomach flipped. Had he bought her a ring? No, of course he hadn't. He was married. Yet her whole body buzzed as his hand lifted out.

He held the paper bag he'd carried from the hardware store, and Nell's shoulders slumped. Disappointment coursed through her, but also shame that she'd even imagined he might propose after a love affair that had lasted little more than a week.

He handed her the bag.

Nell opened it, peering inside. She spotted a small metal tin and drew it out, reading the label. "'Mouse and Rat Killer.'"

"It's arsenic."

She wrinkled her brow. "I don't under…" But she trailed off because suddenly she did understand. It was poison—not for rodents, but for Alice.

"Michael…" She shook her head. "I don't think I can do it. I… I couldn't live with myself."

"Nell." He moved closer to her, taking the bag and tucking the canister back inside. "You don't have to think about it at all right now. She likes to have a sloe gin fizz on the boat in the evening. You'll make her cocktail and serve it to her. Just imagine you're adding a teaspoon of sugar. It's important that it happens on the boat."

"During the sail this weekend?"

"Yes. You see, that ensures that questions won't be asked. You'll be far away from shore. In all likelihood, you girls won't even know anything is wrong until morning."

"But… how will we get back to shore?"

He smirked and tilted her chin up so she met his gaze. "Darling, since when do any of you girls need Alice to sail the boat? She's taught you everything you need to know. In fact, you don't even need to steer back to our harbor Go anywhere you like. Flag down a passing ship if you see one—after, of course. The key will be to give her this at night so that there's no one around on the lake and then dispose of the bottle over the side. I'll make the dose very strong. She'll go to sleep and never wake up."

Nell's stomach churned. The champagne gurgled in her belly. She stood, sheet dropping to the floor, and lurched to the bathroom. She vomited into the toilet, her entire body shivering.

Michael followed her in. He crouched and rubbed her back.

"Too much champagne too fast," he murmured. "It's okay. Come now, come lie down. I'll go to the vending machine and get you a ginger ale."

~

It was customary for all the girls to get a birthday party, but the house was abuzz with visions of Nell's party. Mildred's own party during the dreary month of March had held none of the dazzle or excitement that Nell's seemed to inspire.

Nell was turning eighteen. It was both a birthday and a transition into adulthood. It would only be a matter of time before Nell flew the nest, as Mrs. Ashwood liked to put it. Nell had been learning to type on Mr. Ashwood's typewriter, and he'd taken her to town that day to help with the ledgers at his friend's book-keeping business. Mrs. Ashwood had connections, secretarial schools around the state, and it was customary for her to place the girls with a job before they left the house.

One day, Mr. Ashwood would load Nell's two worn black suitcases in the back of his pickup and drive away. Nell would likely never return.

Mildred hated the thought. Nell was nicer than the other girls. When she spoke to Mildred, she didn't use the same caustic, irritated tones the other girls used.

At least that was how it had been, but Nell had changed and Mildred knew why. She was having an affair with their guardian. Nell was going to ruin it for them all. If Alice Ashwood discovered the betrayal, they'd all be sent away. Cocoa already had a beau downstate in Detroit. Bitsy could return to her family. Margie's family couldn't afford to keep her, but she was musically talented and Alice had mentioned more than once a special boarding school for girls of her talents if she ever wanted to purse it.

Only Mildred would be left high and dry. Her own family had sent her away. They would refuse her. She might go into an orphanage and spend the years until her eighteenth birthday in ugly gray smocks eating sugarless grits and scrubbing floors.

It infuriated Mildred that Nell could be so selfish. She stared at the gifts piled on the table in the study. Cocoa had set them there after they'd been wrapped, intending to hide them before Nell returned home. Mildred waited until the living room was empty, then she stole into the room, slipped a small gift from the table, and folded it into her dress.

She left the house and cut across the yard into the trees. She ran until her lungs screamed and a muscle in her abdomen pinched painfully.

A large boulder sat at the base of a big oak tree. Mildred sat on the rock and tore the wrapping paper away. Inside, she discovered a small white box. She lifted the lid. A lovely gold peacock comb sat in the box. It had an emerald eye and colored feathers.

Mildred recognized the comb. It belonged to Bitsy and had been given to her by her grandmother. It was a family heirloom, and yet Bitsy was now gifting it to Nell. Mildred slid her fingers along the glittering edge. She pushed the comb into her hair and felt the weight of it, imagined how she'd look with her hair pinned up, wearing a pretty dress and the comb clinging to the side of her head.

She dug a hole and shoved in the wrapping paper, covering it with dirt. Mildred hid the comb in her skirt and started back to the house.

~

When Nell and Michael returned to the house that evening, he joined the other girls in the study as if nothing at all had happened. He sat at the table where they played a card game and asked to be dealt in. Alice was nowhere in sight, but as Nell slipped toward the stairs, she heard Margie tell Michael that Alice was on one of her walks.

Nell hurried to her bed and knelt down. With shaking hands, she slipped the tin of rat poison from the pocket of her dress and shoved it beneath her mattress.

30

Adam hurried to the front door and pulled it open.

Ted held a casserole dish in his hands. "Is everything okay, Adam?"

Adam swallowed, unsure what Ted had heard, but confident he'd caught Adam screaming 'go the fuck away.' He rubbed at his jaw, pulling the door open further. "Yeah, come on in."

Adam stepped aside so Ted could walk the dish to the counter. "Cheryl made ya a ranch chicken casserole. We're all torn up about Holly. Thanks for sending me the message to let us know. How's she doin'?"

"She's good. The doctor said she's got a virus, something's going around, apparently. You'd think this heat would burn away anything, but…" Adam shrugged.

Ted stared toward the living room, and Adam realized the man had a direct line of sight to the Ouija board sitting on the coffee table.

"And how are you holding up?" Ted asked, eyes sliding back to Adam's.

"Pretty good, just… exhausted. You know how it is after a day at the hospital. I was getting ready to go to bed."

Ted's mouth turned down slightly. "Were you yelling?"

"At the TV," Adam explained. "I was watching some action movie where the hero was making one stupid mistake after another." He chuckled.

"Okay." Ted glanced a final time toward the living room and then moved back to the front door. "If you need anything, Adam, even just to talk, don't hesitate to call me."

"Sure, thanks. And thank Cheryl for the casserole. I appreciate it."

Adam watched Ted leave. When the man's taillights disappeared down the driveway, he returned to the living room. He grabbed the planchette and set it on the board, fingers resting on the edge of the plastic dial.

"What do you want?" he murmured.

He closed his eyes and waited. At the side of the room, he heard Marshmallow pacing.

"What do you want?" he said again.

The planchette moved beneath his fingers. It slid again to a single letter: M.

He waited. Seconds turned into minutes and nothing on the board moved. Finally, he took his hands away and eased into the couch.

"M," he said, unsure if it was an answer or merely a trick of his desperation causing the board to move.

Adam woke refreshed and focused. He'd slept surprisingly well the night before and met the day with a clear purpose. He needed to find out everything he could about Michael and Alice Ashwood. Michael had to be involved in the deaths of the Ashwood women, and Adam felt confident he hadn't acted alone. He'd been plotting with a seventeen-year-old girl under his care to murder Alice. Something had clearly gone wrong.

There'd been a desk drawer in the study stacked with folders. The one on top had said a girl's name. He suspected they were the records of the girls who lived at the Ashwoods' house.

Adam brewed coffee and filled a stainless-steel to-go mug, allowing Marshmallow to accompany him to the house. A choice he soon regretted as the dog darted into the forest and came back with burdocks embedded in his fur.

At the Ashwoods' house, Adam left Marshmallow outside. Adam pushed into the house and strode down the hall to the study.

The door stood closed.

Adam gazed at it, but it was his aunt's bathroom door that rose up in his mind, the intricate crystal knob. The cracked pale blue paint that had not quite covered the darker wood beneath. He blinked and cleared the memory. This was not that door. He took a step toward it and then paused.

He'd left the diary in there too, dropped it on the couch and fled. His resolve wavered. He did not want to open the door.

"Stop it," Adam muttered, and twisted the knob.

Nothing shifted in the room.

He hurried to the desk drawer where he'd seen the files. Part of him suspected they'd be gone, as if whatever entity haunted him would have somehow removed them to deepen the mystery. They weren't.

He plucked them out and dug through the drawers, searching for any other documents that might be useful. He found a marriage certificate. Michael Andrew Ashwood and Alice Francine Granger.

He added that to the folders, grabbed Nell's diary from the couch, and darted back on to the front porch. Marshmallow stood barking at the tire swing, which swayed despite the still air. Adam studied it, trying to discern what had agitated the dog, but saw nothing in or around the swing and no squirrel escaping up the trunk of the tree.

"Come on, Marshmallow. Let's go."

The dog stayed for another moment, his bark shifting to a growl, and then he turned and sprinted toward Adam, ran ahead of him onto the forest trail.

At home, Adam laid the folders on the kitchen table and opened the first one. The name on the cover read Bertha Walker.

The first document inside was a birth certificate, which revealed Bertha's date of birth, parents' names and location of birth. Only one other document was inside. A letter.

Dear Mr. and Mrs. Ashwood,

I am writing on behalf of my daughter, Bertha, or Bitsy, as we call her. We would be delighted if you would consider hosting her for the 1956 summer and fall semesters. She learned of your homestead from Jillian Springs, and was delighted at the thought of learning the care of horses and spending some time in northern Michigan. Our family is less fortunate than some and we've been unable to provide her with many of the experiences that young women need to advance in this modern world.

Sincerely,

Sally Walker

He opened Nellie's folder.

Dear Mrs. Ashwood,

My name is Esther Madden. Last summer, my sister-in-law died tragically in an accident. We have taken into our home her only daughter, my niece Nellie. She's a beautiful and intelligent young woman and I fear for her future if she becomes a ward of the state. We simply cannot afford to keep her. Would you consider bringing her into your girls' home?

With our deepest gratitude,

The Madden Family

Each file contained a copy of a birth certificate and a letter. A couple of them included additional correspondence from family members checking on their daughters, though neither Mildred nor Nell had any extra letters from home.

He read the letter in Mildred's file.

Dear Mr. and Mrs. Michael Ashwood,

This past winter we suffered a terrible tragedy when our three-year-old son fell from a second-story window at our home and perished. It has been a painful time. Our daughter Mildred is suffering as we grieve. Might you consider bringing her into your home for the 1956 summer/fall and 1957 winter seasons with the possibility to extend that time if she thrives under your guardianship?

Mildred is a cunning child—intelligent, imaginative, but also helpful. We believe she would an acceptable addition to your group.

Best,

Derek Spalding

Adam considered the material. It was a starting point, but he needed the internet to dig deeper into the Ashwoods and the girls. He had a choice to make, either spend the day at the library or bite the bullet and get a damn computer.

"Screw it," he murmured.

He grabbed his wallet off the counter and climbed into his truck. He drove first to the hospital, visiting with Holly, who sat eating scrambled eggs and flipping through a magazine.

"How was your night?" she asked when he delivered the flowers he'd bought in the lobby.

"I slept hard. Marshmallow was antsy with you being gone, but he survived."

Holly smiled and leaned her head back on the pillows. "I had nightmares that something was wrong," she admitted. "I almost called a few times, but I didn't want to wake you."

Adam smoothed her hair away from her cheek. "You can wake me anytime, Holl. I'll take a few minutes talking to you over sleep any night."

She rubbed his hand and sighed, leaning into his palm. Her eyes welled up.

"Hey, what is it?" He scooted closer and slipped an arm behind her back. Her skin beneath her hospital gown felt cool.

"Nothing. Not nothing, but…" She shook her head and swiped at her tears. "Nothing I can put my finger on. Ever since we moved into the house, you've seemed so far away. This was supposed to bring us closer, give us more time together, but even when you're with me, you're not with me."

Adam swallowed and lifted her hand to his lips, kissing her fingers. When his lips landed on the mother-of-pearl ring, he jerked back, startled.

Her face crinkled in worry. "What?"

He looked away from the ring and then forced himself to meet Holly's gaze. "I'm so sorry, Holly. I am. And you're right, you're totally right. I guess I've been struggling with… the change of it all. Not having the shop, not having the construction of the house. I went from so busy to… unlimited free time. Never in my life have I not had a job."

"I understand that, and I thought it might be hard for you. So, what can we do after I'm out of here? How can we ease you into this transition?"

"I'm working on it. Okay? I'm going to get myself straightened out while you're in here and when you're out, it's going to be picnics and hammocks and beach days."

She laughed. "Don't go driving yourself mad. Let's just try for better communication. Okay?"

"Okay."

Adam picked out a laptop and printer and wheeled them to the checkout. He took out his wallet and pulled his credit card free. A slip of paper fluttered to the floor. He picked it up and read the name Hattie Porter along with a phone number. The pastor had given him the slip of paper. He'd forgotten about it.

As he drove home, he called Hattie Porter. The woman answered on the first ring.

"Hi, I'm trying to reach Hattie."

"You've reached her."

"My name's Adam Tate. I got your number from Pastor Brian at Touchstone Ministries."

"Okay."

"Umm… well, he thought you might be able to help me."

"With what, exactly?"

"With… a… ugh, with some weird stuff that's been happening in my house."

"A haunting?"

"Yes."

"Based on the timing of your call, I suspect I will pass your area around nine tomorrow morning on my way to the Upper Peninsula. I can make a detour to your home."

"That'd be great. Wow, thank you. I really appreciate it."

Adam rattled off his address, thanked Hattie again, and ended the call. He pulled up to a stop sign and watched a family of four carrying beach toys and a picnic basket run across the street. He felt a pang of longing for such a normal day.

31

Adam set up the computer in his study and connected it to the hotspot on his phone. He opened a browser window and typed in 'Michael Andrew Ashwood, Michigan.'

A series of hits came back, which included the two articles he'd read previously about the sailboat that vanished in Lake Huron. He clicked on a site called 'Find A Grave.'

An image of a headstone populated with the name Michael Andrew Ashwood and the dates September 5, 1913-August 11, 1961.

It was him, the same Michael from the photo Adam had seen in the Ashwoods' house. The man had died five years to the month after the women had perished.

He read the obituary that accompanied the photo.

Michael Andrew Ashwood went Sunday to be with his creator after passing from natural causes. Michael was preceded in death by his first wife Alice Ashwood and his daughter Marilyn, his parents Bill and Gail Ashwood and his brother Frank Ashwood. He is survived by his second wife, Charlotte Ashwood.

Flowers or donations can be sent to Charlotte Ashwood at 2864 Copper Avenue, Sault St. Marie, Michigan.

There are no services planned at this time.

Adam found no other sites results related to the Michael Ashwood he searched for. He considered everything he'd learned and then, thinking of Nell's diary, typed in 'Nellie Katherine Madden.'

No hits came back at all for Nellie, but he found one for Jerome

Madden. Again an obituary and Nellie's name appeared. Jerome had died in 1984. He'd been preceded in death by his parents, by his son Warren, his sister Vivian Madden, and his niece Nellie Madden.

Adam read the 'survived by' comments. He then returned to the browser and pulled up Facebook, logging in to the now defunct Daydream Café Facebook Page. There were more than a hundred notifications. Previous patrons had left messages on the page asking how Holly was doing, how the new house was coming. He skimmed them, but navigated to the search bar and typed in the names of people Jerome had been survived by. The first was his wife. No results came back. The second was a daughter named Gloria Madden. When he typed her name into the search bar, a profile appeared for a woman who lived in Rose City, Michigan.

He scanned her page, confident this woman had been Nell Madden's cousin. He sent her a message.

Hi, my name is Adam Tate and I live on Black Mountain Road in Northern Michigan. This is probably coming out of left field, but I wondered if I could speak with you about Nellie Madden, assuming I have the right person and you're her cousin. Please call me on my cell.

He returned to the search bar and typed in 'Alice Ashwood.' No hits other than those he'd previously discovered, including the finding of a body in the Manistee National Forest that was suspected to be the daughter of Michael and Alice Ashwood.

Adam's stomach grumbled, and he headed to the kitchen and fixed a sandwich. He let Marshmallow out and then filled his food and water bowls.

As he started back toward the office, Adam's cell phone rang. He didn't recognize the number.

"Hello?"

"Is this Adam Tate?" a woman asked.

"Yes, speaking."

"This is Gloria Madden."

"Gloria, hello. Thanks so much for calling me back."

"I haven't spoken Nellie's name in"—the woman paused—"so long, so very long."

"I'm amazed that I found you. I was afraid most of Nellie's family might be gone."

The woman released a tinny laugh. "Not yet, but I'm getting up there. I turn seventy-three next week."

"Happy birthday."

"Thank you. I was rather surprised to see your message," she admitted. "Like I said, I haven't spoken of Nellie in years, decades maybe. My sister died in ninety-eight and she knew her better than me. They used to write letters when Nellie went to the Ashwoods' home."

"Why did she end up there?" Adam asked. "With the Ashwoods?" He knew from reading Nell's file that her mother had died, but he didn't want Gloria Madden to know he'd been poking around in her private documents.

"Her mother was killed in a cattle stampede at a county fair. My parents had me, Luanne, and Warren. My dad did odd jobs and my mother didn't work. They barely got by and kept us fed. My mom wanted Nellie, but my dad was adamant we couldn't keep her. His sister, Nellie's mom, was a bit of a loose cannon, and my dad was afraid Nellie might have a similar temperament. She didn't, but he never paid much attention to any of us girls.

"He'd gotten wind of the Ashwoods from someone he worked with and arranged to have Nellie move there with them. He thought she'd have a better life, and he was probably right. We were living hand to mouth those days and it would have been a real struggle if Nellie had moved in. My sister and I already shared a room. My brother slept on the sofa." Gloria sighed. "My mother never forgave herself after Nellie died."

"After the sailing accident?"

"Yes. It was a terrible shock. Nellie was an excellent swimmer. My mother used to call her the family mermaid."

"So, if an accident had happened on the lake, she'd have been able to swim to shore."

"In a perfect world. But obviously it's far from a perfect world, isn't it? Anyway, the boat must have been way out, considering no one ever found any wreckage. She couldn't have made the swim."

"Yeah, that seems to be the prevailing theory."

"Have they found anything? Any evidence of the sailboat or… the bodies?"

"Not that I'm aware of," Adam lied, picturing the remains of the sailboat buried in the woods.

"So, what has you digging into all this, Mr. Tate? I'm assuming you're not a detective."

"No, I'm not. My wife and I recently built a house on Black Mountain Road. I came upon the Ashwoods' old house during a walk. Then I learned about the sailing accident, and it stuck with me. Gloria, just out of curiosity, did anyone in your family ever hear from Nellie after that weekend? Ever receive a letter or phone call?"

"Of course not. How could we have?"

"Just following crazy ideas, I guess. If Nellie had somehow survived, would she have contacted family?"

"She would have reached out to my sister, Luanne, without a doubt," Gloria said. "They were very close. Luanne was heartbroken about Nellie."

"And she never mentioned anything about hearing from her, thinking she saw her after the sail."

"These are unusual questions. Do you suspect Nellie survived the sailing accident?"

"No, not really. I've just… wondered if maybe one of them lived and had amnesia or something, Like I said, chasing some far-fetched theories."

"Yeah, I wish she had. We would have given anything to see Nellie again."

After they ended the call, Adam retreated to the study, finished his sandwich and started searching for living relatives of the other girls. He sent Facebook messages and emails to several, including a possible sibling of Bitsy, and a potential cousin and nephew of Cocoa.

He sat at the computer until nearly midnight and then, having discovered little in the way of new information, wandered to his bedroom, crawled beneath the covers and prayed that nothing visited him that night.

~

Adam slept until nearly eight-thirty a.m. He'd just finished his coffee when he heard a knock on his front door. Marshmallow barked and looked through the window.

Adam opened the door to an older woman with long white hair flowing over her narrow shoulders. She was pale and bony beneath her pink silk blouse and gray skirt. A silver cross hung at her neck.

"You must be Adam," she told him, her voice soft and curious.

"Yes, thanks so much for coming, Hattie or Mrs. Porter." He shook her thin, cool hand.

"Hattie is fine. And you're welcome. It's an unusual way to meet, but it's necessary, I realize."

"I can't believe I caught you as you were driving north. Perfect timing."

"If you pay attention, you'll realize everything in the world is carefully orchestrated and we are not the composers—well, not in the way we think, anyhow."

"I have to admit, I'm not entirely sure what you do."

"I'm a communicator. I speak with the spirits and try to get a sense of what they want." Hattie smiled, bending over as Marshmallow nudged his way through the door. "Look at you, what a lovely creature." She scratched Marshmallow's neck and chest. "He is beautiful."

"Thank you. He misses his mother."

Hattie straightened up and nodded. "Your wife?" Hattie frowned and put a hand over her heart. "She's ill."

"Yes."

"I suspect she misses you both as well, but let's not linger. I have a long drive still ahead. Just to give you a bit of background, my work is subtle. I need to first get a sense of what is here."

"See if I'm making it up?"

Hattie chuckled. "Rarely do I meet a person who is making it up. By the time they come to me, it's no longer about seeking attention. It's a desire to be rid of this thing, whatever it is. Often when a house is haunted, the spirit or spirits are benevolent, friendly even. I've spoken to people who have spirits who fold their laundry, who alerted them when their child was choking. But those are not the only kind."

Adam opened the door and Hattie followed him into the house.

"Can I get you some water? Or tea?"

"Nothing right now, thank you."

"May I ask how you got into this… line of work?"

Hattie smiled and gazed wistfully through the window, touching the little cross at her neck. "I believe I was born to this work, but I needed a lifetime of preparation. For many years, I merely allowed it. I tried not to engage, but I observed the entities that drifted at the fringes of our world. Not all of them do that, though. Some of them bully their way in. They take hold of people's lives as if they are holding a jar filled with lightning bugs, shaking them as a child would to get them to light. It was those people who finally called me to the work. I could be of service to them in a way that I can't be to anyone else in this world.

"That's my gift. An unfortunate one in some ways. I've often wondered why couldn't I be a veterinarian? I love animals. Why couldn't healing have been my special gift?" She shrugged. "Eventually you surrender. If you want to be happy, you surrender and give what you are meant to give. That being said, I waited until my mother passed through the veil. She too was born with this gift and she believed strongly that it ruined her life. She did not want to see that happen to me."

"I can see how it might… complicate things."

Hattie sighed. "It has certainly done that. And you are a caretaker of sorts, aren't you, Adam?"

"Accidentally, yes."

"There are no accidents. My mother was a caretaker. I never was. Which is why I never had children. I never married. I was an artist for a very long time. I painted and painted. I travelled. But you were drawn to love and love demands great sacrifice."

Adam thought of Holly in her hospital bed missing the warm summer's day, unable to gaze out at her garden and see the flowers spilling pink blossoms onto the ground. He sucked in a painful breath.

"I sense that what has happened here," Hattie murmured, letting her eyes drift shut, "arose from that sacrifice, didn't it? You made a choice, and it has had… some unpleasant consequences."

Adam flushed.

Hattie opened her eyes and locked them on his. "Tell me what happened, Adam."

He hesitated, his chest constricting. How could he tell this woman what he'd done? How could he tell anyone?

She said nothing, but something in her expression softened the vice around his lungs. He released a shaky breath.

"I did a terrible thing. I know I did, and this is my fault. I need to fix it, but… my wife is sick. Her heart is failing. This was her dream. This house, this place."

"It's okay, Adam. Just tell me exactly what happened." Hattie walked to the door and stepped outside as if she knew it had begun out there.

He followed her. "In the spring, I was digging the foundation. I made it a few feet into the ground and hit bones. A full skeleton. And then another and another. There were five in all. They were in pieces with clothing and shoes. My first instinct was to call the sheriff's office, but… I knew what would happen. They'd shut down the construction. I figured we'd bought an old cemetery, so old that it wasn't in the records, maybe a family burial plot.

"Eventually, we would have gotten it straightened out, but Northern Michigan has a short season for building. At the very least it would have set us back a year. Holly might not have a year. I'd put everything into getting this place done. Contractors were hired. I poured a huge portion of our savings plus a building mortgage into this. Everything was scheduled down to the day. A month, two months, six months' delay would have meant delays across the board." He heard himself talking too fast, stumbling over his words in a rush to explain the stupid thing he'd done next. "I dug a hole, and I re-buried the bodies."

Hattie nodded slowly. She left him and walked across the yard. He had not pointed out exactly where he'd buried them, and yet she walked right to it. She paused at the pudding stone and knelt, pressing a palm on the ground. Her head flicked up as if she'd heard something. Her eyes moved first toward his house and then away toward the woods in the direction of the Ashwoods' former house.

Hattie said nothing. She stood and strode across the lawn and into the woods. Adam jogged and caught up with her.

"Hattie—" he started.

"Sshhh…" She put a finger to her lips.

He worried about her walking through the tangled forest. What if she tripped on a root? Broke a hip, twisted an ankle? But he closed his mouth and followed. He knew where they were going, though he'd never taken this particular route to the Ashwoods'. It was a bit of a shortcut, he realized, that allowed the walker to bypass the tangle of bushes he'd had to hack away when he first discovered the house.

Hattie stepped onto the weedy lawn. She gazed at the Ashwoods' decrepit house, the grooves of her face deepening as she stared, transfixed, at something that Adam did not see.

"Yes," she murmured, so quiet he almost didn't hear her. "I'll come inside."

32

Hattie didn't consult him as she crossed the yard and walked up the porch steps. She didn't so much as look at him as she pushed open the door and stepped into the foyer.

She touched nothing, but her eyes strayed over pictures and furniture. She took a step toward the stairs, paused and turned instead to the living room. She walked in and gazed down at the stains on the wood floor. Her hand drifted to her throat and her face pinched as if she were in pain.

"Do you see something?" Adam whispered, searching the floor.

"Sshhh…" Hattie frowned and looked at the ceiling.

A door slammed above them. He heard, as he had previously, footfalls marching down the hallway, dragging something heavy. The stomping reached the stairs, and the footsteps started down with a thud as the thing it dragged thumped on each stair.

Adam put an involuntary hand on Hattie's shoulder. She didn't move.

He struggled to breathe, eyes fixed now on the hall where the footsteps were headed.

Instead of the person entering their line of sight, the footsteps abruptly stopped and then started again, dragging the thing down the hall and then down the basement stairs. Thud… thud… thud…

For a suspended moment there was no sound and then a woman cried out and a terrible retching sound followed. The sound emerged from the room they stood in as if a woman lay at their feet choking and vomiting.

Hattie looked toward the floor, and Adam saw something in her face. She could see something down there, someone. She could see the woman making the sound.

The retching stopped. Hattie moved toward the front door, stepped onto the porch and down the stairs. She moved across the lawn, past the pool and barn and into the trees.

He wanted to ask where she was going, but then he knew. As they neared the place, he heard the crackling of fire and his face and hands blazed hot. He gasped and reeled away, but the sensation vanished as quickly as it came.

Hattie studied the ground, gazing at the debris—all that was left of the *Darling Marilyn*.

Several minutes lapsed in silence, and then Hattie nodded as if she'd come to some conclusion.

"Let's return to your house, Adam. I need a rest."

Adam offered Hattie his arm, and she leaned heavily on him as they made their way back to his house. Once inside, she sat at the kitchen table.

"Can I get you some coffee or tea? I think Holly has some herbal stuff?"

"Just water would be lovely. Thank you."

She sipped the water, and Adam studied her face from across the table. It looked more drawn than when she'd first arrived and her eyes, originally clear, were marred with tiny red webs.

"There's a lot of emotion here," she told him. "A lot that is stuck. Confusion, fear, perhaps most of all rage. There is not a single spirit, but several, and they fade in and out, but there's one… one who seems to be the most… here right now."

"Is she, um… is her hair dark?"

Hattie looked at him. "Sometimes."

"What did you see? Can you tell me?"

Hattie took another drink. "I suspect the women were poisoned. Their deaths were… unimaginable. The suffering…" She shook her head. "To inflict that on another human being."

"Do you know who killed them?"

Hattie's mouth turned down. "I wish it were that transparent. Communication with those who are suspended is not black and white.

When a person perishes in high emotion, in fear, what remains is cloudy. They are here and yet they are not here. Often, they don't even seem to know who ended their lives... though..." She frowned again and then shook her head. "I'm seeing a golden comb, a peacock. I don't know what it means. In any case, I suspect the spirits here do know who killed them, but it's rare that they can pass that information to us."

"Do you have any idea why they seem to be here in my house? It makes sense they'd be in the Ashwoods' house. Look at the place, not to mention they died there."

"That's one of the great misconceptions that arises around hauntings. People look at old abandoned houses and think they must be haunted, but spirits are reaching out for connection, they are searching for life, they're desperate to communicate their story, desperate for someone to hear or perceive them. That's why when you encounter one or many, they will follow you home. The more they try to make contact unsuccessfully, the more outrageous and potentially violent they become in an attempt to get your attention.

"The challenge is that they can't communicate in the usual ways. They can't sit down and have a conversation with us. Sometimes they may be reaching out again and again, and we're totally oblivious to it. We're not seeing them, we're not hearing them and so they get louder until they break through and we notice. And once we notice, they get louder to keep us paying attention."

Adam thought of the pounding on the door, the blowing lightbulbs, the apparitions. "They're doing that," he agreed. "But what can I do? How do I make them go away?"

"Adam, they have a purpose. They won't be silenced by my urging. The police need to come out here. These bodies need to be excavated, their families informed and, if possible, their killer identified. The only way to truly silence a spirit who is trapped is to set them free."

Adam walked Hattie to her car. Before she climbed in, she put a hand on Adam's arm. "It's going to get worse, Adam. These spirits are gathering energy now. They know you sense them and their desperation will heighten. It could become dangerous if you don't do something soon."

"Dangerous? How can they be dangerous?"

"You've already experienced that they can influence matter, but there are worse things. Spirits can get inside you, Adam. Holly, due to her illness, would be at a greater risk, but you are as well. You've opened yourself to them on some level. You have to close that door and the only way to do that is by setting them free."

"When you say inside us, are you talking about… possession?"

"Yes."

Adam blinked at her, wanting to refute the possibility.

"Just do the right thing," she told him. "You know what that is."

She climbed into the driver's seat and drove away.

Adam watched her go. As he turned back to the house, his eyes flickered to the pudding stone. He imagined what lay in the ground beneath it. What would happen if he phoned the police? Would it be enough to dig up the skeletons? Would they want to excavate beneath his house? That had, after all, been the original burial place of the girls. Would the police arrest him for obstructing justice or whatever moving murder victims was called?

How would Holly take it?

That troubled him most of all. Imagining the expression on her face, the disappointment. And how would her body handle the news? What kind of stress would be added to her already weak heart when investigators descended on their property and began ripping it to pieces?

He dialed Holly's room at the hospital.

"Holly's House of Happiness."

Adam recognized Cheryl on the line. "Hi, Cheryl, it's Adam. How's it going up there?"

"Adam, hi, how are you?"

He detected something in her voice, a note of concern perhaps, and wondered if Ted had told her about their strange interaction the night before.

"I'm good. How's Holly?"

"Oh, she's fixin' to eat her lunch, some bland-looking pasta thing. I told her I'd be happy to run home and get her somethin' fit to eat, but she won't let me. Here you go, hon."

Holly's voice came on the phone. "Hi there."

"Hey, beautiful. How ya feeling?"

"Better. Fever's gone. The nurses have been spoiling me, not to mention Cheryl and her ladies."

"Good. I'll be up there to spoil you in a bit, too. Can I bring anything?"

"I'd say bring my fluffy boy, but I'm confident you can't smuggle Marshmallow past reception in a duffel bag."

Adam laughed. "I'm willing to try."

"I know Marshmallow too well to think he'd let you. Just bring your handsome self. The doctor is coming around three. Maybe plan to get here then. I know you hate missing the doctor's litany of orders."

"Perfect. I was hoping to snag a doc while I was there, so that will work out."

"See you in a couple of hours," she told him. "I love you."

"I love you most."

He ended the call and dug from his wallet the napkin the man from the diner had given him days before. His son had been a deputy, he'd said. Adam read the name: Rob Donahue. He was reluctant to talk to a cop for fear of some far-flung repercussion, but Hattie's warning rang in his head.

He dialed the number. A woman answered.

"Donahue's," she said brightly.

"Is Rob available?"

She clicked her tongue. "Available, yes, but home, no. He's over at Seagull Point Park with his metal detector. Probably won't come back this way 'til late afternoon when his stomach gets to grumbling."

"Seagull Point, you said?"

"Yep, right on Huron over by Roger's City."

"Great. Thank you."

Adam let Marshmallow out for a pee and then, after returning the dog to the house, he climbed in his truck and headed for Seagull Point.

When Adam arrived at Seagull Point Park, it was largely deserted thanks to gray skies. He spotted a man walking along the lakeshore, sweatpants rolled to his shins, a black metal detector extended in his hand.

Adam cut across the grass toward him. The man looked up, tilting the rim of his ball cap and squinting towards Adam.

"Hi," Adam called out, waving. "Are you Rob?"

The man paused, flipping something on the detector, which killed its steady beep, and strolled down to Adam. "I sure am."

"I met your dad at the diner the other day. I'm Adam Tate."

Rob walked to a picnic table and unclipped a leather bag from his belt loop, plunked it on the wood surface and rested the metal detector beside it. "My dad lives at that diner seven mornings a week. You'd think eatin' all that bacon would have those old geezers keelin' sideways, but I suspect they'll be celebrating their hundredth birthdays at that same table."

"I hope so," Adam said, smiling at the thought of the old men.

"What can I do ya for?" Rob asked.

"My wife and I just moved to the area, and we built a house off Black Mountain Road. I found the old Ashwood place when I was hiking and I've been troubled by it. I'm trying to find out more about what happened."

"Oh, okay. You're that guy," Rob said. "My dad mentioned he gave my number to someone asking about the Ashwoods."

"That's me."

"Found out anything interesting?"

Adam's stomach flipped. He was talking with a retired detective, a man who'd made a career out of interrogating people. "Not really," Adam admitted. "It bothers me that nothing was ever found."

"Sure, yeah. It bothered most of the folks around here. Though fewer and fewer remember the Ashwoods these days."

"You obviously didn't work the case, right? You can't be old enough."

Rob laughed. "No, I was five when the sailboat sank. But I worked under Sheriff Brady. He investigated it and managed the searches on the water."

"What did he say about it? I know some of the information is likely privileged, but…"

"Not really. There's no crime we've been aware of, but Brady said it was hinky. The entire story felt off to him right from the get-go. He couldn't find any witnesses who saw the sailboat go into the bay or out on the lake. Mr. Ashwood said he'd left the house early because he had a business trip. He drove Alice's car and left her with the truck so she could launch the boat."

"Did the sheriff ever question Michael Ashwood? In the years after?"

"He tried to track him down once because a local paper wanted to cover the story a year after the boat disappeared, but the man had gotten remarried pretty soon after the accident. His new wife took the call from Brady. The sheriff said she spoke to him like he'd just thrown a glass of ice water in her face, real mean and nasty. She told him Michael had no interest in participating in a story and not to call again. The sheriff might have if there'd ever been new evidence, but there never was."

"Did the sheriff ever search the Ashwoods' house?"

"Nope. Why would he? They'd gone sailing, after all." Rob sighed. "But later on, I think he wondered if he'd made a mistake trusting that story. Either way, you can't search someone's property without a warrant and you can't get a warrant without probable cause. There are a lot of hoops to jump through before you can accuse someone of a crime, and the bottom line is that Michael's alibi checked out. He was out of town."

"I found an obituary for Michael Ashwood. It looks like he died five years after the Ashwood women went missing."

Rob looked thoughtful. "Huh, I didn't know that. He was a healthy guy, real fit. I'm surprised to hear that. An accident?"

"I'm not sure, but it said 'survived by his wife, Charlotte.' Was she someone from here in town?"

Rob shook his head. "The name doesn't ring a bell, but… like I said, I was five when the sailboat sank. I wasn't exactly a man about town."

"If something had happened to the women, something criminal, what could you do about it now? Would there be criminal charges or…"

Rob took off his ball cap, scratched at his balding head. "Not if Michael Ashwood was behind it—he's dead, after all—but the sheriff's office would follow up. There are likely living relatives of some of the girls. They've waited over fifty years for news about their loved ones."

"Did the sheriff ever wonder if one of the women might have been involved? Alice or one of the other girls."

Rob's eyebrows lifted. "I see you've caught a whiff of a few of the rumors. Brady heard a few. The most popular was Alice had gone off the rails and sunk the boat on purpose, but… again, with no evidence it's hard to chase a lead like that. Not to mention he knew Alice, and he didn't believe she'd have ever hurt those girls."

"What about one of the other girls in the house?"

Rob frowned. "I don't see how or why one of them girls would have done something like that."

33

1956

3 Days Before the Sail

Nell sat on the stump and gazed at the razor blade she'd taken from the medicine cabinet. It glinted in the sun cutting through the trees. Resting one pale arm on her knee, she took the blade to the skin. The silver shone next to the forking blue veins beneath her nearly translucent wrists. She'd always been so pale. Her mother had sometimes called her Snow White, the palest girl in the land.

Biting her lip, Nell pressed the edge of the blade into her skin. The edge bit her flesh, and she winced as a spot of blood ballooned there. How hard would she have to push to reach one of those veins that appeared so close to the surface?

She thought of Michael and his large warm hands and the life he'd promised and she didn't want to go any further, but what it took to gain that life… The tin of white powder lay beneath her mattress and Nell did not think she could go through with it. The guilt would eat her alive and someday it would drive her back here again, but at that future time she'd have the nerve to drive it in deep. Why not do it now? Spare one life by sacrificing her own.

"Nell?"

The voice startled her, and Nell dropped the blade in the grass, cupping her hand over the tiny wound.

Alice watched her. The woman stood beside a peeling birch tree. Her forehead creased and her eyes flicked to Nell's wrist.

"I... I was just... daydreaming," Nell murmured, aware that she'd given no explanation for what Mrs. Ashwood had likely witnessed.

Alice walked to her, bent over, and plucked the razor blade from the grass. She dropped it into her apron, not bothering to wipe Nell's blood from the sharp edge.

She walked a few paces away and sat cross-legged in the grass. It was an odd position to see her in. Mrs. Ashwood often seemed formal. Even when working in her garden, she sat on her knees as if repenting some sin. Now she braided her hands in her lap and offered a sympathetic smile to Nell.

"It's a hard crossroads, Nell. Seventeen to eighteen, moving from girl to woman, facing the big wide world with all of its temptations. I remember that time in my life well, and I don't remember it fondly. There were fun times, of course, exhilarating times, but the uncertainty, my gosh, it was brutal. Would you like to tell me anything, Nell?"

Nell squirmed, crossing and uncrossing her legs, remembering the heat of Michael between them. Her face flushed, and she looked guiltily at the ground.

Alice didn't seem to notice. In the distance, the sound of an axe splitting wood rose in the air, and Alice's gaze shifted toward it. "I was engaged before I married Mr. Ashwood," she said.

"You were?"

Alice nodded. "Elliot Keane. He was a lovely man. Tall and fair-skinned, like you, with dark hair and bright blue eyes. His father owned a furniture company in Lansing. That's where I grew up. He and I were high school sweethearts, made for each other."

"What happened?"

"He died. He was helping a friend with his roof and fell from the scaffolding and just like that he was gone."

"I'm sorry. That's so sad."

Alice nodded. "I've often wondered what my life would have been like if I'd have married Elliot instead of Michael."

"How did you and Mr. Ashwood meet?"

"At a dance," Alice said, her face pinched as if it were not a happy memory. "My girlfriend dragged me along. I was in such agony. I made the wallflowers look social. Michael appeared before me and he… insisted I dance. He took me driving after and… the rest is history."

"That's a nice story," Nell murmured, though nothing in Alice's face looked joyful at the memory.

Alice's fingers smoothed along her own wrist and there on the tanned flesh, barely visible, was a crisscross of pale lines. Long faded scars.

"Did you…?" Nell didn't say the words, but Alice's eyes followed Nell's gaze to her scarred wrist.

"After my daughter…" Alice breathed, clutching both arms suddenly to her stomach as if it caused physical pain to remember.

Nell's eyes widened. "Your daughter? I thought… I didn't know you had children." A tremor of hurt coursed through her that Michael had never mentioned a daughter.

"Marilyn." A tear fell from Alice's eye and cut a path down her cheek.

"Did she die?" Nell asked, trying to soften her words, though it was a question that could not be tempered.

"She's never been found. Perhaps only in death will I know what become of my darling Marilyn."

Alice stood suddenly and rushed away, walking briskly through the trees toward the house.

Nell watched her go, even more unnerved by that little tin of white powder. She could go back to the house, take it from beneath her mattress, and bury it in the woods. She'd tell Michael it disappeared, that someone must have found it.

The scenario played out in her mind, confessing the poison had disappeared followed by Michael's reaction. Or she could make up another lie. Say Alice didn't want a drink during the sail, the tin fell overboard, something, anything.

A twig snapped and Nell looked up to see Michael making his way through the trees.

Michael put his hands on her shoulders and leaned down to kiss her neck. She stiffened, and he turned her to face him.

"Alice was here," Nell said, eyes darting past him. "She could come back at any moment."

"I saw her go into the house. We're alone, darling. Don't worry."

She couldn't look at him. Her eyes welled with tears that would soon spill over.

"Hey." He crouched to meet her eyes. "What's wrong?"

She wiped at her tears angrily. "You… you had a daughter."

He nodded slowly. "Yes, Marilyn. You didn't know that?"

"How could I have known that?"

"I just assumed that all you girls knew, that Alice talked about her."

Nell studied his face, tried to sense if he spoke the truth. "She never has, never, until just now."

"It's hard for both of us to talk about Marilyn. It wasn't intentional, Nell. I wasn't lying to you."

"What happened to her? Your daughter?"

He shook his head. "I don't know. She went into the woods, the Manistee National Forest, with a friend. She vanished. We searched, the police searched, but she was never found. It's possible a bear or a wolf got hold of her, though Alice has never believed that."

"What does Alice believe?"

He frowned. "I can't make sense of her beliefs, but I'm at the heart of it. Of that much, I'm sure. She blames me for Marilyn's disappearance. She blames me for a lot of things."

Alice strode into the house, ignoring the greeting of Mildred, who stood in the kitchen arranging decorations for Nell's birthday party the following day. She pushed into the bathroom and locked the door behind her.

Bracing her hands on the porcelain sink, she fought for breath. Her ribcage tightened around her lungs. She could not get a breath. Black spots swam behind her eyes, and when she looked in the mirror, a corpse looked back. Her skin appeared mottled and black, her lips as gray as the bark of a tree.

She gasped and clenched her eyes shut, sinking to the floor. Something sharp poked into her leg and she reached into her apron and found the razor blade still stained with Nell's blood. Alice gazed at it, head swimming, and considered the aftermath if she finished what she'd started all those years ago.

Michael would have to break down the door. They'd find her in a heap of skirts and blood. Could she perish before they became suspicious and forced their way into the bathroom? No. If she wanted to do it, truly, she must ensure no interruption. Wait until the weekend sail during the night when the boat drifted in darkness and the girls slept below. Fill her skirt pockets with rocks and slip into the black water.

She blinked at the tile floor and imagined how peaceful that would be. Sinking down and down and perhaps before she even reached the cold lake bottom, she'd have left this world and stepped into the next, into the arms of her darling Marilyn.

34

Adam drove away from the park, thinking about the things he'd wanted to ask Rob Donahue but hadn't.

What if someone found the bodies and moved them? What would the sheriff do? He wanted the information, but he couldn't exactly pose it as a hypothetical. It was so far-fetched that it would immediately garner suspicion.

When Adam arrived at the hospital, Holly was alone in her room, and he was grateful that Cheryl had left. He feared she would reveal something about what Ted had seen the night before.

"Hey, gorgeous," Adam said, kissing Holly on the forehead.

"Mmm…" she sighed, tugging him closer. "Get in this bed with me. I've missed feeling you."

She scooted over, and he climbed onto the bed, one leg hanging off the side. He tucked an arm behind her, and she buried her face in his neck and inhaled.

"You smell like pine and beach sand." She brushed her lips along his cheek. "I want to smell like you instead of this funky lotion they keep rubbing on my hands."

He lifted one of her hands to his nose and breathed. "You smell soft and fresh. I love the scent of you."

She smiled up at him. "I have the aroma of old sick people."

He grinned. "You could roll in manure and still smell heavenly."

"Liar," she murmured.

The door opened, and a doctor walked in, clipboard in hand.

"Hi, Holly. This must be the spectacular husband you've been raving about?"

Adam stuck out a hand. "Hi. I'm Adam Tate."

"Nice to meet you, Adam. I'm Dr. Meer. I've been looking after this lovely lady. How are you feeling, Holly?"

"Fantastic." She rested her hand on Adam's stomach. "And ready to be home."

Dr. Meer nodded and lifted his stethoscope to his ears. He held the metal chest piece up. "Let's take a listen, shall we?"

Adam stood and gave the doctor room. He leaned over Holly, placing the dial beneath her thin gown. "Big breath… good… and let it out." He moved the disc to several places on Holly's chest, nodding each time as if confirming something positive.

"Everything sounds okay?" Adam asked when Meer removed the buds from his ears.

"Better," he said. "We could hear a bit of fluid in the lungs when we admitted her. That's cleared up." He directed his words at Holly. "Your heart rhythm is good, though not as strong as we'd like."

Holly rested a hand on her chest. "Story of my life."

Adam went back to her bedside and sat down. He squeezed her hand.

"Nothing major though?" he asked the doctor. "Heart wise? I mean, the new heart seems to be… working well?"

"For now," Meer said. "But illness takes a toll. We've got to be really diligent with keeping your immune system in high working order, Holly. I'd advise against any alcohol. Best to avoid sugar, which depresses the immune system. And also children—if possible I'd stay away from kids for a bit."

Holly's face fell. "I just started helping in the kids' program at our new church."

Adam kissed the back of Holly's hand. "It's not forever, honey."

"That's likely where you picked up the virus to begin with," Meer explained. "Believe me, I love children. I have four of my own, but they can be super-spreaders with colds and flus. They're pretty resilient, but for people with compromised systems, children can be deadly."

Holly smiled sadly. "Guess it's best we never had any," she murmured.

Adam hugged her and kissed the top of her head.

"I don't say any of this to depress you," Meer went on, "and once you're past this, you can go back to working with the kids, but I'd recommend a lot of hand-washing and some extra Vitamin C and zinc when you do. In the meantime, the remedy is staying on top of your meds, drinking a lot of water, and getting plenty of rest."

"We can manage that," Adam said. "Right, Holl?"

"Yeah."

"How's it looking for Holly getting discharged?" Adam asked.

"I think it's safe to say that tomorrow by five, Holly can pack her bags."

Adam stayed with Holly until the nurses ushered him out, citing the end of visiting hours. He almost argued, but Holly insisted he go home.

When he reached the house, he let Marshmallow out and then hurried to his laptop. He had one new Facebook message.

It had come from Blanche Spalding, a person he'd connected to Mildred.

Hi, Adam. My name is Jolene. This is my mother's profile, but I manage it, as she's not very tech-savvy. She's interested in speaking with you. You can reach her by phone at 231-525-0011.

It wasn't quite seven p.m.

Adam dialed the number.

"Hello," a woman's brittle voice answered.

"Hi, is this Blanche Spalding?"

"Yes," the old woman said.

"My name is Adam Tate. I received a message from your daughter Jolene after I contacted you about a family member, Mildred Spalding?"

"Ahh... yes. Mildred was my sister."

"Thanks so much for speaking with me. Ummm..." Adam's mind went blank. He suddenly wasn't sure what he'd intended to ask this woman.

"Mildred was the second-born," Blanche explained. "Cordelia was first, I came third, and then our brother, Edwin. I'm the only one left."

"I'm sorry," Adam said. "That would be hard. Did you or your older sister also spend time at the Ashwoods' house?"

"Oh, no, only Mildred."

"Why is that?"

The woman started to speak and a coughing fit seized her. The sound grew muffled, as if she'd covered the phone with one hand.

"I apologize. I've had this"—she paused and coughed again —"cough for a month now. Hay fever or some respiratory bug. Who knows anymore? It was a tragedy that sent Mildred to the Ashwoods' house. A terrible accident or maybe something much worse."

Adam pressed the phone tighter against his ear. "Can you tell me what happened?"

"Well, as I said there were three of us girls. My parents had longed for a baby boy, but it seemed he was not meant to be. Then, as if by a miracle, my mother, who believed she was going through menopause, discovered she was with child. Lo and behold, it was the little prince they'd prayed for. That's what we called him, the little prince.

"Mildred was about nine when he arrived and she was odd with Edwin. She pinched him to make him cry, and she hid his toys, but when she was in front of others, she acted as if she just adored him. One morning, my mother heard a terrible scream. My older sister and I were playing in the back yard. My mother ran up the stairs, but Edwin wasn't in his room. We lived in an A-frame house that had a third level, with a small room and a balcony that jutted out over our driveway.

"Mildred came out of that room. She seemed surprised to see our mother. Mother demanded to know where Edwin was. Mildred cried, but much later in life, my mother told my eldest sister and I that they were crocodile tears. Mildred insisted Edwin had gone onto the third-floor balcony and fallen over the side. My mother rushed back down the stairs and outside, and there he was on the cement. He was still alive, but only barely. The ambulance came and rushed him to the hospital." Blanche's voice grew thick. "He died later that day."

"I'm so sorry," Adam whispered. "How devastating."

"Yes, it was that. Made harder by the sudden removal of Mildred from our home just weeks after Edwin's death. I was only seven and didn't quite understand what was happening. Our life, which had been so lovely, was suddenly filled with despair. I learned later that Mildred told a story about Edwin slipping through a spot in the wrought-iron rail, but it was hardly big enough for a cat, let alone a three-year-old boy. Mother had to be hospitalized. She was absolutely inconsolable.

She refused to come home if Mildred was in the house. She insisted Father find a boarding school or a home for Mildred."

Adam's pulse quickened. "Why?"

"Because my mother believed that Mildred threw Edwin off the balcony—that she murdered our baby brother."

35

Silence stretched on the line. Adam's eyes flickered to the picture of the Ashwoods' girls. Mildred appeared gray in comparison to the other girls in the picture, with her muted clothes, her slouched posture. He studied her dark eyes and shivered. "Do you believe it's true?"

Blanche cleared her throat. "Yes. I remember how cruel Mildred was toward Edwin, how jealous. But who could fathom how far she would go? Many children have sibling rivalries. Something was wrong with Mildred. My sister Cordelia told me stories when I got older, things Mildred had done to children at school. She was not a good person."

"How did your parents handle… the sailboat sinking, and Mildred's disappearance?"

"My father mourned her. He had forgiven her for what she'd done, but my mother hadn't. I never heard her say a prayer for Mildred. She never forgave her."

"If Mildred had somehow survived the sinking of the boat and… I know this is a long shot, but if she decided to start a new life, do you think she would have contacted your family?"

The woman snorted. "If Mildred had ever contacted us again it would have been for one reason. Revenge."

~

Adam had barely ended the call when a book fell off his shelf and landed with a thud on the floor. Before he could step over to retrieve it, the shelf collapsed and ten more books toppled beside it.

He blinked at the shelf and then at the books. He started to pick them up and heard Marshmallow barking outside. He hurried down the hall and out the front door. Marshmallow stood beside the pudding stone, hair raised, teeth bared.

"What is it, boy?" he asked, though his voice barely emerged.

He couldn't see anything at the stone, but he felt… something. The air seemed thick and alive.

Marshmallow continued barking and then from the house behind them a loud shriek began. The fire alarm.

Adam turned and sprinted back to the house. The fire alarm just outside the pantry door screamed. Marshmallow followed, barking frantically. The door to the crawlspace stood open and something billowed out, not smoke exactly, more like a mist.

Adam kicked the trap door closed and waved at the alarm. Finally, when it continued to blare, he punched it off the ceiling with the side of his fist. It broke free and dangled, the sound dying.

36

The next day dawned bright, and thankfully cooler than the ninety-degree days they'd been having for weeks. Nothing else strange had happened after the fire alarm and the mist from the crawlspace, but Adam had still had a restless night. He'd locked himself and Marshmallow in the bedroom, though he had little doubt that if the thing haunting him wanted in, a locked door wouldn't stop it.

Adam started out of the house, pausing at Marshmallow whining behind him. He had a nearly two-hour drive ahead of him to get to Sault St. Marie, the city where Michael Ashwood had lived with his second wife. Adam had to be back in time to get Holly from the hospital. The dog barked.

Adam sighed and opened the front door.

"All right, you can come, but you're not sitting in my lap. Deal?"

Marshmallow bounded to the truck and launched through the open passenger door. He sat and watched Adam, tongue lolling.

They listened to an oldies rock station as they drove north, crossing over the Mackinac Bridge and heading into Michigan's Upper Peninsula.

Adam had printed Michael Ashwood's obituary, which included a street address. Though he couldn't say if Michael's second wife, Charlotte, still lived there, or still lived at all for that matter, he wanted to find out.

Before driving the last leg of the trip into Sault St. Marie, Adam pulled into a roadside park and let Marshmallow out for a bathroom break. The dog peed on several trees and then started after a squirrel, but Adam called him back to the truck.

The address for the last residence of Michael Ashwood was on a dead-end street with mostly Victorian homes. Some of them were painted in elaborate colors, including one that was pink with white trim. Adam gaped at it. It looked as if someone had blown up a girl's dollhouse.

Michael Ashwood's former house was also a Victorian, this one white with blue shutters. Flower boxes sat in the windows, displaying a rainbow of blossoms that Holly could have named on sight.

Adam parked and left the truck running with the air conditioning on for Marshmallow. "Be back soon, Marsh," he told the dog, scratching his neck.

He walked to the front door and rang the bell, still not entirely sure what he'd say if presented with Michael Ashwood's widow.

A young man, likely in his mid-twenties and wearing a green track suit, opened the door.

"Can I help you?" he asked.

"Maybe. I'm looking for someone named Charlotte Ashwood. She used to live here?"

The man, little more than twenty-five, wrinkled his brow. "My wife and I bought this place two years ago. The previous owner's name was Hart, if I remember correctly."

"Dang, okay. Umm...."

"You can try the pink nightmare two houses down. The lady who lives there has been on this block for like a hundred years."

"Great, thanks." Adam returned to the sidewalk and headed for the dollhouse.

Though he was sure the porch had been empty when he'd driven by minutes before, he now saw a thin old woman rocking in a white wicker chair. He walked the path up to her house.

"Hi," he said, pausing at her porch stairs. "I'm looking for a woman named Charlotte Ashwood. Your neighbor said you might remember her."

The woman continued rocking, eyeing him thoughtfully. "Come on up here and speak a little louder. I thought you said Charlotte Ashwood."

Adam walked up the stairs. "I did. I'm trying to find her. Did you know her?"

The woman slowed her rocking, steadying her feet on the wood floor. She wore slippers in the shape of bunnies the same color pink as her house. Adam noticed her nightdress was a similar shade of pink. Her skin was pale, her hair a shock of white, and her eyes a misty blue. She studied him. "I'll make you a deal. You bring that fluffy critter you're hidin' in your truck up here to see me and I'll tell you everything you want to know."

Adam grinned and glanced back at his truck, where Marshmallow watched them from the driver's window. "I'd be happy to," Adam assured her.

He went to the truck and released Marshmallow, who bypassed him and ran to the woman's house, bounding up the stairs. The woman leaned forward in her chair and sank her bony hands into Marshmallow's scruff, allowing him to lick her face.

"Easy does it, Marshmallow," Adam told him, afraid the dog would jump on the woman and break her already fragile bones.

"Oh, no," the woman insisted. "He's just fine. Give this granny some sugar, Marshmallow. My goodness, you are as sweet as a marshmallow, aren't you?" She gestured at a wicker sofa. "Have a seat."

Adam sat down and watched the woman nuzzle her face against Marshmallow's.

She pulled away, laughing. "What a treat. I haven't had any puppy snuggles in ages. My own pup, Ruby, passed on two years ago. She's still around though." She winked at Adam.

Adam smiled, not sure what to say. "I'm Adam, by the way, Tate. I guess I didn't introduce myself."

"I'm Lola Imogen Walsh, but you can just call me Lola."

"Thanks for talking with me, Lola."

She scratched Marshmallow behind the ears. "I love to talk. Just ask my granddaughter in there. Sometimes I think she puts headphones on to tune me out."

"Does your granddaughter live with you?"

"Oh, no—well, temporarily she does. Iris is studying to become a lawyer, but she's having a spot of trouble. You see, our family has the sight, and it seems the gift has been visited on our dear Iris."

"The sight?"

The old woman tapped the spot just above and between her

eyebrows. "She sees things that others can't." Lola winked at him again and craned back to shout through the screen door. "Iris!" Lola yelled.

A young woman appeared at the door. She had coppery hair, long and curly, flowing over her shoulders. "What is it, Grandma?" she asked. She spotted Adam and narrowed her eyes, stepping quickly onto the porch.

"This is Adam Tate," Lola told her. "And this beautiful baby is Marshmallow. Aren't you, honey?" She leaned her face close to Marshmallow's again. The dog barked happily.

"Can I help you?" Iris asked Adam, her tone cool.

Lola grinned. "Iris is my guard dog. She makes Marshmallow look like… well, a marshmallow." She laughed and slapped her hands on the arms of her rocking chair. "She's more of a Doberman pinscher."

"Hi, Iris," Adam said. "I came to ask your grandmother some questions about a neighbor who used to live nearby."

She looked him up and down. "You're not selling anything?"

"No."

"Okay." She turned to her grandmother, dropping her voice. "Are you comfortable answering his questions, Grandma? It's okay to say no."

Lola shooed her granddaughter away. "You go on and get back to your work, sweetie pie. Your grandma just wanted you to meet this handsome young man, though I see he has a wedding ring on, so I guess he's not available." She cocked an eyebrow at Adam.

He smiled and shook his head. "Happily married, I'm afraid."

Iris gave him a curt nod and disappeared back into the house.

"Whew. She can be a grouchy thing." Lola laughed. "Never to me, of course, but she's more of a 'shoot first, ask questions later' kind of gal, and it don't help that she's coming into her birthright. That's the trouble with birthrights, a lot of times you don't want 'em. But enough about Iris, you're here to talk about Charlotte Ashwood."

"Yes."

Lola started a slow rock again, leaning her head back and closing her eyes. "Let's see… the Ashwoods moved in around 1957, I'd say. It was winter, a cold one. I had a baby, Melody, and another on the way, Donald. I still remember standing at the picture window by the Christmas tree watching them unload their truck. Charlotte looked so young. I thought she was his daughter, Michael Ashwood's, but then come to find out she was his young wife. Probably had been a scandal where they were from, so they moved up here to start fresh."

"Did you become friends with her? Charlotte?"

"Oh, no. She was not a friendly girl. It wasn't just that she kept to herself, which she did. They both did. She was downright rude if you spoke to her. Acted like she descended from royalty. I tried to be friendly with her. I figured it must be lonely moving all the way up here in the dead of winter, but she wanted nothing to do with me. Arthur, that was my husband, got to know Michael a bit, but none too well because that Charlotte would run him right out of there anytime he came around. Arthur told me once he saw the girl slap Michael so hard across the face it left a handprint."

"Really?" Adam imagined Nell's diary. If she was the young wife, she'd undergone quite a personality shift between her final diary entries in 1956 and her move to the Upper Peninsula with Michael in 1957.

"Oh, yes, a nasty girl."

"And they lived here for about five years?"

"She lived here longer than that. Michael passed in… hmmm…"

"1961."

"Was it '61? Yeah, that sound about right. He passed rather unexpectedly and Charlotte didn't have a service at all, no viewing, nothing. It was very strange."

"How did he die?"

The woman held up her empty hands. "The answer to that is about as clear as mud. One day he was out buying a ham for dinner and the next day he was getting rolled out of the house under a white sheet. The coroner called it natural causes, but I'd never known a perfectly healthy man to die for no reason. I believe Charlotte refused an autopsy, which was her right. They buried him at Riverside Cemetery. Arthur and I took flowers out there a couple times, but I'll tell ya something strange. One of those times, I'd forgotten this little cross we'd bought, and I went back the next day and the flowers we'd left were shredded to bits. Like someone had stomped them into smithereens."

"That's disturbing. Were there graves other than Michael's disturbed as well?"

"Nope. None of the flowers on any other headstones had been touched, just the ones we'd left on Michael's."

"What happened to Charlotte after Michael passed?"

"Nothing much for about a year. She stayed in the house, kept to herself. Then in the summer of '62 she took a liking to Morris Flannery.

He was a widower, a delightful man who owned a little carpet store in town. He'd inherited a good deal of money after his wife passed, but he wasn't a spender. Just had his modest little house."

Lola sat up and pointed a finger down the street. "See that house on the corner there? The reddish one with the white fence? That was Morris's place. I started seeing Charlotte walking down there in the evenings carrying casserole dishes and pies. Funny too, because Arthur told me she never cooked a thing for Michael. Michael prepared all the food. Anyhow, she got Morris's attention and not even six months after she started paying him visits, they got married."

"Morris married Charlotte?"

"Yep. For the life of me, I don't know why he married her. She was pretty enough, though she had the look of someone who tried too hard. Thick makeup and strong perfume and far too much jewelry. I didn't know what Morris saw in her, but loneliness does strange things to a man.

"Women get on fine when their husbands die, but men have a harder time with it. They don't realize all the little ways their wife kept their world turning. Dishes and laundry and grocery shopping. I remember when my brother's wife died, he called me one morning and said, 'Where on earth do I buy a carton of boiled eggs? I can't puzzle it out.' Barbara, that was his wife, always made a carton and put them in the fridge and he didn't even know she boiled them herself. He figured she bought them boiled."

Adam thought of Holly, and his stomach grew hollow and tight. He'd pondered the same fears himself. How would he go on without her? How could he greet the world when all the color had drained out of it?

"Charlotte got Morris to sell his house and move in with her. He didn't have children, but he had Angel, this beautiful Pomeranian that had been his wife's beloved dog—caramel-colored and sweet as pie. Let me tell you that dog had a face on her anytime Charlotte came around. Angel was not the type of dog who disliked strangers, either. The neighbor kids could come up and feed her treats. She didn't let Charlotte anywhere near her. She snarled and snapped at that woman like Charlotte was brandishing a battleax. I remember Morris bought a gorgeous gem-studded collar for Angel. One day, when Morris was at work, I saw Charlotte rip the collar right off that poor dog's head. I don't know what she did with it, but I never saw it again."

"Did they stay here for a long time? Charlotte and Morris?"

Lola's face blackened. "Three years. They lived here for three years and then Morris, much like Michael before him, died of so-called natural causes. He'd worked at the carpet store the day before. Went home as fine as Sunday morning and the next day he got carried out of that house in a body bag."

37

1956

2 Days Before the Sail

Nell stepped into the dress Alice had made for her and pulled it up. The bouncy skirt fell just above her knees. Alice had sewn tiny white faux pearls onto the neckline. It was beautiful and brought out the blue in Nell's large almond-shaped eyes. She smiled and spun slowly.

"Nell! I just love it," a voice gushed from the doorway.

She turned to see Bitsy wearing a party dress of her own, though hers was a hand-me-down from Cocoa that didn't quite fit her narrow frame. Cocoa had curves. Bitsy was thin and flat-chested.

Nell too was thin, but her dress accentuated the bit of womanly body she had, giving her a waist and propping up her tiny breasts.

Nell blushed and turned back to the mirror. "Could you zip me up?"

"Sure." Bitsy slipped in and pulled the zipper high. "I'm so excited for you to open my gift! I can't believe you're eighteen." She squealed and hugged Nell.

Over Bitsy's shoulder, Nell saw a shape move in the hall. Likely Mildred eavesdropping, as she often did.

"Are you coming down now?" Bitsy asked, walking backwards toward the door. "Everything's ready."

"I'll be right behind you," Nell promised. She turned back to her dresser, picked up her photo of her mother, and kissed it. "I love you, Mom," she murmured. Her eyes fluttered to the bed and her stomach tightened at what lay beneath the mattress.

As Nell walked down the staircase, the door opened. Michael stepped into the house. Nell beamed as his eyes shifted up and caught sight of her.

He froze, and his features darkened. His mouth turned down, and he turned abruptly, making a beeline for the kitchen.

Nell slowed her descent, a self-conscious hand reaching to the pearl neckline. At the bottom of the stairs, she turned and looked into the large oval mirror, searching for what had upset Michael. For a moment, she thought Cocoa had overdone her make-up—maybe she looked trampy—but no, her eyes were a bit brighter beneath the mascara and her lips a soft pink. Her hair was still in place.

Her lower lip trembled. If she cried, her makeup would be ruined and they would all be able to see the tracks of her tears. Nell steadied a hand on her chest, took a few deep breaths and quelled the emotion bubbling up.

"Hey, birthday girl!" Cocoa boomed, coming up behind Nell and tickling her sides. "Look at you in that dress. You look like a princess."

Nell blushed and touched her hair. "It's not too much?"

Cocoa put a hand on her hip. "Are you kidding me? There's no such thing as too much. Come on, let's get out there before Mildred eats all the cake."

A long table sat outside near the garden covered in a white linen tablecloth and adorned with vases of fresh flowers. The girls had made taffeta bouquets and hung them from the trees along with streamers. Balloons were tied to the back of the chairs and bumped gently in the warm breeze.

Nell caught Michael's eye. He no longer looked angry, but she sensed some disquiet in him when he gazed at her.

They ate the dinner Alice had prepared especially for Nell, beef stroganoff and a garden salad. After they'd finished eating, Alice walked to where Nell sat at the head of the table. She handed her an envelope and returned to her seat.

"We're doing gifts before cake?" Margie asked, surprised.

"Yes," Alice said. "Go ahead, Nell. Open it."

Nell's eyes flicked to Michael, but he seemed equally curious about what lay inside the envelope.

Nell opened the envelope. She slipped two cardboard rectangles out and studied them. She held two train tickets from Traverse City to Detroit. She cast a questioning gaze first toward Michael, who seemed unaware of what she looked at. It was Alice who stared back at her, a waxy smile on her lips.

"Two train tickets to Detroit. You and Cocoa will leave on Monday after we sail this weekend. I've made all the arrangements."

Nell's mouth dropped open as Cocoa swooped in and grabbed her in a hug.

"Isn't it divine? You and I as city girls with our very own apartment," Cocoa gushed, pulling Nell from her chair and twirling her in the grass.

Dizziness swept over Nell and she tripped over Cocoa's feet, nearly plunging face first into the grass, but Michael leapt up and caught her, grabbing her around the waist in a gesture so intimate she immediately felt the eyes of all the girls on them.

She quickly stepped away, smoothing her hands down her dress. She forced herself to meet Alice's eyes.

Alice smiled. "A birthday gift for Nell and a departing gift for Cocoa. Everything has been arranged. An apartment with two bedrooms, a position for you both at an office."

"I thought…" Nell trailed off, feeling Michael's eyes on her. "I thought Cocoa couldn't go until December because there were no apartments."

"I made some phone calls. I can see you're both ready. There's no benefit to the two of you staying tucked up here in the wilderness. It's time to spread your wings and fly."

"Thank you," she stammered. "This is a wonderful surprise."

She walked on wobbly legs to Alice and leaned down, kissing her cheek. Alice smelled of strong soap. As Nell pulled away, Alice caught her wrist and gripped it in her hand. Her fingernails dug into Nell's flesh.

"You look so pretty in that dress, Nell," she murmured, caressing the full skirt of Nell's dress with her free hand.

Nell curtsied, wanting to jerk her wrist away. A lump of terror formed in her throat. She recognized something in Alice's eyes, but couldn't name it. Hatred perhaps.

"It's a beautiful dress," Nell said. "Thank you so much for making it for me."

Nell opened the rest of her gifts, painting on a smile, though inside her guts writhed. A new journal from Cocoa, magazines from Margie, a copy of *Jane Eyre* from Mildred.

Bitsy frowned and searched the table. "Did you open my gift, Nell?" she asked.

Nell looked at the wrinkled wrapping paper and the scatter of gifts. "I don't think so…"

Bitsy looked beneath the table. "Maybe it fell in the house. I'll go look." She disappeared into the house and emerged a moment later, her face blotchy. "It's not in there."

The girls stood and searched the grass and crisscrossed the yard, but they found no sign of Bitys's gift.

Bitsy started to cry.

"Oh, Bitsy, it's okay. I'm sure it will turn up," Nell assured her.

"But… it was my grandmother's peacock comb. The one you always loved. I wanted you to have it… to… to remember me." Her voice shook.

Nell hugged her, rubbing her back. "I could never forget you, Bitsy. We'll write letters every week, and when you're eighteen, you'll come to the city to live with me and Cocoa."

Bitsy sniffled and wiped at her eyes.

"Now, now," Alice said. "Let's not spoil Nell's party with tears, Bitsy. I'm sure once we put everything away, we'll find the present laying in plain sight. That's how these things go. Come now. Let's light the birthday candles."

Michael lit a match and carefully held it to each of Nell's eighteen candles. His eyes flicked up and held hers. She stared at him, transfixed, and then broke the gaze when her eyes filled with tears. She fought them back as the girls started to sing. Nell leaned in and closed her eyes.

I wish… She thought of what she wanted most in the world. Michael. She wanted to be with Michael. *I wish to be free.*

She blew out the candles, unsure of why she'd made the wish, but knowing she could not wish to be with Michael. It came at too great a cost.

~

After they'd cleaned up the party things, Nell loitered in the backyard hoping to catch Michael's eye, but she was unsuccessful.

Mildred circled her, head tilted, smiling her mischievous little smile. Cocoa had once commented to Nell that Mildred reminded her of a weasel with their dark eyes and always-perked ears. For the first time, Nell saw the resemblance.

"I'm tired, Mildred. What do you want?" She was normally kinder to Mildred, softer. She knew the girl had no friends. But that evening, Nell had no patience for her. She wanted to sneak away and meet with Michael, but Alice was keeping him busy, and Nell feared she was trying to ensure he didn't have a moment alone with any of the girls.

"The fabric on that dress is so lovely. Do you know where Mrs. Ashwood got it?"

Nell sighed. "I'd imagine she bought it from the store in town."

"I don't think so," Mildred told her in a sing-song voice.

"Get to the point, Mildred," Nell snapped.

Mildred reached into the pocket of her smock. She held out a photograph for Nell to see.

It was a photograph of Mr. and Mrs. Ashwood, younger, both smiling. Between them stood a beautiful girl, a young teenager. She held a bouquet of tiger lilies in her hands. She wore a dress that looked eerily like Nell's own.

"It's not exactly the same..." Mildred said, leaning over to peer at the picture. "She had to add a bit to make it fit you, plus the tulle beneath the skirt."

Nell's fingers shook as she handed the photo back. "So what?"

"Well... do you know who the girl is in the photo, Nell? It's their dead daughter."

38

Adam's mouth fell open at Lola's revelation. "Charlotte's second husband died out of the blue as well?"

"Yep. Morris was thirty-nine years old. No health problems. Poof—dead."

"Was there an autopsy performed?"

"What do you think?"

"No."

"Right you are. Charlotte said it went against her religious beliefs, though not a soul in town had ever seen her attend services."

"Holy crap," Adam whispered, mind racing. "Do you think—?"

"That she killed him? Him and Michael both? You bet I do, and so did Arthur. He even went to the police department and told them as much. Trouble was, he didn't have any proof and Charlotte put on a good show of being the grieving widow. Still, I think she sensed the tide had turned against her here in town. A few months after Morris passed, a 'for sale' sign went up in her yard and by the next fall she was gone."

"Do you have any idea where she went?"

"Not a clue. Arthur kept at the police for a few years after she left, but eventually he gave up hope of anything ever getting done."

"Did she take Morris's last name? Flannery?"

"Yep."

"So, if I wanted to track her down, I'd be looking for Flannery, not Ashwood."

"If God is good, anyway, but if she kept up her antics, who knows what name she'd be carrying."

Adam thought of the photo of the Ashwood girls. Why hadn't he brought it with him? Here was a woman who could have identified Michael's second wife if perhaps she had been Nellie Madden.

"I have a picture of a bunch of girls Michael used to know. I think one of them might have been his wife. If I were to email it to you, do you think you could identify her?"

"I could identify her. It's the email I'll have a problem with. I don't have one myself."

"What about Iris? Maybe I could send one to her?"

Lola nodded. "Oh, yes, she's tapping away at her little computer seven days a week. Iris!" she called.

Iris appeared. "Yes?"

"Adam needs your email."

"What for?" She looked through the screen towards Adam.

"I have a photo I'd like to show your grandmother, but I forgot it at home. I'm hoping she can identify someone who's in it."

"Okay, hold on." She stepped out a moment later with a card in her hand. "This is my work email. I rarely check the personal one."

As she stepped toward him, her eyes widened and her gaze locked on something beside him. He turned, expecting to see someone or something standing there, but there was nothing there.

"Here," she said quickly, dropping the card in his lap and turning abruptly to walk back into the house.

Adam looked at Lola, who offered him a conciliatory smile.

"Don't worry, Adam. It's not you who spooked her."

~

Adam drove to the hospital, contemplating Lola's allegations. Both she and her husband had suspected Charlotte Ashwood of murdering not one, but two of her husbands. What had begun as a curiosity was spiraling into a murderous rampage that had potentially taken the lives of over seven people.

When Adam arrived at the hospital, the discharge papers had been completed and Holly was ready to go home.

He pushed her in a wheelchair to the truck, despite her insistence that she could walk.

"Humor me," he told her.

When she spotted Marshmallow, she sprang out of the chair and jerked open the passenger door. Marshmallow leapt out, but he was careful not to jump on Holly. He landed beside her and pressed his face into her outstretched arms.

"Oh, there's my baby boy. Mama missed you."

Marshmallow licked her hands and face.

Back at the house, Holly settled on the couch and propped her feet on the table. Adam slid a pillow beneath her heels.

She leaned back and smiled. "I could get used to this."

"Good." He kissed her. "Hungry? I could make burgers on the grill?"

"How about your famous grilled cheese? I was craving one of those."

"I can do that."

He went to the study first and pulled out the photo of the Ashwoods' girls. He took a picture of the image with his phone and attached to an email and sent it to Iris's address. He made grilled cheese for Holly and himself, and heated some of the leftover casserole from Cheryl as a side dish.

They attempted a movie, but Holly nodded off minutes after opening credits.

"Bedtime," he murmured in her ear.

She started to sit up.

"No, I've got you." He lifted her and carried her to the bed.

After he'd tucked her in, he checked the laptop. No return email from Iris. He thought of sitting down and opening the search bar, typing in Charlotte's name and trying to track her movements after she left Sault St. Marie. But then he thought of Holly alone in bed and closed the screen, returned to the bedroom.

Adam woke in the dark room and listened. Something sighed in the house, a floorboard, or perhaps something living. He rolled to his side away from Holly, where he had a direct line of sight to the door. A dragging sound emerged in the hallway as if someone were walking down the hall but had one injured leg. A little thump and then a drag, thump… drag.

Adam swallowed and a cold sweat prickled between his shoulder blades.

Unbidden, the memory of a story arose in his mind from the book *Scary Stories to Tell in the Dark*. It had been called 'The Big Toe' and in it a young boy had discovered the toe of a man on the roadside and added it to the family stew, but that night as the boy lay in bed the corpse had returned to take back what was his.

The sound grew closer. Thump… drag.

Adam sat up and swung his legs over the side of the bed. His heart rapped against his breastbone and he put a steadying hand on it, a move he'd done on Holly infinite times, counting heartbeats, urging them to slow down. Despite his best efforts, adrenaline surged through him at the next thump… drag.

He gritted his teeth, stood and walked to the door, jerked it open, prepared to face the thing approaching.

The hall was empty. No one awaited him.

Adam checked every room in the house, turned on lights, peered into closets. He found nothing, but when he stepped back into his own room, moonlight spilled in from the open curtains. A figure stood over the bed, gazing down at Holly. The woman's eyes were black hollows in her face and her black lips pulled away from her rotted teeth. Her eyes, blazing, were locked on… what?

Adam's gaze dropped to the bed where Holly's hand lay on top of the comforter. The mother-of-pearl ring shone in the moonlight.

The figure stretched its pale arm toward Holly's hand.

In the bed, Holly gasped and her eyes flew open. She sat up, blinking into the room. She swiveled her head, squinted. "Adam?"

He couldn't move, couldn't speak. The woman, the dead thing, continued to stare in open fury at his unsuspecting wife.

Adam opened his mouth to speak, but nothing emerged. Holly pushed the covers off. As if the slight shift in the air were a gust of violent wind, the entity quaked and disappeared.

Holly crawled across the bed. "Adam, what's happening? Are you sick?"

"No…" he breathed, finally feeling his feet, his hands. He furled and released his fingers, took a halting step toward Holly. He sat on the bed and hugged her. She buried her face in his neck.

"Why are you up?" she asked.

"I had a bad dream, got up to use the bathroom."

"I had a bad dream too," she murmured, breath hot against his neck. "I dreamed I was in the woods outside and someone was chasing me, a woman, I think, but I was so terrified. What was your dream?"

"I don't remember it."

"Lie back down with me. Come here." She pulled him down beside her and snuggled into the shape of him.

He lay and stared into the shadows, sure he would not sleep again that night.

39

1956

1 Day Before the Sail

"I tried to get to you, but Alice wouldn't let me out of her sight," Michael told Nell, pushing her against the tack room wall and kissing her.

"What are we going to do, Michael? I have a ticket to leave Monday."

He pulled away. "You don't have to worry about that, Nell. After this weekend everything will be different."

Nell frowned, that familiar sick feeling growing inside her. "I'm… I'm just not sure."

"I put the gin in the boat. I disabled the radio just in case. If you put enough arsenic in her cocktail, she'll never get to the radio anyway, but just in case…"

"Michael—"

He pushed his mouth against hers, cutting her off. When he pulled away, Nell was breathless and dizzy.

"Here, darling. Happy birthday." He shoved a small box wrapped in shiny red paper into her hands.

Nell's fingers trembled as she opened it. Inside a black velvet box, she discovered a gold necklace with two circles intertwined.

"It's the infinity symbol," he told her. "Because soon we're going to be together forever."

Tears poured down Nell's face. She hiccupped.

Michael wrapped his arms around her. "We're so close, Nell. We're so close to doing this anytime we want."

~

Alice lay in bed and stared at the shadows on the ceiling. The shape morphed as she watched it transforming from a benign nothing into the silhouette of a grim reaper, scythe raised as he sniffed the darkness for her.

"Come here," Michael's husky voice commanded her in the black room.

A dark revulsion poured over Alice at his touch, but she didn't squirm away. As still as a statue, she lay and allowed his fingers to glide down her belly. Her nightgown stuck to her skin. The humidity of the day lingered into the night. His breath added to the heat as he climbed on top of her, breathing harder, forcing her legs apart with his own.

She tilted her head, escaping the hot wetness of his breath, tuning out the sound of his grunts.

She stared through the window at the rising moon through the branches of the big oak tree. Above her, the reaper shifted. It sensed her now, sensed the writhing, and it drew ever closer.

40

Adam paused, watching Holly from the doorway. She gazed into her oatmeal, eyes solemn, her shoulders folded forward like a bird shielding its breast. It was a down day. She rarely had them. Holly was a woman who always managed to find shards of gold amid the rubble.

"Hey, beautiful," Adam chirped.

She looked up and replaced her frown with a smile. "Hi, honey. How'd you sleep?"

Terrible. "Great. Like a log after the bad dream. You?"

"Pretty good." She mirrored his lie. A network of red webbing marred the whites of her eyes.

"Are you feeling sick this morning, Holl?" he asked, flipping the knob on the stovetop to heat the kettle.

"No, just… a little tired."

He ripped open a packet of oatmeal and dumped it in a bowl. "Refill?" He lifted the coffeepot and filled his mug.

"No more for me," Holly sighed, poking her spoon in her oatmeal and then setting the utensil aside.

"I could make scrambled eggs, or how about an egg sandwich?" He paused behind her and massaged her stiff shoulders.

She rubbed his hand. "Not this morning. I think I'll go sit in the garden for a bit. I thought this afternoon we could take Marshmallow for a long walk. I haven't explored the property at all."

Adam paused with his mug halfway to his lips. "Yeah, sure." He glanced through the window toward the pudding stone and then beyond to the trail that led to the Ashwoods' house.

She stood, shot him another falsely cheery smile, and slipped out the kitchen door. He watched her, Marshmallow trailing, as she disappeared around the side of the house.

Adam took his coffee and went to the study, opening his laptop and flipping it on. He maneuvered to his email.

One new message from Iris Walsh. Subject: Charlotte Ashwood.

He opened it.

Adam,

My grandmother looked at the picture. She circled Charlotte Ashwood. I've attached the image.

Iris

He clicked the image. It loaded slowly, and he bit his lip, fighting the urge to refresh the screen.

"Adam?" Holly's voice startled him from the doorway.

He slammed the laptop closed. "Oh, crap, Holl. You scared me. I didn't hear you come in."

She tucked a lock of dark hair behind her ear and looked at the computer. "You bought a laptop?"

"Yeah, I…" He searched for a reason. "I wanted to research transplant stuff."

She sighed. "You were supposed to use the time I was at the hospital to rest."

He stood and walked to her, pulling her into a hug. "You know me better than that."

She smiled sadly. "I thought we could take a walk now? I need to stretch my legs after being in that hospital bed."

"Sure, definitely." He stood, resisted the impulse to open the laptop and view the picture first, and followed Holly from the house. He tried to guide her in the opposite direction than the trail that led toward the Ashwoods' house, but Marshmallow bounded onto the path.

They held hands as they walked, both quiet. Holly's eyes drifted from the tall prickly stalks of stinging nettles and up into the leafy trees. She paused at a blackberry bush and plucked one from a branch, handing it to Adam. As he slipped it past his lips, he thought of the Ashwoods' girls. *Poisoned,* Hattie had said, and Nell's journal had revealed as much. The berry tasted bitter, and he spit it out, grabbing Holly's hand as she lifted one to her mouth.

"Don't eat that," he said.

"Why? It's a blackberry."

"Mine tasted funny. Let's not risk putting anything in your body that might make you sick."

She nodded, but her face grew more drawn. Normal Holly seemed absent, as if she'd retreated somewhere and a shell of her former self had stepped in.

When they arrived at the clearing to the Ashwoods' house, Adam's pulse quickened. He stared at the house and for perhaps the first time he saw what it was, a murder house, a tomb of sorts. It contained a horrible secret. The windows looked like black accusing eyes, the sagging porch like a scowling mouth.

"Wow..." Holly breathed. "It's so sad, isn't it? There's something heartbreaking about this house out here in the forest, the vines pulling it down, taking it back, and the house resisting, continuing to stand as if... it has a story to tell."

Adam stood rooted to the edge of the property, Holly's hand tight in his own, but she pulled free and walked toward the house. Marshmallow ran to the backyard. Holly followed, and Adam reluctantly walked behind.

She paused when the view of the pool and stables came into view.

"You've already seen all this?" she asked him.

"Yeah." His throat had thickened. He couldn't seem to gather any spit. He needed a drink, desperately, a glass of water, but what popped into his mind was a shot of something, vodka or gin.

The murky water of the pool didn't look like water. It looked like vomit, black bile. What the women had spewed on the floor—what someone had cleaned in an attempt to hide the evidence, and then they'd hidden the bodies. Bodies that were meant to be found. Why else would he and Holly have chosen that of all spots to build their house? The dead girls wanted their justice, and Adam had stolen it from them. He'd dug another hole and dumped them into it.

Holly released a little moan and staggered forward, too close to the pool. Marshmallow darted in front of her and Adam grabbed her from behind, pulling her back before she could topple into it.

"I felt..." She put a hand to her heart. "As if something pushed me just now. Not a hand... but... a wind. Did you feel that?"

He shook his head. "Let's go back, okay? You're pale."

She nodded, closed her eyes for a moment. Her face had grown shiny and moist. Adam lifted his t-shirt up to wipe at the sweat gathering at her hairline.

"It's hot out here," she breathed.

"Yeah. Here, come on." He supported her, arm around her waist. "I can carry you," he offered.

She shook her head. "No, I'm fine. Had a little dizzy spell, but it's passed."

~

Holly drank a glass of water and climbed into bed. When she closed her eyes, Adam returned to the study.

He opened his laptop. Only the top edge of the picture had loaded. He'd interrupted it when he'd closed his computer. Marshmallow sauntered into the room, circled him once and then left, likely to nudge open the bedroom door and join Holly.

The photo loaded, grainy and pixilated. Gradually, the girls took shape. One of them had been circled in red marker. Adam sat forward in his chair, gazing at the photograph of Michael's second wife, the girl who'd likely murdered them all.

41

Mildred. It was Mildred who had a large red circle drawn around her head. The sixteen-year-old girl suspected of murdering her own brother. Had she acted alone when she killed Alice and the other girls? Or had Michael been in on it?

Lola had implied that Michael himself had died under unusual circumstances and then Mildred's next husband just a few years later.

Adam opened his search engine and typed in the name Mildred had taken on after her supposed death.

'Charlotte Flannery, Michigan.'

The top result was a wedding announcement. He clicked it and an image materialized of Mildred in profile, older, her hair dyed blonde and stacked in curls on top of her head. Her eyes looked dark and small, surrounded by heavy makeup. A gold peacock comb with a jewel eye held her hair in place.

He leaned closer to the grainy image, thinking of an entry Nell had made in her diary. He stood and went to the box where he'd hidden Nell's journal. He tugged it out and flipped the pages. The second-to-last entry described Nell's birthday and how upset Bitsy had become when the gift she'd wrapped for Nell, her grandmother's antique peacock comb, had disappeared from the gift table and not been found.

Adam returned to the laptop screen and read the wedding announcement.

Ms. Charlotte Flannery was married to Bart Warren Robinson on July

13th, 1974, in the Maple Leaf Chapel. Chaplain Gregory Palmer performed the ceremony. The bride wore a chiffon gown with lace-trimmed sleeves and a lovely comb, a family heirloom passed down by a great-grandmother.

Following a honeymoon in the Poconos Mountains in Pennsylvania, the newlyweds will reside in Alpena, Michigan.

Adam looked at the picture of the bride. Her smile looked flat, her eyes equally lifeless. Her groom was just the opposite with lively features, kind, bright eyes and a smile that imbued an otherwise dreary photo with joy.

Adam opened another browser bar. His fingers trembled as he typed the man's name.

Bart Warren Robinson.

Above the former wedding announcement, he found a different news announcement regarding Bart. An obituary.

Adam clicked it and read.

Bart Warren Robinson of 759 Monroe Street in Alpena, age 46, died Sunday at home. He was born on March 8th, 1931, in Erie, Pennsylvania, to parents Jillian and Harold Robinson. He was the owner of Bart's Heating and Cooling.

He is survived by his wife Charlotte Robinson, his brother Bill Robinson (wife, Judith) and two nieces, Melanie and Katie.

Bart was an active member of the Masonic Lodge and the Indigo Golf League.

Funeral services will be held at Kasson Funeral Home on Wednesday at 11 a.m. Burial will be at Autumn Pond Cemetery.

"Holy crap..." Adam rubbed both hands over his cheeks. A third dead husband, this one forty-six years old.

He returned to the search bar, but found no additional marriage or death announcements connected to Charlotte. He did, however, find a single recent article dated just months earlier.

An Author in Our Midst

Charlotte Robinson considers herself your run-of-the-mill lady down the block (her words, not mine). However, this lady down the block has a secret that has only recently come to light. Behind the scenes, Robinson is a prolific author who has penned over two hundred short stories and novels under several pseudonyms including N. Madden, B. Walker, and A. Ashwood.

Robinson's work runs the gamut from science fiction to murder mysteries. When asked how she got her start as a novelist, Robinson said, "I took the advice 'write what you know' and then twisted it until it made for good read-

ing. I've always believed that if we pay attention, the stories reveal themselves in the world around us."

If you're interested in reading Robinson's harrowing tales, you can find her latest release Dark Waters *in stock at Books and Things on Main Street.*

Adam studied the acronyms Charlotte had used as pen names. N. Madden, B. Walker and A. Ashwood.

"Nellie Madden, Bitsy Walker, and Alice Ashwood," Adam murmured.

Charlotte had used the initials of girls from the Ashwoods' house as well as Alice herself as her pseudonyms. Adam looked at the address of the newspaper article. It was located in Alpena, Michigan—the place where her last husband had perished. She lived little more than an hour's drive from where he sat.

A sensation like clammy fingers lighted upon his neck, and Adam jumped to his feet. The room had grown cold—so cold his breath plumed from his mouth. The coffee mug he'd set on the desk that morning trembled and cracked, spilling cold coffee across the surface.

"Shit!" He stopped the liquid with his hands before it reached the laptop and then dragged his shirt over to sop it up.

Something knocked against the floor beneath him, a steady tap-tap-tap, and then it changed to scratching and clawing as if something were trapped beneath the house.

Adam looked at the door where Holly slept across the hall. Could she hear what was happening? Would she come rushing in at any moment?

"Please stop…" he murmured.

The clawing grew louder, frantic. Above him the ceiling fan started a slow spin and then gained speed, shaking. The light flickered on, then burned out with a sizzle. The room got colder and Adam watched a layer of frost streak down the window.

As he gazed at it, a large crow pummeled toward the glass. Adam leapt back as the bird struck the window, shattering the glass and plummeting into the room. It writhed on the floor, wings flapping, and then grew still.

From beyond the room, he heard Marshmallow bark, a high-pitched warning sound that somehow spooked Adam more than the dying crow.

Adam ran into Holly's room, but she wasn't in the bed. He raced down the hall and into the kitchen. Marshmallow stood at the door, barking and scratching at the frame.

"Where is she, Marsh?" he demanded, flinging open the door and plunging outside. The heat of the day shocked him after the icy temperature in the study.

"Holly!" he screamed.

He searched the porch—no Holly—and started around the side of the house toward the garden.

She sat crouched by the pudding stone, her face glistening as she clawed at the dirt. Her eyes looked blank. Dirt coated her arms from fingertips to elbows and she tore at the earth, flinging handfuls of soil over her shoulders. It struck her in the face and landed in her hair. She didn't make a sound as Adam approached her, didn't look up.

For an insane moment, he thought she would shove a handful of dirt into her mouth. She didn't.

When he touched her shoulder, cold sweat met his fingertips beneath her t-shirt. She was soaked.

"Holly."

She didn't respond, hunched further over and kept digging.

Adam scooped her up. Her body went rigid, and she fought him, scratched her fingernails across his neck.

"Stop," he shouted. "Get out of her!"

For another moment, she thrashed and then her body went limp in his arms. He ran back to the house, Marshmallow trailing him, whimpering.

Adam carried her to the bathroom and laid her on the floor, turning on the shower. He stripped off her clothes and then his own and climbed into the bathtub with her. Holly didn't respond. Her eyes had closed and her breath grew heavy. He turned the faucet cold, wincing at the icy spray.

Holly's eyes flew open, and she gasped, pulling away from him.

"Adam!" She twisted in the tub, and he yanked the knob back to warm.

"It's okay, we're in the shower. I put you in."

She sputtered and shook her head, blinking. "Why? Why?"

He held her and after a moment, her breath slowed and she leaned into him.

"You… you were sleepwalking. You went outside and were digging in the dirt."

She twisted around to look at him, incredulous. "What? No."

"Yeah."

She looked at the drain where dirt swirled with the water and disappeared.

He soaped her hands and arms. She shivered despite the heat of the shower. He thought of the doctor's warning about Holly getting sick, the strain on her heart.

After they'd dried off and he'd helped her into clean athletic pants and a long-sleeved t-shirt, Holly settled on the couch. He took her temperature and checked her pulse. Everything was in the normal range.

"Did you take your pills this morning?" he asked her.

Eyes troubled, she nodded. "All sixteen of them."

"I'll make you some tea and then we should talk."

He made the tea and carried it into the living room. His hands trembled so badly he'd slopped half the cup onto the wood floor before he got there. Holly had pulled a blanket up to her neck and fallen asleep on the sofa. Marshmallow lay at the foot of the couch, a spot he was not allowed to be, but Adam said nothing. He smoothed Holly's wet hair away from her face.

Adam watched her sleep, his throat full and thick with unshed tears, or perhaps it was unshed words. He'd kept so much from her lately; a mountain of secrets had been built between them in the weeks since they'd moved into the house.

He'd been ready to reveal everything, but as he watched her sleep, he couldn't bear to wake her up. Everything would be different once he told her his terrible secret.

He crept from the room and returned to the study. The coldness had left it, but the bedlam remained—his broken mug and the mass of black feathers where the crow lay on the floor.

Grimacing, he picked up the bird and dropped it out the shattered window. He gathered the shards of glass and put them in the wastebasket. He'd plastic the window later, otherwise they'd have a house full of mosquitos at nightfall.

Adam took out his cell phone and dialed Hattie's number. It went to voice mail. He left her a message and then sat heavily behind the desk wishing he could erase the vision of Holly, blank-faced, digging at the place where he'd buried the bodies. The spirits had made her do it. He didn't understand how, but it was true.

Everything in his body told him they'd somehow gotten inside of Holly.

He returned to the search engine on his laptop. He wanted to type in 'possession,' but he wasn't ready to tackle what might arise if he put the words into the world. He searched instead for the B. Walker pen name listed for Charlotte in the article. A series of books—mostly science fiction—appeared under the acronym. A. Ashwood revealed ten short story collections. The final pseudonym, N. Madden, brought up fifteen novels and ten short story collections. He clicked one title and read the description, frowning.

Janie is seventeen when she poisons her abusive parents and flees to Mexico to start a new life…

He clicked another title and discovered yet another story that involved a woman poisoning her deadbeat boyfriend. They didn't all include descriptions of poisonings, but over six of the titles did. He ran a hand through his hair and returned to the original article.

The reporter had added contact information at the bottom of the page, which included a website for the local author. Adam navigated to the page. It was a simple website with a listing of Charlotte's books. He went to the contact form and paused with his fingers above the keys.

Hi, Charlotte. I came upon your interview in the Alpena Daily News. *I hoped I could interview you for a series I'm doing on Michigan authors. Please email me at daydreamcafe@gmail.com. Thanks!*

Adam returned to the living room. Holly still slept, her hands tucked beneath the side of her head as if in prayer. Adam turned a movie on low and settled onto one end of the large couch, drifting into sleep.

~

A high-pitched howl from Marshmallow jerked Adam awake. He sat up, struggled to get his bearings, and then remembered he'd fallen asleep in the living room beside Holly. Except her end of the couch lay empty, her blanket discarded on the floor.

Marshmallow howled again. He stood at the picture window, paws braced on the ledge.

Adam floundered toward the glass, the stupor of sleep fogging his brain.

Night had fallen, and a steady rain pattered against the roof. The porch light illuminated the lawn.

Adam spotted Holly outside. She stood in the center of the yard, arms outstretched, face tilted up, with her mouth open to catch the falling rain. It was a very Holly thing to do and yet…

As he watched her twirling slowly, her body seemed to shudder and her features changed. For an instant, it was not Holly's face he saw, but Alice's and then she too dissolved and Nell replaced her. Still, she moved, slow and ecstatic, but the features of another woman, Cocoa, flickered. Holly's face reappeared for an instant, but her expression twisted as if in fear.

Adam slapped both hands on the glass, shouting. "Holly!"

He turned and raced through the house and into the rain.

"Holly!" he screamed.

She stopped twirling and her head righted, but it was not Holly looking back at him. Alice stared out from his wife's face. She looked furious and reached her fingers, Holly's fingers, toward her face as if she intended to gouge out her own eyes.

Adam lunged toward her and snatched her hands down, pinning her arms against her side.

Holly's mouth opened and a voice he didn't recognize shrieked in his face.

He shook her. "Get out, get out of my wife," he screamed as Marshmallow circled them and barked.

Alice's features on Holly's face distorted and she snapped her teeth at Adam. He held her tighter.

"Get out, get out!" he told her.

Holly's head flung back hard, and she collapsed, limp in his arms.

For the second time that day, Adam carried Holly into the house. Wet, he sat on the couch and cradled her, reaching for the blanket she'd dropped and wrapping it around her. He rocked her and whispered.

"You're okay, you're okay…"

Her arm lay limp on the couch and he stared at the mother-of-pearl ring. Gently, he pried it off of her finger. He wanted to get rid of it, throw it outside, toss it in the trash, but he needed to sit with her. Her lips and eyelids had turned purple.

Slowly she warmed up, and the color returned to her face. He eased her onto the couch and peeled off her wet clothes. In the hall closet, they had a heating blanket. He plugged it in and wrapped it around her naked body.

For a half hour he sat holding his fingers to her wrist, counting her pulse, pressing a hand on her chest to monitor her heart. It was steady.

When he felt he could leave her for a moment, he went to the kitchen and opened the crawlspace. He flung the ring into the black hole.

"Leave her alone," he hissed. "I'm going to fix this, but you have to leave Holly alone."

Nothing stirred beneath the house.

42

Holly seemed to have no memory of what had occurred the night before and when she asked Adam how she'd ended up naked in a heating blanket, he told her he'd spilled water on her when walking to the couch. It was a flimsy, terrible lie, but she believed him. Shame made it nearly impossible to meet her eyes during breakfast.

Charlotte, aka Mildred, had messaged him back, and they'd agreed on an eleven a.m. meeting at a coffee shop near Mildred's home.

"Cheryl's coming for a couple of hours," Adam told Holly. "I've got to run to the Home Depot and meet with a guy about a prefab shed I'd like to get put on the property."

Holly looked up from her oatmeal. "A shed?"

"Yeah, I thought we could have it set right by your garden, put all your planting stuff in there."

She smiled. "That sounds nice."

His oatmeal curdled in his stomach. He walked the bowl to the sink and dumped it into the garbage disposal.

He did intend to stop at a Home Depot and talk with someone about a shed, but he was doing so on that morning because he needed a justifiable reason to sneak off to his meeting with Mildred, and a shed was something Holly could use.

When Cheryl arrived, Adam kissed Holly goodbye and headed for his truck.

As he pulled onto the main road, his cell phone rang.

"Hello?"

"Adam, it's Hattie. I got your message about your wife. I'm sorry I didn't see it sooner. What happened?"

Adam frowned at the memory and explained the previous day's experiences of first finding Holly digging in the yard and later discovering her spinning in the rain.

"I see," Hattie murmured. "I know you said Holly suffers from heart issues. Has there been anything lately that might have weakened her hold on her body, allowed for something to slip in?"

"When you were here, she was in the hospital because she'd caught a virus. She collapsed here at the house."

"Okay. That's likely when they got ahold of her."

"What do I do? How do I get them out?"

"In all likelihood, they're coming and going. Sleep is a time when spirits can sneak in because the sleeper is often travelling in dreams."

"So, what then? Keep her awake?"

"No, Adam. That's not healthy for her or you. What you need to do is call the police and get those skeletons out of the ground."

Adam sighed. "I'm going to. I am. I just have to do something else first."

Hattie said nothing for a long moment. When she spoke again, her voice was grave. "Time is not your friend, Adam. Do it soon."

~

Adam recognized Mildred immediately, though the girl from the photos at the Ashwoods' house had changed dramatically. Mildred sat in a corner booth, aged hands thick with rings wrapped around a mug. Makeup lay thick on her face. Her hair, now dyed black, was short and bushy around her head. She wore a navy blue blouse with buttons high on her neck. It was her eyes that gave her away, black empty eyes, shark's eyes.

A copy of one of her novels sat on the edge of the table.

"Hi, you must be Charlotte?" Adam said, offering his hand.

She gazed up at him and smiled. The lipstick on her dry lips cracked.

"Pleasure," she told him.

Adam slid into the booth across from her. He nodded at her book. "May I?"

"By all means."

He picked the book up and read the title, *No Remorse*. The cover depicted the silhouette of a woman walking away from a burning house.

"Compelling cover," he told her. "This is your newest pen name?"

"Yes. They're thrillers."

"And if I read correctly online, they're written from the point of view of the villain? A murderess?"

She stared at him, unblinking. "Yes, Violet McGuire, though whether she's the villain is in the reader's perception. To Violet she's bringing a little more justice into the world."

"It sounds really interesting. I ordered a copy," he lied. "I did a bit of digging on you, Charlotte. Your story is fascinating. And I have to tell you I found something really bizarre that I hoped to talk to you about. Get the scoop on, so to speak."

Her expression didn't change, but he thought her hands tightened on the mug.

"Go ahead."

"I read about one of your former husbands, Michael Ashwood. You used to be an Ashwood, right? Before your second marriage?"

She nodded curtly, lips pressed tightly together.

"I read about the tragedy that befell his first wife." Adam shook his head dramatically. "What an insane story. A whole sailboat full of women that disappeared on Lake Huron. Have you ever considered writing that tale?"

"It's not my story to tell."

"Sure, sure, but… he must have told you about it. Right?"

"No. Michael was a very private man."

"I see. I live up in that area, to tell you the truth. After I read about the sinking of that sailboat, I went and looked for the old house, the Ashwoods' place. It's still standing. Isn't that bizarre? This big old house left rotting in the northern Michigan forest. I wondered who owns it?"

"Well, I do, of course. It went to me after Michael's death in 1961."

"Oh, okay. Have you ever been there?"

"No."

"Really? It's a neat house. I'm sure it was beautiful in its prime, big pool and horse stables."

"You're aware that it's private property?"

Adam nodded. "Yeah. I figured I could get away with a little poking around. I hope you don't mind."

"Not at all."

"So, Michael passed on in 1961 and then you married..." He fumbled a notebook out of the backpack he'd brought, pretending he'd forgotten the name of her second husband.

"Morris Flannery."

His eyes flicked up to her. Nothing had changed in her face and yet... he felt the tension building in the surrounding air.

"That's it, Flannery. And he passed as well?"

"Sadly, all of my husbands are deceased. It's the curse of many women to outlive their men. I've always thought men run themselves to death, always chasing. Money, women, notoriety. They can't sit back and enjoy their lives. They always want more. Are you that way, Mr. Tate? Always chasing something?"

He thought of Holly at home, savoring the gift of just breathing, and a blush rose into his neck. "I try not to."

"Hmm... You should try harder. Death comes much sooner for the insatiable man."

"Do you mind if I ask how your other husbands died?"

She studied him, but said nothing for a long moment and then she reached into her purse and drew out a silver cigarette case embossed with tiny jeweled stars. She took a slender cigarette from the case, propping it between her thin lips.

"I don't think you can smoke in here."

"I'm aware of that. You can't smoke anywhere these days, but I take pleasure in feeling it, smelling it." She waved it in front of her face and inhaled the unlit cigarette. "My husbands died of their own dissatisfaction." She laughed at the look of surprise on his face. "Or maybe they simply ran out of time. Who can truly say what kills a man? They died, and that is all."

"Were you sad?"

She tilted her head. "What an odd question."

"I don't mean to pry."

"Don't you?"

He smiled. "Well, maybe a little. It's just that... my wife is sick." He hesitated as he confided such an intimate detail to this despicable woman, but he wanted to soften her, wanted to slip into her confidence.

"Is she?"

"Yes, congestive heart failure."

"That must be difficult."

"It is. It's horrible. Some days I don't want to get out of bed, it's so terrible."

She looked at him, bemused. "You're loyal to her, then. Some men have that trait. Some do not."

"I am completely devoted to my wife."

She smirked. "For now, but when she is dust, what will your loyalty be worth?"

He recoiled at her words, but she offered no apology.

Mildred gazed at him with shrewd, watchful eyes, but her face remained unmoved.

"When did you start writing, Mildred?" It had been a slip of the tongue, what psychiatrists might have called a Freudian slip, and the moment he'd uttered the name her entire demeanor changed. She grew erect in her seat, her eyes narrowed and her face hardened as if into stone.

"What did you call me?"

He considered his next words as the charade he'd been playing at unraveled around him.

"I know," he told her.

"You know what?"

"I know it was you, Mildred."

A look of disgust rose and fell away from her face at the second mention of her given name.

"You killed them all, Alice Ashwood and the girls, and I think you killed your husbands too."

She raised an eyebrow, lifting the cigarette beneath her nose and sniffing. "You have a vivid imagination, Mr. Tate. When people we care for are on the brink of death, we're very good at creating stories. It's as if we need fiction to survive the truth of this dark and disturbing world. It's a feeling I know well.

"Mr. Ashwood never recovered from the loss of his wife and the other girls. He said he should have gone on the sail; he should have insisted they not go. All the what-ifs. His tales grew wilder and more reckless. You know what he once told me?"

She leaned in closer and he caught a whiff of her acrid breath. It smelled as if there was something decayed deep inside of her.

"He told me he thought Alice was behind it. Sunk the boat on purpose. Maybe she even murdered the girls before it went down. She was losing her mind that summer, he said. Her daughter had vanished many years before and she no longer wanted to live. If his blame eventually shifted to himself, that is merely a symptom of his grief, his inability to accept that this world is not kind or beautiful, there is no grand purpose, no reason behind every tragedy. He couldn't bear it so he sought to blame."

"I found the bodies, Mildred. The skeletons. There was no sail. I found the burned boat."

Again, she said nothing, but she'd grown very still. When she spoke, her voice had dropped lower. "Mr. Tate, I think you may need to seek professional help. If you did find bodies, I can only imagine that Mr. Ashwood had more guilt on his conscience than he admitted. A disturbing thought truly, but the man has been in the ground for nearly half a century. I don't think you'll be able to ask him."

She pushed from the booth, leaving her book forgotten on the table.

As she walked toward the door, Adam called out. "They're not gone, Mildred. Alice, Nell, Cocoa, Bitsy and Margie are still there. They won't leave until you're brought to justice."

She gazed at him with false sympathy. "For your wife's sake, I hope you get some help."

She stepped through the door and disappeared into the parking lot.

43

1956

The Day of the Sail

Dark clouds smoldered above the trees, but in the distance, blue peered through. The sail would go on as planned, though Nell had secretly hoped it would not.

Her stomach curdled at the thought of the tin of white powder tucked beneath her mattress. Could she possibly go through with it? No. Of course not. Alice wasn't beloved amongst the girls, but she was a good person. She did her best despite the mental issues that plagued her. That was what it came down to for Michael—taking mercy on his poor, insane wife. If they killed her, she could be free from her mental prison. Otherwise, she might be institutionalized. He'd said it repeatedly in the previous days.

Michael said he'd recently woken in the night to Alice standing at his side of the bed with a butcher's knife. Another time he'd caught her lighting matches next to the curtains. He suspected she was contemplating lighting them on fire, allowing all of them, girls included, to burn. Nell had not seen these things, but Alice would likely hide such behaviors from the girls in her care.

Nell rolled to her side. Cocoa still slept in her bed across the room. Her chest rose and fell. She'd set her hairpin curlers the night before and one of them had unraveled and fallen to the floor. A spiral of hair hung loose on her pillow.

Nell could leave with Cocoa on the train on Monday. She could step out of this world and into a new life and Michael could follow her if he pleased, but what if he didn't? What if Nell left and Alice burned him and the entire house to ashes? How could she live if she lost Michael forever?

~

Alice sat in a rocking chair beside the window. She'd rocked Marilyn in the same chair, fed her, sang to her. Alice could almost conjure the image of Marilyn's tiny little hand resting on Alice's chest as she slept, wrapped in pink blankets, murmuring in her sleep.

Through the window, thick clouds textured the sky, but rays of sun poked through, casting long beams of light over the forest. Life was like that sky, gray and muted with a few bits of light to keep people moving, stumbling forward hoping to catch another shred of illumination.

Alice pushed against the wood floor with her bare feet and closed her eyes, humming a song she'd sung to Marilyn.

After Michael had finished his business the night before, Alice had felt something shift within her, a sudden urge to start again, somewhere far away from Michael and the forests of Northern Michigan.

Alice had a cousin who lived in the Florida Keys. Twice a year, she sent Alice postcards of palm trees and sandy beaches. Alice thought perhaps she could be happy in a place like that. She could live in a little apartment near the beach, take walks on the sand rather than isolated tree-lined roads. If Death wanted her, he'd have to catch her first.

~

Mildred woke early and slipped from her attic room and down the two sets of stairs to the first floor.

The other girls hadn't yet risen. Mildred locked the doors in the house and wedged bits of wood beneath the frames, making them difficult if not impossible to pull open.

She lit the burner on the stove and added a pot of boiling water, poured oatmeal in the water and set the little egg timer. She spooned oatmeal into the line of bowls on the counter, adding a healthy dose of cinnamon and honey. She slipped the tin from the pocket of her dress.

~

"I made it special," Mildred announced, handing Alice her bowl of oatmeal first and then passing another to each girl at the kitchen table.

"I'm not hungry," Nell mumbled. "I think I'll go change."

Mildred smiled and shrugged. "Maybe a bit later you can have some."

Nell walked to her room, shoved off her nightgown, and pulled on her sailing dress. A figure appeared behind her in the doorway. It was Mildred.

"I brought you an orange juice," Mildred told her, "and don't say no. You have to eat something before the sail or you'll be lightheaded." She set the glass on Nell's vanity.

"Thanks, Mildred."

Mildred watched her, waiting.

"What?" Nell asked.

Mildred gestured at the glass. "Come on. Drink up. I'm not leaving until you do."

Nell frowned, not used to Mildred being so pushy, but she wanted the girl to leave her alone. She lifted the glass to her lips and drank it in several large gulps. It had a bitter aftertaste, and she wrinkled her nose.

"I think that orange juice is going bad," she told Mildred.

Mildred took the glass, a satisfied look on her face, and slipped from the room.

Nell had barely sat down when her stomach rumbled and spasmed.

In the house beneath her, she heard a strange sound. Cocoa, she thought, was moaning loudly from the first floor. Nell started toward her bedroom door. Her stomach cramped, and she doubled over, falling to her knees.

~

Alice didn't understand. All the girls were on the floor. Their moans came in between violent bursts of vomiting. Alice's own stomach churned and her mouth flooded with saliva.

She started toward the bathroom and then saw Cocoa on hands and knees. She was vomiting blood. It splashed across the wood floor and she shrieked in pain, curling into a ball.

"Help..." Alice mumbled. "We need help." She stumbled into the kitchen to the phone and lifted it to her ear. No dial tone.

Black spots danced behind her eyes, her stomach rolled and she pitched sideways, crashing into the wall. A sailing picture fell and smashed on the floor. She groped along the wall, fighting the vomit trying to rise within her. She had to get to the truck, get help.

She turned the knob and tried to push out the kitchen door. It didn't budge. She fumbled at the lock. It was unlocked, but still the door wouldn't open.

Mildred stepped into the kitchen behind her. Only she seemed okay.

"Mildred..." Alice moaned, sinking down the wall to the kitchen floor. "Hurry... get help."

Mildred said nothing. Alice's stomach twisted, and she threw up into the folds of her nightgown. Her breath came out in shuddering gulps.

"Mildred..." she tried again, tilting her face to look at the girl.

Mildred watched Alice with black, flat eyes.

44

Adam spent an hour talking with the guy at Home Depot about the ideal garden shed. It had been a difficult conversation for Adam to follow.

His mind drifted repeatedly to Mildred. He wondered what she'd do next. Race home, pack her bags and flee? As he considered the possibilities, he realized he'd made another error in judgment confronting her. He'd severely damaged any case police would have against her, ruined their element of surprise.

He suspected she would not run. She believed too much in her own cunning. She'd gotten away with doing horrible things for so long she probably believed she could go on doing it forever.

As Adam climbed into his truck, a car pulled into the parking lot. A shiny, navy-blue Corvette Stingray parked in a spot across from him, a 'for sale' sign stuck to the passenger side window. It was Holly's dream car.

Adam jumped from his truck as a man climbed from the Corvette.

"Hi, hey," Adam called out, walking towards him. "Your car is for sale?"

The man grinned and slapped a hand on the hood. "She sure is. V8 engine, three hundred seventy horsepower. This baby is a monster on the open road. Course I've only ripped her wide open a handful of times. My wife prefers we stay under fifty." He chuckled.

"What are you asking for it?"

The man cocked his head to the side. "I'm asking eighteen, but I'd take—"

"Sixteen?" Adam asked.

The man pulled in his cheeks, gazed at the car for a long moment and rocked back and forth on his heels. "Okay, yeah, sure. I could do that."

"I'll go to the bank right now and get a cashier's check. Could I meet you back at your place to pick it up in, say, an hour?"

"Whew-ee, you're hot to get behind this wheel, aren't ya? Okay, yeah. Just runnin' in here to buy some painter's tape. Wife's got me painting a baby room for our new granddaughter. Let me tell you, she's going to be tickled pink I've sold this car. She's been hassling me about getting a pontoon. I guess I'll be doing some fall fishing."

Adam turned the Corvette into his driveway and pulled to a stop in front of the house.

Holly and Cheryl sat on the porch. Holly's mouth fell open and she screamed.

Adam climbed out of the car as Holly leapt off the porch and ran toward him.

"Hold on, hold on. Take it easy, gorgeous." He caught her around the waist and planted a huge kiss on her mouth.

"You bought me a Stingray? Adam… oh, my God."

"It was meant to be, honey," he told her.

Cheryl came down the porch steps slowly. "Isn't that more lovely than a spring day? Goodness, Adam, you just won husband of the year."

Holly circled the car, hands sliding over the hood and along the roof. "It's the color of a full moon night," she said. "It's so beautiful."

"You like it?" Adam asked.

Holly opened the driver's door. "It's a dream."

"Why don't you take Cheryl for a drive?" he suggested.

Cheryl smiled and shook her head. "I've gotta get home. Ted has a few people from the ministry coming over. You're welcome to stop by for dinner or dessert."

"I think we'll drive this beauty up the coast for dinner." Holly beamed.

Holly turned onto a long empty country road. She accelerated hard and the car shot forward, gaining speed. Adam glanced at the speedometer and watched as they exceeded sixty, seventy, eighty…

"Honey…"

Holly's hair blew wild in the wind and her smile filled her face. At eighty-five she let off the gas and they slowed. Holly turned and drove to Freeway 23, which ran along the Lake Huron shoreline.

They ate at a little Italian restaurant that looked out on a rocky pier jutting into Lake Huron. Afterward they walked to the beach and everything felt so right in the world, Adam wanted to wrap it in glass and preserve it. He had to shatter it soon, tell Holly what he'd done, tell police. It took his breath away to think about it.

Holly picked along the rocky shoreline, bending now and then to pick up a rock, examine it and toss it into the gray water. Occasionally she tucked one into the pocket of her shorts. She held up a large gray rock, tilting it so he could see the underside was sparkling quartz.

"Come walk with me," she told him, extending her hand.

He slipped his hand into hers and they walked.

Unlike the morning before, Adam woke to find Holly in high spirits. They'd driven home the previous night, made love and fallen asleep in a tangle of limbs.

Adam hadn't woken in the night a single time. It had been the first good night of sleep he'd had in days.

Holly stood in the yard with a bucket of soapy water and a sponge. The hose lay coiled by her bare feet.

"It's eight a.m. and you're already washing the car?" he called from the front porch.

"I'm giving her a bath, getting the sand off. I think I'll name her Midnight. What do you think?"

"Love it. I'm going to make coffee."

He retreated to the house and brewed his coffee, listening. The airy morning felt too happy, too easy. When would another bulb blow? The trap door fling open? He turned at a sound, but it was only the washing machine down the hall.

He'd gone to bed the night before determined to tell Holly everything that morning, but now... he hated to ruin an otherwise perfect morning. He could stretch it a little further. That afternoon, he'd tell her.

Holly poked her head in through the kitchen door. "Want to do me a huge, gigantic favor?"

He sipped his coffee. "Your wish is my command."

She grinned. "Run down to the hardware store and get a bottle of wax and maybe some of that leather seat cleaner. Ooh, and the windshield stuff that makes the rain slide off."

He laughed. "You're doing a full detail job on that car, aren't you? Are you sure you're up for all that? Feeling good?"

"I feel like I could swim the English Channel, like I could climb Mount Everest, like I could swing from vines in the jungle."

Adam raised an eyebrow. "What'd you put in your coffee this morning? I need some of that."

"Just a tablespoon of whip cream and a heaping spoonful of gratitude. Thank you, Adam. Not just for the car, which is... so amazing. Thank you for living this extraordinary life with me."

Adam stood and opened the door fully, pulled Holly into a hug. "I love you, Holly."

"I love you most."

~

Adam picked up the car wash supplies and added a bottle of tire foam and a pack of microfiber towels. He plucked a rawhide bone from a bin by the counter for Marshmallow.

"How's the day treatin' ya?" the man behind the counter asked. It was the same man Adam had met previously.

"So far so good."

"That's what I like to hear." The man handed him his bag of supplies and his recipe.

As Adam maneuvered toward home, he passed the sheriff's office and glanced at the small brick building. He could pull in right then, get it over with.

No, he had to tell Holly first. He'd make lunch, something she loved. He swung the truck into the grocery store. He'd pick up fresh fruit and stuff to make Cobb salad, one of Holly's favorite meals.

When Adam returned home, a sleek maroon sedan sat in the

driveway next to Holly's new car. Adam parked and walked into the house, an uneasy feeling spreading through him.

He dropped the bags on the counter next to a bowl of shiny red apples that hadn't been there when he left.

They sat in the living room. Holly held a plastic cup in her hand. Mildred sat on the opposite end of the sectional couch.

"Adam." Holly brightened and stood. "This is Charlotte." Holly's face paled slightly and she sat back down.

Adam's entire body tensed. He strode across the room and snatched the cup from Holly's hand, raised it to his nose and sniffed. It smelled like apple cider, something they didn't have in the house, which meant Mildred had brought it with her.

"What the fuck is this? What's in this?" He stepped in front of Holly, glaring down at the old woman.

The woman feigned surprise, but he saw the secret pleasure his outburst gave her. Somehow, she knew he hadn't told Holly.

"Adam, what on earth are you talking about?" Holly struggled back to her feet and tugged at his shirt-back. "I'm so sorry," she told Mildred.

"Get out," he said to Mildred. "Get out of my house right now."

Mildred stood, gave Holly a significant look as if she'd prepared his wife for the very scene that was unfolding.

"Lovely to meet you, dear," Mildred told her. She moved slowly from the room as if frail, but he'd seen how she stormed from the restaurant. There was nothing weak about Mildred.

Adam strode after her, watching her climb in her car.

"My God, Adam. What was that about? You were so rude to that poor woman. She stopped by to say hello. She used to live in the area. She—"

"We need to go to the hospital, to the emergency room, right now." Adam grabbed Holly's purse from the kitchen table and slung it over his shoulder. He stepped to the window and peered out.

Mildred's car was gone, but some piece of him feared she hadn't gone far. She was parked in the driveway blocking their exit, doing whatever she could to give the poison time to take hold.

"Adam, what are you talking about? Are you sick?"

"No, but the apple cider, where did it come from?"

"Charlotte brought it as a gift along with the apples." Holly gestured at the bag of apples.

Adam snatched the bag from the counter and tossed them into the trash bin.

"Adam, you're scaring me."

"Mildred put something in the cider, Holly. We have to go to the hospital."

"Who's Mildred?"

"Come on, honey, here, take my hand. Let's just… I'll explain on the drive."

"Adam, I'm fine. We don't need to go to the hospital."

"Trust me, okay?"

Holly sighed, but allowed Adam to guide her outside to the passenger seat of his truck. He climbed behind the wheel and rolled slowly away from the house, eyes fixed on the driveway as it cut through the trees. He waited to see Mildred, her car parked sideways to block their exit, but they made it the main road without a sign of her.

As he pulled out of the driveway he released a whoosh of breath, adjusting his rearview mirror and half expecting to see Mildred sitting behind them. He peered into the backseat.

"Okay," Holly said. "Explain."

45

1956

The Night of the Sail

Mildred sat on the porch swing. The chain on the swing creaked and groaned as she drifted back and forth.

Night had fallen and with it came the not-so-far-off howling of a pack of coyotes. Mildred thought of what lay in the house. Coyotes could be a handy means of disposal, but not yet. It wasn't time for that yet.

Michael Ashwood arrived home after eleven p.m., but Mildred had not moved from her seat on the swing. Her legs and butt had grown numb. The sounds from within the house had subsided hours before, replaced by an eerie quiet.

He strode across the lawn and up the porch steps, pausing when he caught sight of Mildred out of the corner of his eye. He did a double-take and then offered a flick of his hand likely meant to be a wave.

"Hi, Mildred. How are you tonight?"

"I'm lovely, Michael," she murmured.

He stared at her for a moment, perhaps unnerved by her use of his first name or possibly that she was home rather than sailing, but he continued on, pushing open the door and disappearing into the house.

Several minutes passed before she heard the sounds—his voice yelling Alice's name, then a string of cries. "No! My God. What is this?"

Mildred stood and walked to the car. She opened the driver's door and pulled the keys from the ignition, slipped them into the rim of the tire swing.

Michael rushed from the house. "Mildred, my God, Mildred. What's happened? They're... they're all... We have to call the police. Where's the phone? The phone, Mildred!"

His eyes were wild, his voice high-pitched and rising. He stumbled down the porch steps, staggered across the yard and dropped to his knees.

"What have I done?" he groaned.

Mildred smiled. "I got rid of the phones, Michael. And I have all the automobile keys. There's no help. It's too late anyway. They've been dead for hours."

He stared, mouth agape, at Mildred. She watched the tumult of emotions ticking across his face. Despair, fear, panic... The color had drained out of him, not only from his face, but his entire person. He looked smaller, weaker, little more than the carcasses lying in the house behind him.

"What are you saying... what? What did you do, Mildred?"

"Don't you mean what did you do? What did you do, Michael? I have the receipt from the arsenic. I have your and Nell's letters, all in a safe place, of course, should you decide to do to me what you had every intention of doing to Alice."

Somehow his already-wide eyes opened further. They seemed to bulge from his face and then he closed them. He teetered on his knees, but put his hands out before he fell forward on his face in the grass.

"Oh, God... oh, God..." He moaned and rocked back and forth.

"Michael, get ahold of yourself. We have things to do. There's plenty of gasoline in the barn. We're going to burn the boat and we could also burn the bodies..."

He stood and staggered to his truck, yanked open the door and climbed inside. He sat there for a long time, perhaps searching for his keys, but Mildred didn't think so. He knew she'd taken them.

She gave him a few more minutes and then went to the passenger door and climbed inside. It was dark in the truck and smelled of sweat and perfume. Mildred suspected he'd taken Nell on the very seats in which they now sat, maybe other women too.

"There, there…" She smoothed a hand down his back. His shirt clung to his skin. "It's a lot to take in. Don't try to speak now, just listen. You were plotting with your seventeen-year-old lover to kill your wife. There's a lot of proof of that. I have it all. What's done is done. They're all dead. There's no bringing them back.

"You have a choice now. You can go on, you can live—*we* can live—or you can run screaming to the police. I will produce proof of your conspiracy, and I will say I didn't eat the oatmeal that Nell fed to everyone this morning. In her guilt, she then consumed the oatmeal herself. I had been in bed sick. I didn't wake up until evening when you returned home. It was all so horrible."

He groaned, but said nothing.

"Tonight, we're going to burn the boat and then we're going to bury what remains, so there's no proof it didn't go into the lake. We also need to get rid of the bodies. We can burn them too—"

"No!" he shouted, jerking his head up. "Alice must be buried. They all must be. The spirit can't move on if the body is destroyed."

Mildred smirked. "Whatever you say, Michael. You pick the spot and I'll get the shovels."

"No one will believe it," Michael muttered, dropping his head into his hands. "No one… the sailboat never left. No one saw it get launched."

"Because we sailed early, so very early. You helped us launch the boat at dawn and then drove the boat trailer back here before you left for your business trip. We slipped in when no one was at the dock. It's happened before. I've paid attention. Plenty of early mornings when there's not a soul around."

"They'll know. They'll come out here and see the fire… the upturned ground."

"Why would they come out here, Michael? The girls, all of us, went down in a sail. You were gone. You even have an alibi to prove it."

"I… the boat's on the trailer. If we burn the trailer, they'll know."

"We're not going to burn the trailer. You have the jacks, remember? In the barn. We'll put the jacks and boards under the boat just like you did in the spring when you touched up the paint on the bottom. It's easy, Michael. Stop making it so difficult. Come on now. Get up. We have work to do."

~

All night they worked. The flames from the sailboat seemed to touch the sky. Surely the police would come, the firemen summoned by the blaze. They didn't.

Michael thought once of throwing himself into the fire, burning alive, but cowardice kept him away. When he felt the blistery heat on his face and arms, he turned and followed Mildred back to the house.

He stood in the living room and stared at the bodies. Cocoa lay in the fetal position in a pool of her own blood and vomit. Bitsy was sprawled near the fireplace. Alice lay in the kitchen. She looked as if she'd tried to go out the door, but had been unable to escape. He heard the sounds of Mildred on the second floor. She was dragging something.

Stomach churning, he stepped into the hallway and recoiled when she appeared at the top of the stairs. She dragged Nell's lifeless body behind her. Nell's head thumped over each step. Her hair was streaked with vomit.

"Oh, God." He turned and threw up, braced a hand against the wall and started to heave.

"Go to the bathroom," Mildred snapped. "We have enough to clean up already."

~

Mildred watched Michael carefully in the weeks that followed. She stayed hidden in the house, but she insisted a grieving husband would not venture far and so he stayed home as well.

He drank and drank and sat on the porch swing rocking maddeningly. Mildred took him to bed and though he resisted her, the man in him rose to the occasion. He cried like a woman when he'd finished.

"Michael," she told him one night as he lay naked and sweaty beside her. "I've given everything that implicates you to a dear friend. I had to, not because I don't care for you. You know that I do." She traced her finger along his cheek and he shuddered. "I had to do it for my own protection. We will be together now, you and I. We'll move away from this place, get married and begin our new life. The old life dies here in this house. Do you understand? We will never speak their names again."

In the moonlight she could see tears shining on his cheeks.

After a long silence, he nodded.

"I need you to say it, Michael."

"Yes," he whispered.

And so it would be.

46

"Holly…" Adam started. He gripped the wheel and stared straight ahead, unable to look at her. "I've been keeping a secret from you, a huge, horrible secret."

He felt her tense beside him. "Okay."

"When I dug the foundation for the house in the spring, I found… bodies, skeletons."

"You found skeletons?"

He risked a glance at her. Her eyes were wide.

"Yes. Five of them. I thought it was an old family burial plot. I was afraid if I told anyone, the sheriff or whatever, they'd put a stop to the construction and we'd lose months, maybe longer. I pulled the skeletons out and dug another hole at the edge of the property."

"Oh, Adam, no. You buried them somewhere else?"

"Yes."

"Jesus. I can't believe you didn't tell me. Why didn't you tell me?"

"You were so happy. I didn't want to ruin it, bring this big ugly mess into our dream."

Holly sighed. "Adam, the minute you found those bodies, the big mess was in our lives. The only thing hiding it did was make it worse and put all the pressure on you. My God." She put her hand to her throat. "No wonder you've been so distant."

"I'm an idiot," Adam said, leaning his head hard against the back of the seat.

"Stop. That's not true. It's never idiotic to try to protect someone, but I hope you're beginning to realize you can't protect me, Adam. Not from life, not from death. And frankly I don't want you to."

He blinked back tears and focused on the road. "I know."

"I don't understand what that has to do with the woman who was at the house."

Adam thought of all that he'd discovered between that long-ago damp spring day when he'd found the skeletons and the moment he now occupied, hurtling down the road afraid his wife had been poisoned. And if she had been, it was his fault.

"How are you feeling, Holly? Stomach upset?"

"No, please don't change the subject. What's the woman have to do with the bodies you reburied?"

"I believe she killed them, murdered them."

Holly's mouth fell open. "What? Wait, but you thought it was a family burial plot."

"It wasn't. The house in the woods, the Ashwoods' house—"

"The whose house? Who are the Ashwoods?"

"A couple owned that old house in the woods. Michael and Alice Ashwood. In 1956, they had five girls living in the house. People called it a finishing school or whatever. The belief was that Alice and the girls in her care went sailing and never came back. The police believe the boat sank. Everyone in town believes it, but I started doing some research on what happened and then... and then I found what was left of the sailboat burned in the woods."

"The boat didn't sink then? What does that mean?"

"The skeletons in the ground belonged to Alice Ashwood and four of the girls in her care: Nell, Cocoa, Bitsy and Margie."

"You said there were five girls in her care."

"The fifth was Mildred, aka Charlotte—the woman you just met."

"So she survived?"

"Mildred killed them all. She poisoned them. I'm almost positive. Then she married Michael Ashwood, and she killed him along with two additional husbands."

Holly shifted, pulling her legs onto the seat. She clutched her knees. "That's... are you sure? How do you know that?"

"Because when I put all the pieces together, it became crystal clear. Not only did everything point to her, she's been writing under pseudonyms for the last few decades, initials that belonged to the other girls at the Ashwoods' house. A lot of the books are about women poisoning their enemies."

Holly put her fingers to her lips. "And you think she poisoned me?"

Adam risked a glance at his wife. Her eyebrows drew close together.

"Probably not." He grabbed her hand and gave it a reassuring squeeze. "If she wants to poison anyone, it's me. But better safe than sorry."

Holly's face was troubled. "If she killed all those girls and faked their death on a sail, how did she end up married to Michael Ashwood? Why didn't he turn her in?"

"He was plotting to murder his wife with another girl in the house, a seventeen-year-old he was having an affair with. I think Mildred blackmailed him."

"Adam." Holly put a trembling hand on his arm. "This all sounds—"

"Far-fetched, made-up, insane. Yeah, I know. But it's not. The ring you found in the yard, it fell off of the hand of one of those skeletons. I found a picture of one of the Ashwoods' girls wearing that ring. Her name was Cocoa. For fifty years, everyone in town has believed those girls disappeared during a sail. They didn't. And..." He gritted his teeth and thought of the other things, the things he couldn't point towards logic to explain. "They're haunting us, Holly. They followed me home from the Ashwoods' house. They're angry that I hid their bodies."

He felt her eyes on him, feared what he'd see in her face if he turned to look.

"Why do you say that?" she asked.

"Because I've seen them, felt them."

Her hand drifted up to her chest.

"What is it?" He faced her. "Your heart?"

She shook her head, blinking back tears. "No... it's just..."

He recognized something in her face. "You've felt them too?"

"I think so."

~

After a nurse led them to a room, Adam sat on the bed beside Holly.

"I'm so sorry. I'm sorry I didn't tell you sooner, that I didn't do the right thing when I found the girls. I'm sorry I've screwed everything up."

She put her hand on his thigh and leaned into him. "You didn't, Adam. Nothing is beyond repair. You're going to call the sheriff's office and then... we'll go with the flow. If we have to rent a hotel for a while, then so be it."

He hung his head. A part of him didn't want her easy forgiveness. He wanted her to get angry at him, to shout at him for being so stupid. He'd made so many mistakes and here she was being Holly, the woman who lived in the moment, who held no grudges, whose huge, kind heart was ticking down the moments of her life.

"Hey... look at me." She tugged on his hand.

He lifted his eyes to hers.

"I believe you, okay? I believe every single thing you've told me. I've been feeling something too. I figured..." She laughed and put her other hand on her heart. "I thought it was the donor. You know how I sometimes had dreams that felt like they came from the consciousness of that first heart?"

He nodded.

"Well, I've been having a lot of dreams lately, mostly since we moved into the house and a few times... I saw a figure, a woman, but... barely long enough to register and then she'd be gone. One night I felt as if someone was holding my hand." Her eyes welled up with tears. "I had this thought that it was the woman whose heart I had, but now... now I think it was one of them, the Ashwoods' girls. I don't think they want to hurt us, Adam. I think they're terribly lonely."

Adam thought of Holly spinning on the lawn, the way her face had shifted. Maybe one of them had held Holly's hand, but some of them were angry.

"Hello again, Mr. and Mrs. Tate," Dr. Meer announced as he stepped into the room. "Susan just let me know you were here. Has something happened? Are you feeling ill again, Holly?"

She smiled and shook her head. "I ate something that... might have been mislabeled. Could we do blood work? Make sure there's nothing strange in my system?"

Adam and Holly spent most of the day in the hospital waiting for the results of the tests. Dr. Meer hooked Holly up to the monitor, but her heart rate and blood pressure appeared normal.

It was after five when Meer reappeared.

"No trace of anything usual in your blood work, Holly, but it wouldn't be terrible to stay overnight for observation. Your choice, but if there's something that hasn't shown up, this is the safest place for you to be. I wouldn't recommend this to most patients, but considering your heart situation, I prefer to err on the side of caution."

Holly frowned. "If… I'd been poisoned, how long would that take to affect me?"

Meer shot a concerned look at Adam.

"I don't think I have," Holly added quickly. "I just… I ate something that might have been contaminated."

"We did a full toxicology screen. If you'd consumed poison, we should have seen it on that test."

"And you didn't?" Adam asked.

"No."

Adam looked at Holly. "I think you should stay the night," Adam told her, though he could see Holly didn't want to. "Just in case."

Holly sighed and leaned back against the pillows. "All right. Only tonight, though. And before you go, you're getting me some of that chocolate pudding from the cafeteria."

~

Adam parked and started into the dark house. Marshmallow barked anxiously. Adam scratched him behind the ears and then let him out. The dog ran to the truck and put his paws on the driver's side door in search of Holly.

"She's not here, bud," Adam called. "She'll be home tomorrow."

Adam flipped on the lights and opened the refrigerator. He took out the pitcher of water, grimacing at the jug of apple cider. He drank a large glass of water and then grabbed the cider, poured it down the sink.

Marshmallow barked, and Adam let the dog back inside. Exhausted, Adam slumped into a kitchen chair and rubbed Marshmallow's belly as the dog rolled on his back.

Above them, the light flickered.

"Go away," he muttered.

He was too tired for this shit tonight. He wanted to kick off his shoes and crawl into bed.

The vase of wildflowers in the center of the table fell sideways and rolled off the opposite end, smashing on the floor before Adam could catch it. Glass, water, and yellow flowers skittered across the wood.

Marshmallow jumped to his feet and barked.

Adam stared at the ceiling. "I said go away!" He screamed it. "GO AWAY!"

The lights flickered again and two of the dangling bulbs above the kitchen island exploded, raining thin glass onto the countertop.

Adam stood and grabbed the back of his chair, caught between wanting to plead with the spirits and wanting to shout at them. On the table, he saw the clipboard that held the Five Wishes sheet and he had a sudden urge to rip it to shreds.

Marshmallow ran into the pantry and pawed at the crawlspace. Something slammed against the floor. The banging and scratching started beneath him. Adam put his hands over his ears. Marshmallow barked and lunged against the floor.

A cupboard opened, and a glass tipped off the shelf and smashed on the floor. Another followed, and then a third.

"Stop!" he screamed as the temperature in the room dropped. In the thick, frosty air, a shape materialized. A face stared out from deep-set, despairing eyes—Nell's face—and though her form shuddered, her arm lifted and she pointed out the window toward the Ashwoods' house.

Adam suddenly sensed that Mildred was there. She was in the Ashwoods' house at that very moment.

He should call the police, send them to pick up the woman who'd murdered all those girls, but his earlier compulsion to enter the house swept over him. He wanted to go back inside. He wanted to confront Mildred about what she'd done.

Adam grabbed a flashlight and strode from the house. He ran through the trees, slapping away branches as they struck him in the face. As he hit the edge of the property, he grew winded and dizzy, but he forged on when he spotted a light glowing in a first-floor window. Adam could see the shadowy hulk of Mildred's car parked beside the house and was surprised the car had navigated the overgrown driveway.

He flipped the flashlight off and crept up the porch stairs. The door opened with a groan, giving him away. He stepped into the archway that led to the living room.

Mildred sat on a chair in the living room. Three tall red candles flickered from a candelabra sitting on a side table. She held a framed photograph in her hand and when she looked up, there was no surprise on her face.

"Ahh... Mr. Tate, I thought you might join me." She smiled, her face strange in the candlelight, like a face in a wax museum with those flat black eyes watching him.

He panted, blinking away the shimmering dark spots pricking his vision. A tremor of nausea seized his stomach. He grimaced, and the sensation passed. Had she brought a gun or perhaps set a trap?

She looked amused, as if she knew precisely what he searched for. "How's Holly?"

"Don't say her name."

She laughed. "Oh, no, names are *your* thing, aren't they? You thought you were very clever, revealing my given name."

His eyes drifted to the stains on the floor and he cringed. "Why were you in my house?"

"To meet your lovely wife, of course. And my, she is lovely. What a bright light, but you know what they say about bright lights, don't you? The brighter they shine, the more quickly they burn out."

He glared at her, another little cramp in his gut. He'd never in his life wanted so much to attack another human being. It was an odd feeling tempered by his inability to catch his breath, to bring the room into sharp focus. It blurred in the low light.

"Why? Why did you kill them, Mildred?" he asked.

She tossed the photo on the floor and the glass shattered. He lurched back as a shard skittered toward him. It was the framed wedding photo of Alice and Michael Ashwood.

"Why? That is always the question, isn't it?" she mused. "The question people most want to know. The question I've always wondered is how. How do I make people love *me*? Pay attention to *me*? Notice *me*?"

"You murdered them because they didn't pay enough attention to you?" he scoffed, stumbling sideways and bracing a hand against the doorframe. Another wave of dizziness swept over him and he held tight to the wood until it steadied.

She watched him. "You'll never understand, Adam Tate. You'll never comprehend the terrible loneliness of the ugly girl, the homely girl. The girl with the most clever, cunning mind who is never seen as more than a lump in a dress in the corner. Brushed aside, talked over. Well, I showed them, didn't I?"

"And now me?" he wheezed. "You're trying to hurt me by getting to my wife. Why?"

She reached into the pocket of her blazer.

Adam recoiled, expecting a weapon, but she merely held her cigarette case.

Mildred produced a cigarette, inhaled it, and then leaned forward and held the tip to a candle. It lit, and she brought it to her lips. She released a puff of smoke, watched it drift toward the ceiling.

"I didn't come searching for you, Mr. Tate, did I? I didn't show up at your door with theories and accusation? If you don't want the bear to follow you home, then I'd suggest you don't poke it with a stick."

"It's interesting to me that you think you'll get away with this," he grunted, sweat dripping into his eyes. He wiped it away. "That you'd dare to come here, back to the place where you committed five murders. It's insane. Are you insane?" He meant the words to be sharp, cruel even, but she was unmoved.

"You forget the critical difference between you and me, Adam. You are full of your own grandiosity. Barreling forward on an emotional high. You're Superman flying into the wreckage because you've deluded yourself into believing you are invincible. But I am invisible and that's even better. I am an old woman with no past. I am the furthest thing from a killer they could see.

"As a child, I thought it was a curse, this plainness. No one saw me, but in truth, it is a gift. I am as ethereal as the fog passing over Lake Huron. You could hand me to them in handcuffs with a long list of my transgressions and they'd look at you as if you'd lost your mind."

"I have evidence, Mildred. I have the bodies."

"The skeletons, you mean. Let's not pretend they're something they're not. Do you think the poison would still appear? Do you know that if it did, I have my own evidence? I have letters between Nell and Michael. I have receipts from his purchase of arsenic. I have reasonable doubt for days, but come now, they wouldn't bother taking me to trial. I am seventy-three years old—hardly worth prosecuting. And if they did"—her eyes glinted—"I have money, Adam. Money you can't imagine. I'd build a defense that would leave them looking foolish for targeting a sickly old woman. The only way you're going to get me, Adam, is if you kill me with your own hands." She gazed at his hands and smirked. "And you won't. You might be more afraid of death than you are of me."

"I'm not afraid of you."

"Aren't you? You should be. I have a way of making people go away, Adam. And I want you to go away."

"How do you intend to do that? You think I'm stupid enough to eat your poison?" But even as he spit the words out, his mouth filled with saliva. His stomach spasmed again, and this time the pain nearly brought him to his knees.

He'd dumped the apple cider, thrown away the apples. He'd not consumed anything she'd given Holly. He thought of the pitcher of water in his refrigerator. The cider had been right next to it.

A smile spread slowly on her lips. "Don't worry, Adam. Eventually, the pain becomes so great you pass out. At least that's what happened to Nell. Alice took much longer to lose consciousness."

He turned and started out of the room. A cramp spasmed across his stomach and he braced two hands against the wall. Dark spots skittered across his vision. More sweat came. It poured down his forehead, tasted hot and salty on his lips, and bile rose into his throat. He clutched his gut and stumbled toward the front door.

Mildred followed him into the foyer. He pushed through the door, collapsed on the porch, and vomited.

"Oh, God…" Another spasm gripped his abdomen and squeezed.

She stood in the doorway, candelabra in hand. He felt her watching. She'd watch until the end. It was her favorite part.

He puked again, cried out for Holly.

Mildred laughed.

From the corner of his eye, he saw the tire swing rock slowly from side to side in the darkness.

Mildred's candles snuffed out. From the house, a riot of noise emerged. The voices of women crying, screaming, pleading.

He twisted around as Mildred spun back to face the stairway.

Suddenly, violently, she was jerked out of the doorway and back inside. The front door slammed.

Another spasm rocked him.

Mildred's scream shattered the night and something in the house splintered.

Adam crawled forward and rolled down the porch steps onto the lawn. He fumbled his phone from his back jeans pocket. It was dead.

"Ugh…" He groaned and rolled sideways, threw up again. He'd

dropped his flashlight, but it made little difference. Flecks of light and dark spotted his vision.

More screams erupted from the house.

Another cramp seized him, but there was nothing left to throw up. He dry-heaved and when the muscles in his abdomen went slack, he pushed onto hands and knees and crawled forward.

He had no sense of direction, but inched toward what he hoped was the Ashwoods' weedy driveway and eventually the road beyond. That was his best chance of surviving. He'd never make it through the woods back to his own house.

Another sound emerged from the house, scratching. He thought Mildred was at the front door, clawing at the wood with her fingers.

Adam's stomach clenched. He moaned and curled into the fetal position. He'd never experienced a comparable pain, as if hot metal pliers twisted his guts. The world beneath him rolled.

He drifted down. Yes, that was what he wanted—to black out, to escape the pain—but then the world swam back into focus. He felt the blades of grass against his cheek, heard something crashing through the woods. A wolf maybe, a pack of coyotes, come to finish him off.

"Adam! Adam, where are you?" A man's voice, Ted's voice.

Adam tried to call out, released a gurgle and then heaved again.

A beam of light crisscrossed the forest.

"Adam!" The voice was closer now.

Ted broke through the trees. Adam felt hands on his back.

"Oh, Lord. Come on, we've got to git you help."

Ted hoisted him up, got him on his feet, but Adam collapsed.

The heaving started again. Adam buried his face in the grass. He heard Ted on the phone.

"We need an ambulance faster than a prairie fire."

Adam lost track of what Ted was saying. His ears thrummed and his body shook.

Ted clutched Adam beneath the armpits and dragged him down the driveway toward the road. "Don't you go anywhere, Adam. You stay with me, hear me? Don't even close your eyes."

Adam heard the words, but his eyelids, so heavy, slipped closed. His pain subsided and all the sensations—the clenching in his stomach, the weight of his heels dragging through weeds, the sound of Ted's voice—faded away.

47

Adam woke in a hospital room. He opened his eyes, and Holly was there, hands on his face, kissing his cheeks and forehead.

He'd died. The memory of where he'd been, that glorious place beyond, still shimmered in his mind, but it faded as he gazed at the stark room.

"Adam... oh, Adam..." Tears dripped onto his face. She wiped them away.

"Holly," he croaked, wincing. His throat felt as if someone had poured gasoline down it and lit it on fire. His stomach was hollow and sore.

He'd left his body, forgotten the heaviness of the physical world, and now that he was back, he longed for that other place. But here was Holly, his Holly. How could he have left her without saying goodbye?

She rested her forehead against his. "Oh, God," she murmured. "I was so afraid."

He swallowed, which hurt more than speaking.

Holly grabbed a cup of water and guided the straw to his lips. "It's okay. Don't talk."

He sipped a drink of icy water and cringed as if his esophagus was lined with blisters. His stomach lurched painfully.

"I called Ted," she said. "After you left my monitors started going haywire, the lights were flashing on and off. It was nuts and then... I just had this horrible feeling that she was there, Mildred. That you'd gone home and she'd been waiting for you. I called Ted and insisted he go to the house. Thank God, he got to you in time. She poisoned you with arsenic. They pumped your stomach, but…" More tears. "They said it didn't look good. They said… that your heart stopped."

"For how long…?" he whispered.

"Four minutes."

Had it only been four minutes that he'd been in that other place? It had felt like a lifetime.

"Holly." He put her hand against his cheek. "Holly, it was so beautiful. My mother was there and your mother…"

Her eyes sparkled and she smiled. "I always knew they would be."

~

On Adam's second day in the ICU, a detective from the Presque Isle County Sheriff's Office arrived.

With Holly by his side, Adam told the man everything that had occurred, beginning with the spring day when he'd made a terrible choice. He didn't offer the otherworldly things, but he outlined his research, beginning with Nell's journal. How he'd searched for the names of the girls online, found family members and gradually connected the crimes to Mildred.

"Did you find her?" Adam asked. "Mildred?"

The detective nodded. "This hasn't been released to the public, but Mildred didn't make it out of the house, Mr. Tate. She must have fallen down the basement stairs. We suspect when your friend Ted appeared she panicked and tried to hide."

Adam thought of the door slamming, and Mildred's screams. She'd fallen down the stairs all right, but it hadn't been an accident.

~

Adam sat beside Holly on the porch swing. They'd shut Marshmallow in the house because he got a bit too excitable with the commotion. Crime scene tape stretched along the edge of the property and more than ten investigators moved between the Ashwoods' house and the grave Adam had dug by the pudding stone.

As long as they found all the skeletons, they didn't believe they would need to excavate beneath Adam and Holly's house.

In Sault St. Marie, investigators were discussing the exhumation of Mildred's former husbands. A similar talk was happening in Alpena, where Mildred's last husband had perished decades before.

"Hey," Adam said, leaning over and grabbing the clipboard off the porch rail. He held up the Five Wishes living will paperwork. "I thought we could get this taken care of. I printed a second one for me."

Holly smiled and snuggled into him. "I'm ready when you are."

EPILOGUE

It was November when Alice Ashwood and her girls were laid to rest. Adam had jumped through hoops to have Marilyn Ashwood's remains sent from Manistee, so that she could be buried with her mother. The graveyard occupied a little hill, and if the wind blew the trees just right, they saw Lake Huron through the forest.

Six coffins, side by side, were lowered into the ground. Holly had brought bushels of autumn flowers. Pastor Brian said a blessing, a parting farewell.

People who'd once known the Ashwoods and several family members of the deceased girls attended, as did Cheryl and Ted and other parishioners from Touchstone Ministries.

Adam noticed a man and woman who looked vaguely familiar picking their way across the cemetery. They stopped at the edge of the mourners. As Adam studied the woman's face, he made the connection. These were the people who'd found a group of girls' bodies, including Marilyn Ashwood's, in the Manistee National Forest. He'd seen their photo in the newspaper when he'd been tracking down Marilyn Ashwood's remains.

As people filed away, Adam took Holly's hand and walked to the couple.

"Hi," he told them. "You're Lori and Ben, right?"

Lori nodded. "Yes. Hi." She extended her hand.

"I'm Adam. This is my wife, Holly."

They shook hands.

"This was an admirable thing to do, Adam," Ben told him, nodding toward the graves. "Reuniting Marilyn with her mother."

Adam looked back at the coffins. "It felt right."

"You guys found her?" Holly asked. "Marilyn Ashwood?"

Lori glanced at Ben and something passed between them. "Yeah," Lori said. "In the Manistee National Forest. She'd been murdered."

"Was the killer ever caught?" Holly asked.

"We're confident they're deceased," Ben said.

Holly shuddered, and Adam hugged her closer.

As Adam and Holly drove home, he sensed a kinship with Lori Hicks. He'd seen something in her eyes, some familiar haunted quality, and he suspected that Lori, like Adam, had gotten a glimpse of other-worldly beings that walked among them.

~

"Everything looks good, Holly," Dr. Hansen told her and Adam, perching on a stool in his office.

They'd spent the previous two days at the Heart Transplant Center in Grand Rapids for her annual check-up. She'd undergone labs, chest x-rays, an echocardiogram, a coronary arteriogram and an intravascular ultrasound.

"Nothing unusual at all?" Adam asked.

"No." He looked at Holly. "Your body seems to be accepting the transplant as we'd expect. You know what to look for—shortness of breath, swelling in the feet and legs, change in heart rhythm. You're an old pro at this by now." He winked at her. "As are you." He shifted his attention to Adam. "But I'm happy to say that as of this moment everything looks fine."

Holly rested a hand on her heart, taking a big breath in. Adam put his hand over top of hers.

"Let's go home," she said.

THE TRUE STORY THAT INSPIRED ASHWOOD'S GIRLS

Between 1920 and 1954, a woman with such a friendly face she was known as the 'giggling granny' poisoned and murdered four of her husbands and allegedly murdered multiple additional family members, including several of her own children and grandchildren.

The woman's devious behavior was fueled by an obsession with her search for the perfect mate, which arose in part due to her voracious reading of romance novels and the *lonely hearts* newspaper column. Though she claimed money was never a motive in her crimes, she received large life insurance payouts for most of her husbands' untimely deaths.

The woman was finally found out after the murder of her fifth husband in Tulsa, Oklahoma, in 1953, when an autopsy revealed a large amount of arsenic in the man's system. During an interrogation, the woman confessed to killing four out of her five husbands.

Read the full story at www.jrericksonauthor.com

ALSO BY J.R. ERICKSON

The Troubled Spirits Series

Dark River Inn

Helme House

Darkness Stirring

Ashwood's Girls

Still Falling

Or dive into the completed eight-book stand-alone paranormal series:

The Northern Michigan Asylum Series.

Do you believe in ghosts?

ACKNOWLEDGMENTS

Many thanks to the people who made this book possible. Thank you to Team Miblart for the beautiful cover. Thank you to RJ Locksley for copy editing Ahwood's Girls. Many thanks to Will St. John for beta reading the original manuscript, and to Emily H., Lea P., and Doreen F., for finding those final pesky typos that slip in. Thank you to my amazing Advanced Reader Team. Lastly, and most of all, thank you to my family and friends for always supporting and encouraging me on this journey.

ABOUT THE AUTHOR

J.R. Erickson, also known as Jacki Riegle, is an indie author who writes ghost stories. She is the author of the Troubled Spirits Series, which blends true crime with paranormal murder mysteries. Her Northern Michigan Asylum Series are stand-alone paranormal novels inspired by a real former asylum in Traverse City.

These days, Jacki passes the time in the Traverse City area with her excavator husband, her wild little boy, and her three kitties: Floki, Beast, and Mamoo.

To find out more about J.R. Erickson, visit her website at www.jrericksonauthor.com.